The Detonation Series! – Book 2

HARRIS

Eldon H. Kellogg

https://www.eldonhkellogg.com/
contact@eldonhkellogg.com

ACKNOWLEDGEMENTS

To my wife Patricia: my editor and best friend; whose critiques continue unabated as she fights through cancer and recovery.

To sweet Abby: sashay, sashay, little cat. Life is chill. Just have her kibble ready in the evening. Or else . . .

For almost 30 years the Shearon Harris Nuclear Power Plant has been the spent fuel repository for three other nuclear plants in the utility. Brunswick Units 1 & 2 and H.B. Robinson ran out of spent fuel storage space during the 90's. Harris, with spent fuel pools designed to support four nuclear plants, was the place to go. Now, over 3000 tons of spent fuel sits in the two major pools at Harris.

"I am become death, the destroyer of worlds."
J. Robert Oppenheimer, the "Father of the Atomic Bomb"

Recommendations by the Union of Concerned Scientists after 9/11:
- All spent fuel should be transferred from wet to dry storage within five years of discharge from the reactor core. This can be achieved with existing technologies.
-The NRC should upgrade existing regulations to require that dry cask storage sites be made more secure against a terrorist attack.
- However, these measures do not go far enough to ensure the safety of the pools under a wide range of accident and attack scenarios.

"When the document was presented (in March, 2011), a discussion ensued about keeping its existence secret. The content was so shocking that we decided to treat it as if it didn't exist."
(Comments about a document written by Japan Atomic Energy Commission Chairman Shunsuke Kondo, on evacuating Tokyo after the Fukushima accident.)

Harris Nuclear Plant

Harris Nuclear Plant

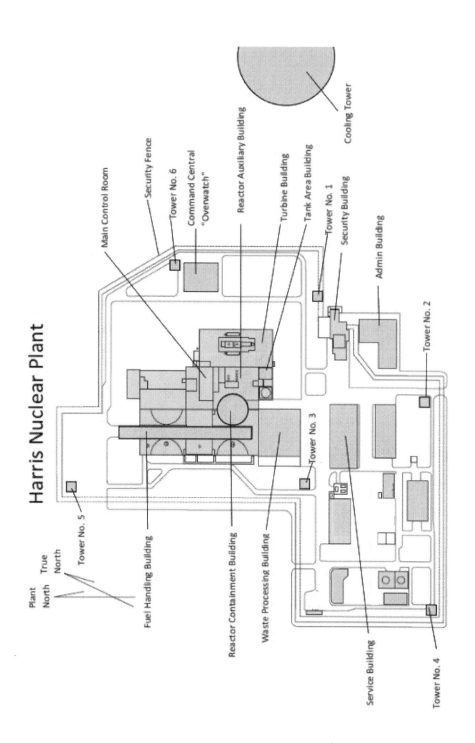

Plant North
True North
Tower No. 5
Fuel Handling Building
Reactor Containment Building
Waste Processing Building
Service Building
Tower No. 4
Main Control Room
Security Fence
Tower No. 6
Command Central "Overwatch"
Reactor Auxiliary Building
Turbine Building
Tank Area Building
Tower No. 1
Security Building
Admin Building
Tower No. 2
Tower No. 3
Cooling Tower

CHAPTER 1

Inova Alexandria Hospital
Room 501
4300 Seminary Road
Alexandria, Virginia, USA
April 19, 1830 hours EST

Lieutenant Gong Aiguo lay in his hospital bed staring at the drop ceiling. The tile directly above his head was painted with a colorful scene of some mountain range. The foreground contained elk and a cabin of western design. It wasn't China, but it drew his mind elsewhere . . . to a place that he loved. He could feel the bitter cold of the Taihang Mountains on his cheeks. Each breath of sub-zero air seared his lungs. Each step through the deep snow was more difficult than the last.

"I . . . am a Siberian Tiger. I . . . am a warrior for the People's Republic of China. I will not yield. I will not surrender," he moaned, as he struggled against the steel cuffs that bound each of his limbs to the hospital bed.

He had been drifting in and out of a drug-induced stupor for days as his body tried to heal from the surgery. The damage caused by the impact of two .45-caliber bullets had been extensive. Steel rods protruded from his left thigh, immobilizing his surgically repaired femur. The right side of his chest was still heavily bandaged. The pain told him that he was still alive and at the mercy of his captors.

"I have not failed my country. As long as I can still breathe, I can still destroy America," he mumbled, as he drifted back into the roiling turmoil of his dreams.

The American's face was always there. The searing hatred in his eyes, the barely restrained fury as he bent low over his prey, the spiraled tunnel held in his hand, that presented itself as a relief from so much pain and torment.

. . . .

Hallway outside Room 501

"So, we're moving him tomorrow?" Alexandria Police Officer Ted Barlow asked, as he stared through the glass at the Chinese Special Forces Operator.

"We aren't doing shit. Our bodyguard duties end tomorrow when the Feds come and transport this guy to some federal hospital," Sergeant Marshon Morehead replied, as he glanced up and down the hallway of the 5th floor.

"Ten days of this shit is about all I can take," Sergeant Morehead said, as he and Officer Barlow nodded and fist bumped in agreement.

"I still can't believe they emptied the whole floor just for this guy. Not like he's going to get up and walk out."

Two other police officers stood at each end of the hall. Another four officers were stationed near the elevators and stairwells. All the officers had been told was that the man they guarded was extremely dangerous and a threat to the nation. All they saw were metal rods sticking out of his left thigh and a heavily bandaged right chest.

"I heard they're taking him to Walter Reed . . . better security up there," Officer Barlow said.

"Yeah, we get off at 6 AM, and that's it. Day after that, we're back at the precinct on day shift. Anything's better than being cooped up in here all night. The floor's empty, with only male nurses to look at," Sergeant Morehead replied, as they both laughed.

As if on cue, a male nurse of Asian descent exited a storage room to their left and headed for Room 501.

"Relax officers, you know the routine. I change the dressings on his chest once a night, and verify the tension on the leg bolts," Nurse Walter Yin said, as he wheeled his cart up to the entrance.

"It's chill, Walter. I just didn't notice you entering the storage room," Sergeant Morehead said, while visually checking the contents on the two-tiered cart.

"That's because there's a door that connects to the nurses' station," Walter said, as he pressed the large square button to give him access to the room.

2

As the cart rolled past and the glass door shut, Sergeant Morehead said, "I'm not sure about that guy."

"Marshon, that sounds like racial profiling . . . and from a brother! I am seriously disappointed," Officer Barlow said, while grinning at his partner.

"Fuck off!" Sergeant Morehead said, while staring through the glass door.

.   .   .   .

Inside Room 501

"So how are you feeling tonight, Lieutenant Gong Aiguo?" Walter asked, his back to the door as he checked the tension in the steel rods protruding from his patient's left thigh.

Aiguo ignored the question, his closed eyes and soft breathing feigning sleep.

"Nice try, but you snore when you sleep. Besides . . . one day as a tiger is worth a thousand as a sheep," Walter said, as Aiguo's eyes gently opened.

"Aiguo, I know you don't trust me, but you are leaving here tonight . . . in less than 15 minutes. You have not been forgotten, or abandoned, by your brothers," Walter said, while switching over to the other side of the bed.

Aiguo said nothing as his mind ran through various scenarios.

"*That phrase was from my training as a Siberian Tiger. Would the American's know that? Is this some kind of plan to make me drop my guard? They may think that I know more than I do. A fake rescue, and then I'll tell them everything. I'll tell them nothing! This is just a ruse,*" Aiguo told himself, while staring into the nurse's eyes.

"Patience comrade, Chénmò de lǎohǔ zǒuguòle yīyè (the silent tiger walks through the night)," Walter whispered, while changing the bandage on Aiguo's chest wound.

"*Only my platoon members knew that phrase. We were the Silent Tigers. This is real. They are coming for me,*" Aiguo thought, as Walter secured the new dressing, stared into Aiguo's eyes and smiled.

CHAPTER 2

Ellen Coolidge Burke Branch Library Parking Lot
Alexandria, Virginia
April 20, 0300 hours EST

"Comrades, it's time to go retrieve our brother," Sergeant Wang Jian said, while tapping Heng on the shoulder.

Heng nodded, and started the engine on the Ford Excalibur ambulance. It was painted white, with orange stripes down the side. The distinctive shield logo of the Capitol Building and a purple cross preceded the 'Walter Reed National Military Medical Center' painted in large blue letters on the side.

"Remember, as soon as we leave the ambulance . . . face shields down. Four Asian men dressed in US military garb would draw attention," Jian said, as Heng pulled the ambulance from the shadows behind the library and turned left onto Library Lane.

"Chonglin, prepare yourself! What are you doing back there?" Jian asked, while staring toward the darkened rear of the ambulance.

"Nothing, Comrade. Just focusing on the mission," Chonglin said, while placing his combat knife back in its sheath.

The streets were empty as the ambulance turned left onto Seminary Road. A thick fog had settled in since midnight.

"Two minutes, Comrades. Remember, stay calm, but alert. We are supposed to be transporting a dangerous prisoner. I will be the only one that talks. If we meet anyone, and I decide they need to be taken down, I will point at them. Silence is imperative. Our only chance is to get in and out without starting an alarm," Jian said, as the ambulance turned right onto North Howard Street.

"Remember, Heng, second right, then curve to the left. The loading dock is on the far side of the hospital," Jian said, while laying his hand on Heng's right shoulder.

They had walked through the scenario for days until all five men knew the assignments of every position, but Jian was nervous. He knew that all plans seemed perfect . . . until they weren't. There were always surprises, or holes, in the data used to plan an operation.

"I think the fog's getting worse," Heng said, as he slowed the ambulance, and took the second exit off North Howard Street.

Heng and Jian were dressed in white US Army hospital duty uniforms. The four men in the back of the ambulance were all dressed in green camo US Army Combat Uniforms (ACUs). All four were armed with M4A1's with suppressors. They exchanged glances, and then lowered the dark visors on their helmets.

"Remember! Keep the weapons slung at your side. If you carry them forward, the suppressors are too obvious," Jian said, as they drove past the Emergency Room entrance.

No other ambulances were present. The entrance was a bright glow in the thickening fog.

"Slowly Heng, curve to the right, past the parking deck. The loading dock is on the right, at the end of the building," Jian said, while staring into the dense fog.

"Wǒ kàn bù dào gǒu shǐ (I can't see shit)."

"Just keep going. There's the entrance to the parking deck on the left. Keep going," Jian said, while glancing over his shoulder at the others.

All four men were facing toward the rear of the ambulance, visors down and weapons at the ready. The wheeled gurney they would use to transport their comrade sat between them.

"There, on the right, that's the loading dock. Go a little further, and then start backing up. I'll get out and guide you back," Jian said.

The loading dock had two levels. One was for ambulances and the other, two feet higher, was for tractor trailers. Jian jumped out of the ambulance passenger side, as Heng started to back up toward the ambulance loading dock.

"Good, you're lined up . . . ten meters, go slower . . . five meters . . . one meter," Jian said, while glancing around the loading dock.

It was quiet. No personnel were visible. The loading dock staff only worked two eight-hour shifts, and weren't due at work for another two hours.

With a slight bump the ambulance stopped, and the rear doors swung open. Jian climbed onto the loading dock. Four rifle barrels greeted him as he approached the rear of the ambulance.

With a nod, Jian reached into the ambulance, removed the gurney, and pulled it to an upright and locked position. The team moved in silence. The last member to exit the ambulance shut the rear doors. As expected, the entrance door into the loading bay was locked, but was quickly picked by one of the team members.

The storage area inside was dark, but the exit into the hospital was visible on the back right. Two double doors with glass inserts cast enough light for them to make their way through the storage area.

Jian pushed open the doors with the gurney as they entered the brightly lit corridors of the hospital. He glanced at his watch . . . 0310.

"We should be back at these doors in 12 minutes," he told himself, as they wound their way through the twists and turns that led to the main elevator.

As he navigated a turn to the right, he almost ran into a janitor pushing his cart of cleaning supplies.

"Jesus, dude! You scared the shit outta me. This place is like a ghost town at night. Whoa, what's with the guns?" the man asked, while brushing his long hair out of his eyes.

"I'm sorry. I didn't mean to scare you. We're here to transport a patient up to Walter Reed," Jian said, while nodding at the team trailing behind him.

"Oh, you must mean the dude up on the 5th Floor. I have to have a cop escort me up there. I'm due to make my nightly run in about half an hour. Rumor has it that he's the one that killed all the staff in the ER a few weeks back. I'll be glad to see that SOB gone," the man said, as Jian smiled and began to push past him.

"Sorry about the scare. We've got a schedule," Jian said, as the man nodded, and began to push his cart down the hallway.

Jian turned and stared at the man's back. Then he pointed at the man. Zhang Weimin, the last man in the group, wrapped his left arm around the janitor's neck as the man walked past him. With his right hand he applied pressure. The struggling man was unconscious in seconds.

Jian made a slashing motion across his neck, and pointed at a door leading off the hallway. Weimin and Bingwen carried the man and his cart into the room. Both reappeared seconds later and nodded.

"*Two-minute delay*," Jian thought, while glancing at his watch.

The hospital seemed empty as they walked up to the main elevator and pressed the Up button. When the doors opened, Jian pushed the gurney in, to the far side of the elevator. His four comrades stepped into the elevator and unslung their weapons. Bingwen pressed the button for the 5th Floor. All four men shouldered their automatic weapons, and faced the opening.

CHAPTER 3

Inova Alexandria Hospital
Room 501
4300 Seminary Road
Alexandria, Virginia
April 20, 0315 hours EST

Aiguo could feel the adrenalin coursing through his body. He had always loved the feeling, as it quickened his mind and his reflexes. Everything started to slow down. He glanced at the clock on the wall. The nurse had walked out of his room 16 minutes ago. If something was going to happen, it would happen now.

. . . .

5th Floor
0316 hours EST

When the elevator doors opened on the 5th Floor, two Alexandria PD officers were chatting about basketball. North Carolina had won another national title, and both men hated UNC. They glanced over at the elevator, expecting the nurse to return from the cafeteria. Both men were dropped with single shots to the head.

A wedge was inserted into the elevator doors to hold them open. There were no words as the team exited the elevator, turning left into the main hallway. The four gunners led the way, staggered left and right to give each a clear field of fire. Officers Ted Barlow and Marshon Morehead still stood outside Room 501, 50 feet away. Barlow's head exploded. Marshon flinched, but never felt the bullet crease the right side of his cheek.

There was no time to think, only react. Marshon dove to his left as two bullets thudded into his Covert IIIA protective vest. His vest was not standard issue and would stop a .44 mag. Still, it felt like someone had hit him in the chest with a baseball bat. His 9 mm Glock appeared in his hand and he began firing wildly down the hall. Renshu spun to the floor, hit in the left hip. Weimin was clipped in the left arm. A second round took him in the throat.

Both of Marshon's legs were hit, and he tumbled to the floor. As he raised the pistol to fire again, his right arm was shattered by two more rounds. He slumped against the wall. Glancing to his left, he saw two US Army soldiers advancing on him.

"What the fu . . ." were his last words as a 5.56mm round entered his forehead and blew out the back of his skull.

Renshu struggled to his feet, cursing in Chinese. Jian silenced him with a gesture as the sound of running feet could be heard coming from two adjacent hallways.

The first officer came running around a corner to the left and was dropped by half a dozen shots. The second appeared at the end of a hall perpendicular to Room 501. She dropped to one knee and began placing well aimed shots at the attackers. Chonglin staggered, as two rounds struck him in the chest, but were stopped by his body armor. The second officer's head snapped back, torn apart by the impact of two bullets. Her body jumped and twisted as she was riddled, until she settled into a rapidly expanding puddle of her own blood. Silence, and the acrid ammonia smell of spent gunpowder, lingered in the hall.

"Chonglin, Bingwen, clear the floor. Kill any hostiles," Jian ordered, while turning and staring down at the twitching body of Weimin.

Blood still spurted from a severed carotid artery in his neck. His eyes glazed over as the spurting became a dribble.

"Renshu, can you walk?" Jian asked, as he bent over and closed Weimin's eyes.

Renshu sat on the floor and slit open his pants at the wound site.

"Flesh wound . . . hurts like shit," he said, while removing an emergency bandage from a pouch on his web gear.

"May have nicked an artery. As the Americans would say, I'm bleeding like a stuck pig," Renshu said, while tightening the Israeli-designed bandage.

"Renshu, cover the hall until the others return," Jian said, as he struck the wall-mounted pad that opened the door to Room 501.

"First Lieutenant Gong," Jian said, as he nodded in deference, stepped over to the bed, and inspected the cuffs restraining Aiguo.

"Sergeant Wang, it has been years. I didn't know you were in country," Aiguo said, smiling for the first time in weeks.

"I also was part of General Kung's program, but that story will wait. We need to get you out of here," Jian said.

"The Hēirén (black) has the keys. They hang from his belt," Aiguo said.

Jian nodded, retrieved the keys, and began unlocking the cuffs.

"We have an ambulance at a loading dock. This gurney is smaller and easier to maneuver. Here, I brought you a pistol. After this mess we may have to shoot our way out of here," Jian said, while rolling the gurney over parallel to the bed.

"You'll have to help me, Sergeant. I haven't been out of this bed in weeks," Aiguo said, while trying to drag himself onto the gurney.

The door to Room 501 opened. Renshu limped in and asked, "What do we do with Weimin?"

"Leave him. Take his weapons. We're six minutes behind schedule. If one of the police called for backup, we may not make it out of here," Jian said, while pulling Aiguo onto the gurney.

"Hold the door, we're leaving," Jian said, while pulling a blanket from the hospital bed and draping it over Aiguo.

"The floor is clear. We jammed the other stairwell doors," Bingwen said, as he and Chonglin ran into the hallway outside Room 501.

"Good, back to the ambulance. Silence anyone that we meet," Jian said, as he began pushing Aiguo to the pair of elevators.

When the elevator door on the right opened, Walter's eyes widened as he was greeted with three rifles and two pistols pointed at his head. One shot was fired. Blood and brain matter splattered across the back of the elevator.

"Idiot! He was one of ours!" Jian yelled, as Walter's body dropped across the entrance to the elevator.

"You said silence anyone that we met," Chonglin replied.

The doors closed. Then opened again as they contacted Walter's body.

"Pull him out of the way. He was a loose end anyway," Jian said.

"*This is cleaner. They'll think that he was just another victim,*" Jian thought, as Walter was dumped in the hallway beside the first two officers who were killed.

. . . .

The Ambulance
0330 hours EST

Heng sat in the driver's seat of the ambulance drumming his fingers against the steering wheel.

"Eight minutes late . . . almost nine . . . something went wrong," he said, while lowering the window on the driver's side.

The fog was still thick. He glanced at his watch for the fourth time in the last two minutes and listened.

"No sirens . . . at least there aren't any sirens . . . yet," he said, then jumped as the rear doors to the ambulance were yanked open.

He started the engine while glancing in the rearview mirror and saw the gurney rolled into the back and locked in place. Counting heads, he saw that they were one short.

"What happened? Who's missing?" Heng asked, as Jian leapt into the passenger seat beside him.

"Shut up and drive. Slowly, back out the way we came. Then turn right on North Howard. One missed shot and things got messy. We lost Weimin," Jian said, as the ambulance pulled away from the loading dock.

CHAPTER 4

Inova Alexandria Hospital
Loading Dock
4300 Seminary Road
Alexandria, Virginia
April 20, 0335 hours EST

Heng pulled out slowly, turned left past the parking deck, and followed the road out to the hospital exit.

"Jian, what happened?" Heng asked, as he turned right onto North Howard Street.

"Renshu and Chonglin were leading the team down the hall, as planned. Renshu made his shot, and took down the first guard. Chonglin missed, and it cost Weimin his life. The same guard wounded Renshu before we killed him. Now, be quiet and head for the storage unit."

"Jian, Renshu is still bleeding," Chonglin said, while changing the bandage on Renshu's leg.

"Do the best you can. We have more equipment at the storage unit."

Weimin was the team's trained medic, and he was dead.

"Turn left on the second major street. You won't be able to see the sign in this fog," Jian said, while pulling his phone out of a pocket and turning on Google Maps.

"Shénshèng de gǒu shǐ (holy shit), I can't even see the side of the road," Heng said, while focusing on the double yellow line just visible in his left head light.

Aiguo laid back on the gurney in silence. The pain meds were wearing off and his leg was beginning to throb.

"The pain is nothing. A comrade was lost in rescuing me. I have become soft. They have a plan. Let them finish it," Aiguo told himself, as he began breathing deeply, and placed his mind elsewhere.

"Slow down, Heng, there should be a traffic light up here. Turn left onto North Jordan," Jian said.

"I see the glow. It's red," Heng said, while slowing to a stop.

"Put on your turn signal. Now go, it's green. Be careful, we don't know who's watching in the fog," Jian said, while lowering his window.

"I hear multiple sirens. Keep going. When you get to Duke Street, turn right," Jian said, as the ambulance crept through the intersection in the dense fog.

Each street light was a pocket of illumination as they crept past an endless series of apartment buildings.

"I see a street light . . . a big intersection. The light's green. Do I turn here?" Heng asked, while flexing his hands.

His grip on the steering wheel was so tight that they were beginning to cramp.

"No, keep going. I'll tell you where to turn," Jian said, while staring at the map on his phone.

Jian glanced up. The sides of the street were lined with trees. The naked branches appeared in the fog like hands reaching for them as they drove past. He shook the disturbing image from his mind as the ambulance halted at another stop light. He could see multiple stop lights a short distance ahead.

"The second set of lights is Duke Street. Turn right, there," Jian said, as he wiped his sweaty palms on his pant legs. The adrenalin from the rescue had worn off. He felt tired and shaky. He knew the others would be experiencing similar effects.

They turned right on Duke Street. Heng drove in the center lane. The white ambulance was almost invisible as they drove down the wide avenue.

"The street lights remind me of runway lights at an airport," Heng said, while they continued down the wide street.

He and Jian stared as they passed a runner coming in the other direction. It was a woman, and a strange sight. Multi-colored lights flashed up and down her torso as she ran on the sidewalk beside them.

Behind her, a huge brick building was barely visible in the fog. At first, Jian thought it was a church because of the design. It was a series of connected buildings. In the center was a wall with a huge clock face. It was brightly lit from spotlights below. Jian noticed the time as they slowly drove past.

"It's almost 0400. We're running out of time. We have to get under cover," Jian thought, as a premonition of impending doom struck him.

He had heard occasional sirens as they drove. Now he could hear more . . . many more, and they were coming nearer.

On the other side of the median, six police cars appeared in the fog, blue lights flashing and sirens wailing.

"Jian!" Heng exclaimed, as the police cruisers roared past on the other side of the street.

"Relax, they aren't after us. They're headed to the hospital. Keep going. Stick to the plan. No more mistakes," Jian said, as Chonglin's head appeared between them.

"Jian! Renshu is unconscious. He's lost too much blood. How soon do we get there? He needs a transfusion," Chonglin said.

"Set up an IV. The equipment's in the back."

"I've seen it done, but I've never done it."

"It's easy. Just find the large vein at the bend in the elbow and insert the needle. Use a large needle, size 18. The fluid will go in faster. Have faith, comrade. Renshu is depending on you," Jian said, while glancing at his phone.

"Jian, we are coming to another intersection. Do I keep going?" Heng asked.

"Yes, this is Cameron Station Boulevard. We take the next left onto Pickett."

"I wish this damn fog would lift."

"No, comrade! This fog is saving our lives. We are hidden from the enemy. We have poked a hornet's nest, but they are slow reacting because of the fog. We have to be under cover before they set up road blocks."

They grew quiet as the ambulance glided through the fog. As they approached South Pickett, Jian could see another set of police cars approaching in the distance.

"Quickly, turn left. We must get through the intersection before they see us. Someone may have seen an ambulance leaving the hospital," Jian said, while gesturing for Heng to speed up.

14

As they turned left onto Pickett and drove down the street, Jian glanced back and saw a line of police cars stream through the intersection. None of them turned in their direction.

"*Ah yes, the hornets are buzzing, but they can't see us,*" Jian thought, as his focus returned to the map on his phone.

"Heng, the road will slowly curve to the right, then back to the left. We will turn right onto a small road that heads up to the storage units."

"I have the IV in. The solution seems to be dripping into his veins," Chonglin yelled from the back.

"Good work. We'll be at the storage unit in a few minutes," Jian said, while looking for the entrance on his right.

CHAPTER 5

Public Storage Unit 62
401 South Pickett Street
Alexandria, Virginia
April 20, 0410 hours EST

"Here's the access card. The code is 1949," Jian said, while handing the card to Heng.

Heng lowered his window, inserted the card, and followed the prompts.

As the gate opened, Jian took the card from Heng and said, "Straight to the end, then turn left. It's the fourth double unit on the right. . . . number 62."

"I'll get out and open the unit," Jian said, as they pulled up to Unit 62.

Jian opened the padlock, and raised the insulated roller door. He flicked on the overhead lights and lowered the door, as the ambulance drove in and parked. The double unit had two roller doors. The dividing wall had been removed. On the other side of the bay was a U-Haul moving van.

"Everyone out! Move Lieutenant Gong over to the moving van. Chonglin, bring Renshu back here," Jian said, while walking to the back of the unit.

"After the Lieutenant is moved, change out the Israeli bandage on Renshu. Administer painkillers and morphine. Then get him on the moving van," Jian ordered, while changing out of his hospital garb, and into jeans and a plaid shirt.

"Heng, wipe down the ambulance. No finger prints, no blood. Then spray the inside and outside with the liquid oxygen bleach," Jian said, while slipping on an insulated vest and a University of Virginia ball cap.

"The sun will be up in less than two hours. I want us on the road in 20 minutes. The fog will aid in our escape," Jian said, as he began filling the portable sprayer with the bleach.

With two patients settled in the moving van, the team began discarding their military clothing and storing it in containers. Everything was moved into the U-Haul.

"The ambulance is clean," Heng said, while discarding his paper coveralls, gloves and mask.

"Check the area. We leave nothing behind except the ambulance," Jian said, as he inspected Chonglin and Bingwen.

Fifteen minutes after they had arrived, everyone was on board the moving van except Jian. He walked through the storage unit one last time.

"They will find this place eventually. There must not be anything that will tell them where we have gone," Jian told himself, as he inspected the unit one last time.

"There's nothing left behind. The ambulance has been sterilized. It's time to go," Jian said, while glancing down at his watch.

"0424 . . . "Jian thought, as he raised the roller door, and watched Heng slowly back the moving van out of Unit 62.

Jian turned off the lights and activated the roller door to close, while stepping outside the unit. As he walked past the side of the moving van, he glanced up at the painting on the side. It showed a soldier in an experimental submarine from the American Civil War,

"*A shame that we have to be enemies. They are a very brave and creative people,*" Jian thought, as he climbed into the passenger seat beside Heng.

"Heng, turn right when you get to the bottom of the hill. Keep going until you reach South Van Dorn. Then take a left," Jian said, as he opened the glove compartment and removed a 9mm Glock with the silencer attached.

"Expecting trouble, Comrade?" Heng asked, as he glanced at the handgun.

"American Boy Scouts have a saying, 'Always be prepared,' " Jian said, as he removed the clip and thumped it against his palm to seat the rounds.

Heng chuckled as he stopped at the bottom of the path, glanced left, and then turned right onto South Pickett Street.

"Now we head for South Carolina, my friend," Jian said, while removing his phone from a satchel, opening up Google Maps, and keying in a destination.

CHAPTER 6

5th Floor
Inova Alexandria Hospital
4300 Seminary Road
Alexandria, Virginia
April 20, 0915 hours EST

CIA Agent Amanda Langford exited the stairwell onto the 5th floor of Inova Alexandria Hospital and paused. Three bodies were sprawled in front of the elevator ten feet to her right. Police photographers and forensic specialists were gathering evidence and placing markers by everything of interest. Blood splattered the walls. Pools of blood encircled each victim. As she displayed her ID, and stepped around each bit of evidence, a huge African-American man approached her in the hallway.

"Why am I not surprised that you beat the FBI to the scene?" Detective First Class Angelo Morehead said, as he placed a stick of Nicorette into his mouth and began to chew. The wrapper was carefully tucked into a suit pocket.

"So what happened?" Amanda asked, while glancing around at the carnage.

"Based on the overlay, it happened in two phases. The assault team exited the elevator and dispatched two officers with two shots. The shell casings are in the elevator. That's why you had to walk up the stairs. The last victim had the misfortune of coming up the elevator as the assault team was exiting the floor. They shot him in the elevator, dragged him out and dumped him here. As I said, he was their last victim," Angelo said, while pointing at the male nurse lying face down across the body of one of the police officers.

"After killing the first two officers they exited the elevator, turned left, and fired on the two officers standing outside Room 501."

"That's where the Chinese . . . " Amanda began.

"Agent Langford, they murdered my little brother to get that bastard out of here," Angelo said, while staring down at the diminutive agent.

"I'm sorry. How did they . . ." Amanda began, as Angelo turned and began walking up the hallway.

"They opened fire on the two officers standing outside the room. Officer Barlow was instantly killed with a shot to the head. Officer Morehead . . . was hit five times. He was shot in the legs twice. He managed to fire his weapon four times before his right arm was shattered by two rounds. He was then shot between the eyes at close range. His brains are still scatted on the floor and wall where he was propped up, waiting to die. I have to go tell his wife what happened. Then I have to contact our mother in San Francisco, and tell her why her baby boy had to die today. I'm the one who got him a job in the Alexandria PD. She was never happy about that," Angelo said, while staring down at his brother's corpse.

"The man in the military uniform?" Amanda asked, her eyes welling up as she felt the pain in Angelo's voice.

"Another Chinese agent. I had them slice open the sleeves at both shoulders. Same tattoo on the right shoulder . . . four Chinese characters. Below them was the head of a tiger. Below that was a dagger with lightning bolts over the blade," Angelo said, as he turned and stared at Amanda.

"You owed me before, Agent Langford. Now you owe me big. This is personal, and I don't want to hear any of your 'I'm not authorized' bullshit. Either you tell me what's going on, or you'll be seeing everything I know in the Washington Post tomorrow morning," Angelo said, while sticking his finger in Amanda's face.

"Let's go out in the stairwell," Amanda said, as she turned and began walking back down the hallway.

She glanced over her shoulder. Angelo glowered at her, and then began to follow.

Angelo closed the door, changed out the Nicorette gum, and waited as the two stood in the stairwell.

"You're right, I do owe you. So does the country, more than you can possibly imagine," Amanda said, then stopped, as Angelo turned and reached for the door to exit the stairwell.

"The Chinese have been smuggling nuclear weapons into the US for decades," Amanda said, and knew that she had just placed a noose around her own neck.

Angelo turned and stared at her. His right thumb and forefinger began stroking his thick moustache.

"Jesus . . . that actually makes sense. Our boy gets sloppy and winds up in a hospital after delivering whatever it was that was found down at the Torpedo Factory. Yeah, you Feds leave finger prints everywhere you go. You're not nearly as slick as you think you are," Angelo said, as Amanda's eyes widened.

"We just thought he was a killer . . . an embarrassment to the Chinese government, but he was a whole lot more. He should never have been here this long. We should have had a couple of SWAT units guarding him, not a half dozen beat cops. The cops weren't ready for a military assault. The perps were dressed as US Army. The bullet casings are 5.56 mm . . . M-16s or M-4s. The dead perp had body armor. Marshon hit him with a lucky shot in the throat. The guy bled out in seconds," Angelo said, as he sighed again and shook his head.

"Now, tell me everything or WAPO gets everything I know, including this conversation."

Amanda knew that everything she was about to say was beyond 'Top Secret'. To reveal this information could get her life in a federal prison or worse. She also knew that this man would do exactly what he had threatened to do.

"A nuclear device was found in San Francisco on March 11th. Two more were found near military bases close to Seattle soon after that. The Chinese government tried to blackmail the US into leaving the western Pacific and all of Asia. The President called their bluff and they backed down. We came real close to World War III. We're still tracking down and procuring the nukes they snuck into the country," Amanda said, as a trickle of sweat slid between her shoulder blades.

"Holy shit . . . how many?" Angelo asked, while wondering if he wanted to know the answer.

"We think around 50 . . . more or less. The Chinese government is still investigating."

"I thought you said that it was the Chinese government that was trying to blackmail us."

"They were, but we think it was a rogue general that started the whole plot decades ago. Some general named Kung."

"And our boy worked for him, one of his agents?"

"That's what we think. We're still working out all the details. We were going to move him to Walter Reed today, but they got to him first. I'm sorry. We had no idea they were going to try something," Amanda said, as Angelo turned and rested his shoulder against the cinder block stairwell.

"We're pulling all the video in the hospital. We're also pulling all video in a two-mile radius. As of right now, we don't know how many, what vehicle, or what direction. Road blocks are up, but they weren't established until after 5AM. We think this happened between 3 and 4AM. They probably came in through the loading dock. We found a custodian stashed in a storage room with his throat cut. Estimated time of death was between 3 and 4. A day shift nurse found the mess up here at 4:30. She couldn't sleep, and decided to come in a little early for turnover," Angelo said, as he opened the door and walked back into the crime scene.

Amanda stared at the closed door, then turned and began walking back down the stairwell. She had a call to make before she went back on the 5th floor.

CHAPTER 7

Inova Alexandria Hospital
4300 Seminary Road
Alexandria, Virginia
April 20, 0915 hours EST

Amanda stood on the sidewalk outside the main entrance to the hospital. Word had gotten out about a second series of murders at the hospital. Trucks from every major network were visible in the parking lot on the other side of North Howard Street. The police had set up barricades to keep the press at a distance, and the press wasn't happy. Several arguments were occurring simultaneously at the barriers. The press wanted access to the hospital and they weren't getting it.

The fog was gone. The clear sky and cool breeze promised a beautiful spring day. Amanda barely noticed. Her cell phone hung loosely in her hand, but she hadn't dialed Director Davidson yet.

"*I don't know which was worse, the smell up there or the look on his face,*" Amanda asked herself, while wiping tears from the corners of her eyes.

"This is going to be bad, really bad," she said, while auto dialing the number of Janet Davidson, her boss, and Director of the CIA Mission Center for Weapons and Counterproliferation.

"Davidson here. So what did you find out?" Janet asked, from her office in Manassas, Virginia.

"Gong Aiguo is gone. He and his friends left behind six dead police, two dead hospital staff, and one of their own. They were dressed as US Army personnel. Alexandria PD is pulling all the video from the hospital and the nearby area," Amanda said, as two black sedans pulled up outside the hospital.

Two men and two women got out. Dark suits, sunglasses . . . Amanda rolled her eyes at the stereotypical look the FBI agents presented.

"The press is all over this, and I think the FBI just rolled in. Things are going to get more complicated."

"You let me worry about that. What else do you have?"

"We have a serious problem, and you're not going to like it."

"You mean a problem other than the press, eight murders and a Chinese agent on the loose?"

"Yes, ma'am," Amanda said, and then winced. Director Davidson was a retired Marine Colonel and despised being referred to as "Ma'am".

"The Alexandria PD detective in charge of the investigation threatened to go to the Washington Post with the story about Gong . . . if I didn't tell him everything that was going on," Amanda said, and paused, waiting for the explosion.

"So how much does he know? Is this the ex-basketball pro that you told me about?"

"Yes, Director. He knew some of the details before, and has figured out a lot more. I trusted his discretion before this, but now things have changed."

"How so?"

"His younger brother was one of the officers who were killed. He was responsible for getting his brother a job as a cop. He feels guilty, and he's pissed. It was my opinion that he would definitely go public."

"Oh crap . . . and so you did what? Please tell me that you didn't tell him everything about the . . . items."

"Yes, Director . . . I did. Not every detail, but he has a general idea of what is going on. It was the only thing I could do at the time."

She was surprised at the silence . . . then alarmed at the length of the silence.

"Let the detective know that I am sorry for his loss. Ensure him that he is now an integral part of this investigation . . . on a national level. The murder of his brother, and the other officers, will not go unpunished. But . . . he needs to know that the involvement of the media will complicate the matter and impede the capture and punishment of those involved."

"Director, if I can be frank, this man smells bullshit from a mile away. If I tell him that . . . he'll laugh in my face and walk away," Amanda said, knowing that her career was in the balance.

"Then bring him into the fold. Bring him here. He'll become part of our investigation . . . privy to everything. I'll talk to him personally. Then we'll see how tough he is."

"I'll try, but I can't guarantee that he'll go along. He may just walk away."

"Well, Agent, I would suggest that you convince him that playing with us gives him the best possibility of finding his brother's murderers. Our resources are somewhat better than the Alexandria Police Department. Take some damn initiative and fix this damn mess that you've created," Janet said, and terminated the call.

Amanda stared at her phone while saying, "Well, that could have been worse. At least I still have a job."

CHAPTER 8

230 Harlless Bridge Road
Little Rock, South Carolina
April 20, 1215 hours EST

"We are almost there, Heng. Take the next exit onto Highway 57. It may be called Radford Boulevard," Jian said, as he wiped his eyes and studied the map on his cell phone.

They had been driving non-stop down Interstate 95 for the last eight hours. The adrenalin from their assault on the hospital, and subsequent escape from the area, had worn off hours ago. Both he and Heng had taken a dose of Modafinil as they left the storage unit in Alexandria.

"Here, this exit. Turn right at the stop sign. Use all your signals and obey the speed limit. We don't want some local police to pull us over," Jian said, as the truck slowed for the exit ramp.

"Yes, Mǔqīn (mother). I know how to drive. I have been obeying all the traffic laws," Heng said, while smiling at Jian.

Jian knew from training how each of his men reacted to Modafinil. Heng would say things that he would never say when not on the drug. Chonglin would get hyperactive after a day or so. Bingwen, normally very talkative, would become sullen and quiet. Jian knew that he personally, would become tense and short-tempered.

They exited 95 and drove past Jabs Fireworks, painted a bright red and yellow. Dillon Furniture Manufacturing stood on the right.

"Flat farmland with lots of pine trees. This reminds me of home," Heng said, while looking out the side window.

"Pay attention to the road. You're drifting across the center line," Jian yelled, while checking the side mirror for any following cars.

26

"Lots of farmland, but the fields are empty. I wonder when they plant? And what are these metal homes? I've never seen homes like this," Heng said, while centering the U-Haul in the right lane.

"It is where the poor live. They are called mobile homes. I don't know why. They don't have an engine and they don't seem to move once placed on the ground. This area is part of what the rich elites in this country call 'Fly Over Country'. It means that they just look down on the people that live here," Jian said, remembering his studies of the social strata that existed in the United States.

"Now slow down. The speed limit is 35. Turn right at the next intersection, Harlless Bridge Road. Turn at that building with the brick columns," Jian said, while pointing ahead.

As they made the turn, Jian placed a call on his cell phone.

"Lingli, we will be there in five minutes. Open up the barn so we can drive right in," Jian said, nodded, and turned off the phone.

"The road curves to the right up ahead. Then we cross the Little Pee Dee River," Jian began, then stopped as Heng began laughing.

"Little PD? What is a PD?" Heng asked, while continuing to laugh.

"I don't know. It's just the name of a river. Focus on your driving. We're almost there."

"Yes, Mŭqīn!"

"Slow down and take the next right. It will be a dirt road. Drive all the way to the end and pull into the barn. The door should be open."

Heng nodded while he continued to laugh and kept saying 'PD' over and over.

They drove through a thick pine and red oak forest for over a quarter mile before they reached the end of the dirt road. Jian could see the one story wood home that he had purchased through a third party. A large barn stood behind the house with a smaller storage building to the left of the barn. The dirt driveway went past the front of the house, then curved to the right and stopped at the barn. The large swinging door was being opened as they drove up.

A woman held open the door. Jian nodded in greeting as the U-Haul drove past and parked inside the barn.

"Greetings, comrade! You are all over the news," Lingli said, and shook Jian's hand as he got out of the truck.

"What do they know?" Are we safe?" Jian asked, while stretching his stiff back.

"The FBI has locked down all official information. There were reports that multiple police officers were killed while guarding a mysterious patient. The media call him 'Patient X'," Lingli said, while waving at Chonglin as he climbed out of the back of the U-Haul.

"We lost Weimin, and Renshu was shot in the hip. He's lost a lot of blood. He's on a saline IV and painkillers. We treated the wound with a clotting agent and an Israeli Bandage. Then we have 'Patient X'," Jian said, as the others began offloading the U-Haul.

"Bring them both in here," Lingli said, while walking to the other side of the barn.

The right side of the barn had been converted into an office at some point in the past. She had converted the room into a patient recovery room complete with two hospital beds and basic monitoring equipment.

"This will do. Excellent work, Lingli! I trust you have been discrete," Jian said, as he walked around the room.

It was brightly lit, with white walls. The sealed concrete floor was spotless.

"The medical equipment was bought second hand at a retirement home that was being shut down for abusing the elderly. They had an auction. I paid cash for everything. Everything else was purchased at a Home Depot in Florence. It's a few miles down 95 from where you exited. I always went at night."

"I trust that the other item is still secure?"

"The container is still locked in the other shed. I haven't touched it."

"Good! It will be quite some time before we need it," Jian said, while stepping aside as Renshu was helped into the room.

"Put him in the bed on the left. Then bring 'Patient X' in and transfer him into the other bed," Lingli said, while walking over to a large cabinet on the outside wall.

"Yes Doctor Zhang!" Jian said, while smiling and bowing deeply.

CHAPTER 9

Central Intelligence Agency
Mission Center for Weapons and Counterproliferation
Office of Director Janet Davidson
Manassas, Virginia
April 23, 1045 hours EST

"Detective Morehead, I appreciate you taking the time to come and meet with me," Janet said, while rising from behind her desk, and approaching the two individuals standing just inside the doorway.

"Agent Langford can be real persuasive. But what I want is information. According to her I have to get it from you," Angelo said, while stepping forward and shaking Janet's extended hand.

"Not a bad grip . . . for a woman," Angelo said, while holding the grip and stepping even closer to Janet.

"Twenty-three years in the Marines, two tours in Iraq, a Purple Heart and a Silver Star; I don't intimidate worth a shit, Detective," Janet said, as she stared, unblinking, up into his dark brown eyes.

"Good, neither do I . . . Director," Angelo said, as he released his grip. He had squeezed hard, very hard, and she hadn't blinked or winced. He was impressed.

"Director, I see this as a case of . . . you show me yours and I'll show you mine. The FBI has the info on this case locked up tight. Eventually, you can pry most of it out of them, but that will take lawyers and time. I know from experience that different federal agencies don't play well together, especially if you've already kept them in the dark on this . . . case."

"The FBI has a recent history of leaking information. The President couldn't risk that. So what are you offering me?" Janet said, as she withdrew her aching hand. She suspected that the man had broken something.

"Video of the perps and video of the vehicle they used to exit the hospital . . . for starters."

Janet considered his offer. *"I either include him or have him terminated,"* then decided she had no other legal alternative than to include this man.

"This story starts with a Lieutenant General Kung Yusheng of the People's Liberation Army. In 1990 he was installed as the Commanding General of 22 Base in Baoji, China. Surplus nuclear warheads are stored at the base in a complex buried deep below a mountain range. Sometime after that, Kung conceived of the idea of smuggling nuclear weapons into the United States. He diverted assets from 22 Base, and replaced older Highly Enriched Uranium with material processed in another facility in the same complex. From what we've learned, partly due to the investigations of Agent Langford, his first insertion of a nuclear device was into San Francisco, sometime in 1992. A fire at that particular location led us to other locations scattered throughout the continental US. To put it simply, Detective Morehead, the Chinese had us pretty well screwed," Janet said, while stepping even closer to Angelo.

Angelo stared into her eyes and knew that every word was the truth. Now he had to decide how far into this maze he was willing to go.

"Well Director, if they had us screwed, why are we still able to have this conversation?"

"Because your government, whatever you might think, isn't completely incompetent. Your turn."

"OK, Director, I'll play. At 0310 an ambulance backed up to the loading dock. At 0312 five men exited the vehicle. Four men were dressed in US Army green camo BDUs, armed with suppressed M4A1s, body armor, and face shields to hide their identities. The fifth man was dressed in US Army hospital whites. He was pushing an ambulance gurney. They entered the hospital through the loading dock. At approximately 0313 they met Marty Watkins, one of the night shift cleaning crew, in a hallway just inside the main hospital. He must have said something they didn't like, or they had planned to kill anyone they came across. We found his body in a storage room off the hallway. His throat had been cut. The team exited the . . ."

"Detective, I got the rest from Agent Langford. I'm very sorry about your brother."

Angelo ignored her interruption and continued, his voice becoming louder.

"At 0315 the team exited the elevator on the 5th floor. They killed the first two officers with single shots to the head. They turned left and engaged the two officers standing outside Room 501. One officer was immediately killed with a single shot to the head. The other officer ducked and returned fire. He killed one member of the assault team and wounded another while being struck four times. Then they walked up . . . and executed my brother," Angelo said, his voice rose, shaking with pent up rage.

Janet swallowed hard as Angelo's eyes welled up with tears. She had seen Marines who had lost friends in combat driven into berserker frenzy. They were almost impossible to control. They were as likely to strike out at friends as at the enemy.

"Angelo, we're on your side. That's why you're here . . . to get answers. We need your help to find the men who did this . . . the men who murdered your brother," Amanda said, while stepping between Angelo and Janet.

Angelo's massive frame was still shaking as he glanced down at the diminutive woman standing in front of him.

Janet stepped sideways, to separate herself from the detective.

Amanda placed her hands on Angelo's massive chest, and tried to guide him toward a nearby bench. She might as well have been trying to push an oak tree.

"Angelo, we all want answers. We all want to find these bastards. Just have a seat. We'll talk about what we know and what we're going to do," Amanda said, as she looked up at him and smiled.

Angelo took a deep breath, shuddered, and said, "Sorry . . . Marshon and I were close, best friends, not just brothers. I still can't believe he's gone."

Janet sat at her desk, opened the lower right hand drawer, and debated on whether to pull out her 9mm or a bottle of Laphroaig scotch whiskey. She pulled out two eight-ounce tumblers and poured two fingers in each.

"You're too young to drink this early," Janet said to Amanda, while walking around the desk and handing a glass to Angelo.

"Are you sure she's old enough to drink?" Angelo asked, while swirling the whiskey and taking a sip.

"As of last year, I think. She'll be getting carded until she's 40," Janet said, as she set the glass on her desk, and looked at the dislocated pinky finger on her right hand.

"Whiskey first," Angelo advised, while taking another sip.

"Good idea," Janet said, picked up her glass, downed it, and pulled the finger back into place.

"Sorry about the finger."

"I've had worse. My Purple Heart was from an IED. A sliver of Hummer door frame went through my right forearm. I could have used some whiskey when I pulled that out," Janet said, while returning to her chair.

"Everything we got was from video. The loading dock was covered, and parts of the hospital corridors, including the elevators," Angelo said, while sipping from his glass.

"This is a whole lot better than the stuff I drink. What is it?"

"10-year-old Laphroaig scotch," Janet said, while pouring another finger into her glass.

"Funny. One of my grandfathers was Scottish. Grandpa Jack used to refer to me and my brother as smoked Scotch. He was a good man, but he could be an asshole sometimes," Angelo said, while swirling the rich liquid and breathing in the aroma.

"They left the loading dock at 0315. The fog outside was as thick as pea soup. I learned that phrase from Grandpa Jack. They left the parking lot, and turned right on North Howard and disappeared. We're still pulling video from every camera in that area," Angelo said, while draining his glass.

"Now that's the way to start your day. Your turn, Director, and don't try bullshitting me or that ambulance will stay in the fog," Angelo said, as he reached over and sat the empty glass on Janet's desk.

"Another?"

"No thanks. Start talking," Angelo replied, turned to Amanda and winked.

Amanda understood the game. She had played mental chess with Detective Morehead before. She just hoped that her boss remembered the story.

The whiskey was numbing the pain in Janet's hand. The dislocated finger was only part of it. She could feel something grinding in the hand as she flexed it under the desk.

32

"When Amanda first started working for me, I gave her an analysis to perform. We had some indications that the Chinese had manufactured more HEU than we had estimated, but we didn't have enough data to prove it. As it turned out we had enough data, we just weren't putting all the pieces together properly. Amanda reanalyzed the data and concluded that the Chinese had enough material to manufacture 40-60 more fission devices than we thought they could."

"So, you started all this shit?" Angelo asked, while staring at Amanda.

"No, they started all this shit. I just figured it out," Amanda said, while returning Angelo's stare.

"Amanda told me that you figured out what was going on in San Francisco."

"I'm from the area, I played ball at USF, my mom still lives there . . ." Angelo said, then paused, as he remembered the look on his mother's face when he had Skyped her and told her what had happened to her youngest child.

"I knew it was something serious. I've got connections in the SFPD. I knew the chemical hazard story at a Chinese restaurant was bull. The federal reaction was too strong. It stopped just short of martial law. The Feds wouldn't do that unless it was something big. I figured it was a dirty bomb, but then I heard that the response was quietly expanding to the whole West Coast. Then our Chinese Special Forces boy showed up at Inova and tapped a bunch of folks. Then your girl comes and talks to me. Then the Feds pull a mini-San Francisco shutdown at the Torpedo Factory in Alexandria. Then it all went away. The only thing left was our friend under guard while recovering from getting his ass shot up by Amanda's boyfriend."

"He is not, and never has been, my boyfriend!"

"That's not what I heard from our SWAT Team. I heard he was ready to put down the Chinese agent in that restaurant, until you talked him down. As I remember, he was married to one of the nurses who were murdered at Inova. I'd have shot the son of a bitch myself, if I was him."

"All I did was keep him from committing suicide. Your team would have killed him if he fired again. I was standing right beside him," Amanda said, as a memory of the event flashed through her mind.

"Still, it takes a pretty strong connection to stop that much anger."

"Kind of like the mood you were in when you walked in here."

"Yeah, I get it. I bet the guy's big, a hardass like me. It's a Beauty and the Beast thing. I had to take my girls to that damn movie three times. They just loved it. They were calling me 'Daddy Beast' for weeks. So what's your 'not the boyfriend' up to? Have you recruited him as part of this crew?"

"No, he's moved on. The Army transferred him. He's down at Fort Bragg, in North Carolina."

"So, Director, did you find all the nukes?"

"That's classified!"

"The fog's getting thicker in here."

Janet considered her options, and then said, "As I said earlier, the President and the General Secretary of the PRC reached an agreement on this matter. China provided a detailed list of the devices and their locations. We were able to retrieve all of the devices."

"You're good, very good. You don't have a 'tell'. I'd hate to play poker with you. But her, she fidgets and looks down when she's telling a lie, or, in this case, when she hears one," Angelo said, while glancing over at Amanda.

"You're short one, maybe more," Angelo said, locking eyes with Janet.

"Just one. It was located just outside Fort Benning, in Georgia. We're still trying to figure out how that happened. If we find out that the Chinese government notified one of Kung's agents inside the US, there's going to be a serious problem," Janet said, and gave Angelo a look that told him that he was pushing his luck.

"So why bust our boy out of the hospital? Why take the risk?" Angelo asked.

"That's a damn good question," Janet replied.

CHAPTER 10

230 Harlless Bridge Road
Little Rock, South Carolina
April 30, 0930 hours EST

"Good morning, Aiguo. How did you sleep?" Lingli asked.

"Fine, but I need to get out of this bed. My body is turning to butter."

"She is beautiful. She reminds me of Meili," Aiguo thought, as the doctor began removing bandages from the right side of his chest.

"This has healed sufficiently. It needs to be exposed to the air. We'll start stretching exercises tomorrow. At first it will hurt to move, and you will have little strength."

"How about my leg? When can the rods be removed? I need to get back on my feet."

"The surgeons did a fine job repairing the femur. My x-rays show perfect alignment. The procedure was unusual in that it was a combination surgery. The bullet cracked the femur and left one large fragment. They aligned the bones and attached the large fragment with a small plate and screws. Then they used external fixation to lock everything into place and allow it to heal. I should be able to remove the external screws in a few days. Then you need to get back on your feet. A little stress will help in the healing process," Lingli said, as she finished removing the chest bandages.

"Another fine surgical job. The bullet punctured your lung on both sides, but just nicked one rib. You were lucky. This wound alone could have killed you," Lingli said, while examining the wound site.

"Lucky? I don't feel very lucky. I need to talk to Jian. Are he and the others still here?"

Lingli handed him two pills and a glass of water.

"Here, take these antibiotics and a pain killer, and yes, they are all here. They're in the midst of planning," Lingli said, while taking the glass and turning to leave.

"Planning? Planning what?"

"You need to talk to Jian. You're alert today. I'll let him know he can come for a visit," Lingli said, while removing her surgical gloves.

Aiguo watched her walk away and again was reminded of Meili. He tried to lift his right arm, and grimaced at the pain. The pain reminded him of the American who had almost killed him.

"I was careless. If I hadn't been looking at a picture of Meili on my cell phone, I would have noticed him. A man that big is hard to miss," Aiguo said, then laughed at his own joke.

"I did hit him, but the plastic gun, the Kel-Tec, couldn't stop him. It was a good assassin's weapon, but not suited for a gun fight," Aiguo said, while closing his eyes and remembering the sensation as he sat in the back of the narrow restaurant near the Torpedo Factory.

"I glanced up when I heard a floor board creak. He was 30 feet away. The .45 was leveled and pointed at my head. If he had shot before I looked up, I wouldn't be here. He wanted me to see his face. He wanted that personal contact," Aiguo said, remembering the end of the fight, remembering the man's words as he stuck the barrel of the .45 in his face.

"I killed his wife . . . one of the nurses," Aiguo said, while lifting his right arm and swinging it in a circle. The pain helped him focus, helped him purge the memory of the man's hate-filled face from his mind.

"What is the American term? Collateral damage? That's all she was . . . collateral damage," Aiguo told himself, as he lowered his arm, closed his eyes and drifted back to sleep.

. . . .

The House
1000 hours EST

"Renshu, why didn't you come by this morning? I told you I wanted to look at your wound," Lingli asked, as she served herself a bowl of salty wheat noodles and approached the common table for breakfast.

As she sat down, she reached over and grabbed an egg-filled steamed bun from a bowl in the center of the round table.

"The wound is fine. It is almost healed," Renshu replied from the other side of the table.

"Still, I want to see the wound."

"OK, here is the wound," Renshu said, while standing and dropping his pants.

"Wah! Renshu, you're a pig. Pull you pants up before I lose my breakfast," Heng said, while turning away.

Bingwen and Chonglin both started laughing.

"You're right. It seems to be healed," Lingli said, after glancing at the naked man's wound site, while eating her noodles.

"Renshu, pull up your pants. Quit acting the fool," Jian said, while studying an image on his IPad.

"Jian, what are we doing here? What are your plans for us?" Renshu asked, while pulling up his pants.

"We are still on mission. Try to act like a professional," Jian said, staring Renshu into silence.

"Jian, we all want to know. You told us before we rescued the Lieutenant that you would tell us the long-term goal after we got him. Well, he's here. What is the plan?" Heng asked.

"*I don't have to tell them anything. They will do as I order. That is our way. But they should know. They need to understand, not just obey,*" Jian told himself, while considering his options.

"All right, I'll tell you everything I know, including why we are here," Jian said, pausing to make sure he had their attention.

"When you were sent to the US, each of you was given a new identity. Each of you was assigned to act as a minder of a certain family and their . . . property. You weren't told why, because you didn't need to know. We have all been trained, that as Special Forces operators, we are to obey the orders of our superiors . . . period. And that is what all of you have done. I pulled you away from your assignments for a specific reason. We were all part of a plan developed by Lieutenant General Kung Yusheng. He was the commander of 22 Base," Jian began, then paused, as they all stopped eating and stared at him.

"*That got their attention. They all know what's located at 22 Base,*" Jian thought, then continued.

"Decades ago General Kung devised a plan to insert multiple nuclear devices into the United States. He was a devoted follower of the principles of Sun Tzu. He knew that a direct confrontation with the United States was suicidal. He felt that these weapons would give China the leverage it needed to remove American influence from Asia," Jian began. The room was silent. Even Renshu had stopped fidgeting.

"I was assigned to oversee our devices in the southeast US. I had 21 devices in my responsibility. There are many large military bases in this part of the country. Each was targeted with at least one nuke. We had five agents inside the US at my level. I had more devices than any other agent. Each of us was assigned to oversee a different section of the country. My West Coast counterpart informed me of a problem before he was captured. One of his devices in San Francisco was discovered, and the whole program began to unravel. There was a confrontation between our government and the Americans. I don't know the details, but for some reason our government kowtowed to the Americans. General Kung was executed, and we were given up as part of the deal. I pulled Heng and the rest of you from your assignments, and had you remove the device that Heng was monitoring. It was the least vulnerable, and the easiest to remove. Now we have one device still under our control. The last device is located in the crate inside the locked outbuilding beside the barn," Jian said, pausing once again, as he gauged the impact of his words on each individual sitting around the table.

"Why didn't you pull everyone in your area if you knew the Americans were coming after us?" Heng asked.

"I tried. Some of them were already captured or killed, but more on them later. We were all part of General Kung's great plan in some way. We all thought that we were here on assignment with the blessings of the leaders of the People's Republic of China. Well, our supposed leaders have betrayed the nation and the people of China. Our government has told the Americans the location and identity of every one of Kung's agents in this country. If we are captured, the Americans will squeeze every bit of information they can out of us. Then they will return us to China, where we will be summarily executed, if we're lucky."

"You still haven't said why we are here; other than the fact that we have nowhere to go. What is our mission now?" Heng asked.

"We are going to complete the mission that General Kung gave us. He wanted to bring the United States of America to its knees . . . to make them kowtow to us . . . to the people of China."

"But our government? We should obey them, even at the cost of our lives," Bingwen said.

"I am the senior agent left in this country. I can order your obedience or shoot you if you disobey, but I won't do that. We are past such things. If we go on, we go on together. All of us must agree to continue with the mission, or we separate and finish our lives as each of us sees fit."

The screen door swung open. Lieutenant Gong Aiguo stood in the doorway, silhouetted by the mid-morning sun.

"Are you insane? What are you doing out of bed?" Lingli said, while jumping up from the table.

"My chest is healed. I need you to remove these damn rods from my leg," Aiguo said, while hobbling into the room. The screen door slammed shut behind him, with that unique sound that only a screen door can make.

"The femur will not be completely healed for months. You need to be back in bed," Lingli said, as she rushed over to his side.

"Enough, Doctor! You said that the surgeons had done an excellent job, and that they had attached a plate inside to fix the bones in place. I want these rods out now," Aiguo said, as he pushed her aside and headed for a sofa on the other side of the room.

"While the doctor is removing the rods, I want to talk to Jian and the others. I stood outside and overheard most of your conversation. Jian is correct. We have been abandoned by our government. Before I was wounded, I was in touch with my grandfather, Colonel Peng Zihao, General Kung's adjutant. He told me about San Francisco. He also told me that my mission was a failure. After the Americans had captured me, and I had recovered from surgery, they started to interrogate me while I was in the hospital. They were going to move me the day that you arrived to rescue me. For that, I am truly grateful," Aiguo said, while looking at each person, and bowing his head.

"They were going to take you to Walter Reed. It is more like a military base than a hospital. We would never have been able to get you out of there. That night was our only chance," Jian said.

"The nurse, what happened to him? He was one of your agents?" Aiguo asked.

"He did not make it. He was killed during the assault," Jian said, while glancing at Chonglin.

"Chonglin, what are you carving now?" Jian asked, distracted by the scratching sound of a knife carving into the table top.

"Ahh, don't mind him. He just does it to occupy his mind," Bingwen said, while slapping Chonglin in the arm.

Chonglin scowled, but returned his knife to the sheath on his waist.

"The rods, Doctor," Aiguo said, staring at Lingli.

"If you insist. But it will be done the right way, not here. Help him back to the surgery," Lingli ordered, while pointing at Chonglin and Bingwen, by far the largest and strongest individuals in the group.

Jian nodded, and the two men began to help Aiguo back to the surgery.

"Jian, please walk with me. We have much to discuss," Aiguo said, as he was helped back to the surgery.

CHAPTER 11

Central Intelligence Agency
Mission Center for Weapons and Counterproliferation
Office of Amanda Langford
Manassas, Virginia
April 30, 0945 hours EST

"Daddy, I can't believe that you and Momma are thinking about selling the farm. You've lived there for over 30 years," Amanda said, her cell phone in one hand as she sat behind her office desk.

"Almost 40 years, Amanda, and our bodies are telling both of us that it's time to move on. The population in Wake County is exploding, and we've been fending off developers for years. We just got an offer that may be too good to refuse," Will Langford said.

"But what will you do? Where will you go?" Amanda asked, as another call came in on her cell. The face of Detective Morehead popped up.

"Well, we haven't decided yet if we're going to take the offer or not, but we're leaning that way. As far as where we'd live, well, we're both natives of North Carolina, so I doubt we'll leave the state," Will said.

"Daddy, I've got to go. It's a call I've got to answer, but I'll try to call tonight. I love you both," Amanda said, as she terminated the call.

"Detective Morehead, I haven't heard from you in a while," Amanda said, as she answered the call.

"I said I'd be back when I had something. Meet me in Alexandria at the corner of South Pickett and Osprey in an hour. I think we found the ambulance."

"How did you find it?"

"Just get here. I hate talking on these things."

"I'll be there," Amanda said, and hung up.
After texting her boss, she was out the door.

CHAPTER 12

Public Storage Unit 62
401 South Pickett Street
Alexandria, Virginia
April 30, 1115 hours EST

"So, what led the police to this place?" Amanda asked, as she and Angelo walked up the driveway leading into the Public Storage facility.

Angelo stopped, and pointed across the street.

"See the three power poles beside the back entrance into the Home Depot? There's a pole right beside the entrance. That's a security camera mounted on top. It was installed to cover the back of the store, where everything is delivered. It also rotates to cover the road and the exit. At approximately 0410 on April 20th a white ambulance was recorded pulling into this driveway. The fog was thick as hell, but the guy hit his brake lights as he pulled in. All you could see were the tail lights and the word 'ambulance'," Angelo said, as the two continued to walk up the curved driveway.

"We've been here about an hour, and we're ready to enter one of the units."

"Why do you think it's this particular unit?" Amanda asked, while walking beside Detective Morehead.

"We don't know for sure if it's this unit, but the dogs are mighty interested."

The alley between the two long rows of storage units was filled with police cars, equipment and people. South Pickett Street had been blocked off for two blocks in each direction, much to the frustration of the assembled media. The second set of mass murders in the same hospital, combined with the strange incident at the Torpedo Factory, had left the whole DC Metropolitan area on edge. Rumors of chemical weapons, dirty bombs and terrorists were openly discussed on the local news programs and newspapers.

"So why not cut it open?" Amanda asked, as they reached the unit.

"Waiting on a call about a court order."

"Court order? Don't the dogs give you probable cause?"

"Yeah, but my boss isn't taking any chances on screwing this case up when it goes to court. Just like you, I've got a boss I have to answer to," Angelo said, as his cell phone began to ring.

"That's a different ring," Amanda said, as Angelo removed the cell phone from his coat pocket.

"Miles Davis . . . 'All Blues'. He was the best. 'The sea, the sky, the you and I. The sea, the sky, for you and I. I'll know we're all blues, all shades, all hues, all blues.' The man was a genius," Angelo said, while reading the text message.

"Cut it open. We got the warrant," Angelo said, to the officer standing beside him.

"Everyone, back away," the officer yelled, as a SWAT Team stepped forward and faced the rollup door.

Angelo and Amanda retreated behind a van and watched as the first member of the SWAT Team removed the large padlock with bolt cutters. The SWAT team crouched behind two officers carrying transparent polycarbonate shields, then walked as a unit toward the door. One officer reached between the shields and grabbed the bottom of the door.

"Ready, pull," the officer shouted, as he pulled the door up.

The back of an ambulance was clearly visible on the right side of the double unit.

As the door rose up, the officer yelled, "Secure the area."

After verifying that no personnel were in the storage room, a dog handler entered with a large male German Shepard. Five minutes later the handler exited with the dog and shook his head.

"Man, I can smell the bleach out here. No wonder the dogs were going off. This is the part I hate. Now I have to squeeze my big ass into 3XL paper coveralls to get in there," Angelo said, as other officers began roping off entry into the storage unit.

"I've got the opposite problem. I flop around in a small set like I'm wearing a sack . . . if they have any smalls," Amanda said, as they walked over to the back of the Forensics van.

44

"I'm surprised they didn't booby trap the unit," Amanda said, while sitting in a folding chair and slipping on her white paper booties.

"They just wanted to get out of the area. This was an assault with a specific objective. These guys aren't terrorists, they're soldiers. They just wanted to grab their boy and exit the area," Angelo said, while struggling to pull the white paper coveralls over his right shoulder.

"Damn, I feel like a stuffed sausage," Angelo said, as he finally squeezed into the papers.

Amanda snickered while looking at him.

"Can you even walk?"

"Yeah, but I can't bend over. I'd blow out the backside for sure."

"Mind helping me with the booties?" Angelo asked, while leaning against the van and raising one foot.

"Your shoes are as long as my arm," Amanda said, as she stared at the raised shoe.

"Spare me the comments and just put them on."

As they walked into the unit, a bespectacled older man walked up to Angelo and said, "Remember the rules, Detective Morehead. Keep your hands to yourself. That goes for you too, young lady."

"Meet Doctor Wilton Janson, Head of Forensics for the City of Alexandria. Doctor, this is Amanda Langford, CIA."

"Nice to meet you, Doctor Janson," Amanda said, while reaching out to shake his hand.

He looked at her as if she had just dipped her hands in excrement.

"Oh, sorry," Amanda said, while withdrawing her hand.

"A Southerner. You don't hear that accent in this area very often anymore. I've read that it is slowly becoming extinct. Yours isn't deep South, not that pronounced, not enough drawl. My guess is the Carolinas, probably North Carolina, but not Eastern, not the mountains. They are both quite distinctive, which leaves the Piedmont," Doctor Janson said, while staring at Amanda like she was a specimen under a slide.

"I'm sorry, that was rude, but linguistics is part of my trade . . . more like a hobby. I speak 15 languages fluently, a smattering of another 30," Doctor Janson said, while turning away as if he had lost his interest in the specimen.

"He's known for his winning personality," Angelo said, as Amanda looked up at him, the irritation obvious.

"He's also the best forensic scientist and profiler on the East Coast. His wife is buried over in Ivy Hill Cemetery, off King Street. She died six years ago, and he won't leave the area. A couple of years back, I was in a meeting with him and our Chief of Police. The Doc looked at his watch, got up and walked out. Didn't say a word to either of us. He goes to his wife's grave every Wednesday at precisely 11:15. That's the day and time that she died. I think it almost killed him. They had been married for over 30 years. His work and his studies keep him going. I think he's also an adjunct professor at American University. He has a lot of energy for an old dude," Angelo said, while walking up to the back of the ambulance.

The door had been opened. One of Doctor Janson's assistants was slowly working her way through the rear compartment, cataloguing and photographing everything she found.

"Anything interesting?" Amanda asked, the young woman in the back of the ambulance.

"Can you smell?" the woman asked, turning to stare at Amanda. Her face was a pale white with no makeup. Her thin lips looked as if they would crack if she ever smiled.

"Claire, this is Amanda Langford, CIA." Angelo said.

"Whatever," Claire said, returning to her work.

"Claire is the daughter of Doctor Janson."

"And that's 'Doctor' Claire Janson, Detective Morehead," Claire said, while photographing a wad of gum stuck to the side of the bench on the right side.

"If this is fresh, we may have something. Most gum starts to solidify in 72 hours. Within two weeks, it's firm. Fossilization occurs in a month to six weeks, depending on temperature and humidity. Yes, this is fairly fresh. I'd say less than a week. Damn, I need the temperature and humidity in here with the doors secured. I see an article in the Journal of Forensic Sciences in my near future," Claire said, as she used a scalpel to scrape the gum into a plastic sample container.

"So you think you'll be able to get DNA from the gum?" Amanda asked.

"Of course! If not, why would I bother?"

"Is her father like this?' Amanda whispered, as she and Angelo walked away.

"Worse. Much worse. We are intruders who are barely tolerated in their world. But the results they get, and their ability to withstand vicious cross examination in the courtroom . . . absolutely amazing!"

Amanda's eyes wandered to the far wall as they walked across the double storage unit. At first she saw oil on the concrete from a leaking vehicle. Then, while circling the oil spill, she glanced at the surface of the workbench built onto the side of the storage unit.

"Angelo, look at this, scratched into the paint," she said, while walking up to the workbench.

Angelo followed her and stopped, glancing over her shoulder at the strange scratching.

"Looks like Chinese," Angelo said.

"It is. That's the character for 'Tiger'. It's pronounced . . . Hŭ, like the sound an owl makes," Amanda said, while taking out her cell phone and taking a picture.

"To me, it's a gang sign. Like . . . we were here, screw you!"

"You mean like a marker, a calling card?"

"Exactly! This is arrogant and sloppy. Everything else is precise, professional. These guys are Special Forces. I don't get it," Angelo said, while turning and continuing his inspection of the storage area.

"I think they have a problem. They have an outlier who likes to do things his way," Amanda said, while continuing to stare at the character carved into the surface.

"Sounds like you're starting to develop a profile for this guy."

"Gotta start somewhere," Amanda said, looking at the character one last time, and then turning away.

"Hey, Wilton! What have you got? My girl found a clue and you haven't got shit," Angelo said, while walking up to Doctor Janson.

"What, the tiger scratching? It's already catalogued. There's another one in the back of the ambulance," Wilton replied, as he removed a hair from the mat on the driver's side of the ambulance.

"The inside was wiped down and sprayed with bleach, but they should have used a vacuum cleaner. We retrieved one finger print from the inside of the glove box, a wad of gum, and now, a hair; and we're just getting started. Now, if you two would leave and quit fiddling with my crime scene, things might progress more quickly," Wilton said, while waving his hand for them to leave.

Amanda began to respond, but found herself being guided to the exit by Angelo's huge arm.

"That man is an ass, and his daughter is no better," Amanda said, as they were removing their outer clothing.

"Yeah, but in 48 hours they'll produce a report that will give us more insight into these people than you can possibly imagine," Angelo said, while bending over and ripping the suit.

"I'm still thinking about the Tiger. He carved the character on a table top and in the ambulance. To me that looks like compulsive behavior," Amanda said.

"Trust me. Walter will include that as part of his report. That pair doesn't miss anything."

"Did the camera at Home Depot show them exiting?" Amanda asked, straightening her suit.

"We weren't that lucky. It rotates on a 90-second cycle. They left while the camera was pointed away."

"Other cameras? There couldn't have been that much traffic on this road at four in the morning."

"We're still looking, but so far, nothing."

"If we can't find a picture of the vehicle, then they've won. They'll disappear into the country," Amanda said, as they reached the base of the driveway leading up to the storage units.

"They had a guy on a gurney. They couldn't transport him in a sedan. It had to be another truck or a van. We'll find them. I'll contact you if anything new comes up," Angelo said, as he nodded and turned away, heading back to the storage units.

Amanda heard an argument in the distance, and saw a woman in a running outfit being restrained at one of the barricades.

"Listen, I don't care if this is your normal route. Today you're going to have to go run someplace else," an officer told the woman.

"Runners! That's it! Rain or shine . . . or fog, they're going on their run. It's like a religion for some people," Amanda said, as she removed her cell phone and began texting Angelo.

CHAPTER 13

230 Harlless Bridge Road
Little Rock, South Carolina
May 5, 0930 hours EST

"I can't believe that he can walk on that leg," Jian said, while standing beside Lingli.

Aiguo had just completed his fourth lap around the barn. The team had cleared and leveled the ground to minimize the chance of him tripping and falling.

"The doctors had to slice his thigh from the hip to the knee to repair the femur. The rectus femoris, the large muscle above the knee, was punctured by the bullet. Several other muscle groups and ligaments were damaged by bone and bullet fragments. Both legs have atrophied, but are healing. If he can take the pain, this will help. Physical therapy will speed up his recovery."

"If you think this is impressive, you should see his routine in the gym," Heng said, while crunching on an apple.

"Oh, didn't you know? Chonglin and Bingwen have set up a gym of sorts inside the barn. They said they were bored and getting soft," Heng said, as Aiguo came around the side of the barn and stopping, bent over, and threw up.

"I hate this weakness," Aiguo said, as Lingli ran over to him.

"The exercise is good for you; but if you tear something, you'll just set back your recovery. That's enough for today, Doctor's orders," Lingli said, as she handed her water bottle to Aiguo.

"She's right, you know. Let your legs recover. Come in and we'll work on your upper body," Chonglin said, appearing at the entrance to the barn. He was stripped to the waist, his muscled torso glistening with sweat.

Aiguo nodded, drained the water, and limped toward the barn.

"There are parts of plows and other farm implements in the barn. They use them as weights. There are also horizontal poles that the farmers must have used to hang things, perfect for pullups," Heng said, while mimicking Chonglin's heavily muscled physique.

"It's good for the Lieutenant to be around his old team again. After he left for 22 Base, we never thought we'd see him again. He wasn't happy about the transfer out of the 'Tigers', but he knew it was his duty," Jian said, as he and the doctor stood in the warm sun.

"How did you wind up here? It seems a strange assignment for Special Forces," Lingli asked.

"A year after the Lieutenant was reassigned, so were we. We didn't know it at the time, but we were all part of General Kung's plan. He had a special connection with the Siberian Tigers. All of his agents were recruited from our ranks."

"If Kung has been executed and discredited, where does that leave the Tigers?"

"I don't know for sure, but I'm sure that there were changes made in the leadership cadre. They may have joined General Kung and his ancestors."

"I was not a Tiger. I was recruited from the Female Special Operations Company. As American women became more involved in combat operations in the Middle East, I think our government felt challenged to reply. So they created us. They would not dignify us with a proper unit name. We were given silly names like 'Advanced Company of Overall Construction at the Grassroots Level' and 'Female Civilization Post', whatever that means."

"But you are a doctor. How did you wind up there?"

"Ninety percent of us had degrees. There were other doctors and PhD's, a few engineers, mathematicians, nurses. It was a fine group. They recruited me from the 301 Hospital in Beijing. I was trained as a trauma surgeon. I was not the best, only in the middle of my class, but I am still a very good surgeon," Lingli said, while looking at her hands.

"And now you are standing outside a barn in America, associating with agents of a failed General."

"It was my choice. Just like you, I was recruited by General Kung. This safe house was established to support the medical needs of any agents who required medical assistance. I suppose that there are other sites like this, but I don't know for sure."

"Probably so, I only know the heads of the other regions. I don't know the details of their areas. I have the team here and one other," Jian casually replied.

"Another team? You have said nothing about another team."

"Habit, Doctor . . . compartmentalization is the American term for it."

"Where are they? Are they coming here?"

"The reason I am telling you, is that they are coming here today. Our true mission continues, and I need all of the remaining agents for us to succeed," Jian said, while glancing at the position of the sun.

"They should arrive late tonight. We have to make room for six more," Jian said, as he started walking toward the barn to tell the others.

CHAPTER 14

230 Harlless Bridge Road
Little Rock, South Carolina
May 5, 2145 hours EST

The driver and the passenger in the front seat exchanged nervous glances as the brown truck turned onto the unpaved driveway.

"Are you sure this is the place?" Chong Yunru asked, while pausing just off the pavement.

"Positive, look at the oak tree on the right side of the road," Guan Xing replied, as he opened his window and shined a flashlight at two ribbons hanging from the lowest tree branch. One ribbon was yellow, the other red.

"That's the sign. Have you met this Wang Jian before?" Yunru asked, and began heading down the drive.

"No, he was in a different unit back in China. I do remember his name, though. He was a Sergeant Major First Class and had a reputation as an excellent soldier and leader. Like us, he is a Siberian Tiger. He is our leader now, and has summoned us all here for a reason. We'll find out why when he sees fit," Xing said.

. . . .

The House
2150 hours EST

"I hear a vehicle coming down the road," Bingwen said, sticking his head inside the front door of the farm house.

Everyone rose from their seats and walked outside to the porch. The night was warm. The tree frogs and crickets were holding a non-stop conversation. The cicadas chimed in at regular intervals. A waxing moon cast dark shadows from the surrounding trees. The headlights from the truck could be seen winding down the dirt road toward the house.

Jian gestured with his hand. Chonglin and Bingwen slipped off the porch and into the shadows. Both were armed with automatic assault weapons.

The brown truck pulled up to the front of the house, turned off the lights, and silenced the engine. A man on the passenger side opened the door and stepped out. The interior light did not come on.

Jian stepped forward from the porch and greeted the man from the brown truck.

"Zuòwéi yī zhǐ lǎohǔ huó dé gèng hǎo yī nián (Better to live one year as a tiger) . . ." Jian said, in Mandarin.

". . . Bǐ miányáng hái yào zhǎng dá yībǎi nián (. . . than a hundred years as a sheep)," Xing replied.

"Greetings, brother tiger," Jian said, as the two men shook hands.

The van and the porch both emptied at the same time. Chonglin and Bingwen secured their weapons, and stepped out from the shadows on either side of the porch. Greetings, handshakes, and bows abounded as the reunited Siberian Tigers walked into the farmhouse, deep in the South Carolina countryside.

Doctor Zhang Lingli stood to the side, alone, as a sense of dread crept up her spine.

CHAPTER 15

Central Intelligence Agency
Mission Center for Weapons and Counterproliferation
3rd Floor Meeting Room
Manassas, Virginia
May 6, 1000 hours EST

"Ladies, gentlemen, we have one remaining problem," Director Janet Davidson said, while pacing at the head of the long walnut table.

"As most of you are aware, during the last six months, we, along with significant help from our brothers and sisters in Homeland Security, have secured 49 nuclear devices smuggled into the United States. Based on information reluctantly provided by the People's Republic of China, there is one remaining device. Agent Langford, if you would, please provide an update on where we stand with the last device."

"Based on the information provided by our Chinese 'friends', the one remaining device is a Chinese Type 6 weapon dating from the early 70's. It was designed to be dropped from a bomber, but was stripped of its fins and modified. The outer shell was removed, and anti-tampering devices and a remote controlled trigger were added. It should be identical to the original device that was found in San Francisco. That device was disarmed by a contract company working for the Department of Energy. That puts it in the 30-40 kiloton range. To put that into context, the Hiroshima device had a yield of 16 kilotons. For example, if a weapon of this size was detonated in Alexandria, Virginia, the impact on the Mid-Atlantic States would be devastating," Amanda said, as she brought up a map of the eastern United States on a large screen located behind her. She then keyed in some data and pressed enter.

"As you can see, the immediate deaths would be approximately 11,000. Another 20,000 would be severely injured and would probably die within 24 hours. That's just from the initial effects of the blast, the ionizing radiation and thermal effects. The greater impact would be from the fallout. Within about eight hours, residents of Washington and Baltimore would be exposed to levels of ionizing radiation that would quickly be fatal, approximately 100 Rem per hour. Those areas would be uninhabitable for decades. This software only shows fallout areas exceeding 1 Rem per hour. The effects of the plume would extend all the way up to Maine. The entire Northeast would be contaminated to some extent. The panic would be incredible. The economic impact . . . ," Amanda said, and then paused, letting the significance of the one remaining missing device sink in.

"Personally and professionally, I find this whole thing appalling. The Federal Bureau of Investigation has been intentionally left out of the loop during this entire event. The fact that I am just now being briefed on an event of such national . . ." Assistant Director James Allen, of the FBI's Weapons of Mass Destruction Directorate, began.

"Spare me the theatrics, Director Allen. The FBI has become a sieve. To be blunt . . . you couldn't be trusted with the information," Janet said, tiring of his tirade.

"Who couldn't trust us? You?"

"No, the President," Janet said, then smiled.

"I don't believe it! Clarisse, is this true?" James asked Clarisse Beaumont, the National Security Advisor, who sat across the table from him.

"Yes, James, it's true. The President felt that the FBI could not be trusted to keep this information from the press. The only reason you're sitting here now is the latest event at the hospital in Alexandria. Your agents on the ground were quick enough to gain classified information before we could shut the whole thing down."

"Well, good for them. This should be out in the open, at least within the Federal government."

"James, the Chinese were blackmailing the United States. They threatened to go to the press with information about the 50 nuclear weapons they had smuggled into our country. Even you must be able to imagine the impact that information would have had if it had become available to the general public. The markets would have crashed, and there would have been a national panic. The country would have become ungovernable. This was way beyond 'Need to Know'," Clarisse said.

"I am in charge of the FBI's Weapons of Mass Destruction Directorate. I have 35,000 people that report to me. I needed to know!" James said, while standing up and slamming his fist onto the table.

"Well . . . you know now. If the FBI wishes to discuss it with the President, feel free. The FBI has gone through three Directors in the last 18 months. I suppose a new Assistant Director of WMD could be arranged."

"Are you threatening me?"

"No, I'm telling you that if the information you are now privy to leaks, it will endanger the nation. The individual or individuals responsible for the leak will disappear into federal detention for an extended stay. As of today, there have been no leaks during this entire event," Clarisse said, upping the ante from an implied threat to a direct one.

Assistant Director Allen sat down. Clarisse nodded at Janet to continue. She nodded at Amanda.

"As I said, the Chinese provided a file containing all the locations of the devices and the individuals involved. This particular device was stored behind a restaurant named the Fusion, three miles southwest of Fort Benning, in Fort Mitchell, Alabama. The odd thing about this location was the age of the restaurant. The restaurant is only one year old. Every other location used to store one of these devices had been in place for a decade or longer. The only thing I can surmise are the changes initiated at Fort Benning as part of the base consolidation process initiated back in 2005 and completed in 2011. The Armor School was moved there from Fort Knox, and the Maneuver Center of Excellence was established. This translates as more troops and more senior leadership in one location. The Fusion restaurant was a perfect place for a device. The initial blast would take out South Fort Benning, and the plume from the fallout would have swept across the remainder of the base, rendering it inoperable and killing thousands of combat troops and their families." Amanda said.

"So where is the device now?" James asked.

"The family that owned the restaurant was found dead inside their home. The home had been burned down. Local fire investigators determined that the fire had been set. Autopsies verified that the family had been murdered. Their throats were cut. Homeland verified the analyses," said Assistant Secretary Max Lopez, of the Countering Weapons of Mass Destruction Office of Homeland Security.

"You have no clue where the weapon is, do you?" James asked, while looking around the table.

"At this time . . . no. We think that the assault on the hospital in Alexandria to rescue the Chinese agent is related to the disappearance of the final nuclear weapon. We're hoping that if we can find him, we'll find the device. We're following leads at this time," Janet said.

"The only significant thing you said was, 'At this time, no,' the rest was smoke. Who in the Senate and the House of Representatives knows about this?" James asked.

"The President has had private discussions with the Speaker of the House and the Majority Leader in the Senate," Clarisse said.

"So . . . the vast majority of the federal officials duly elected by the people of this nation have no idea what's going on. This is treasonous . . ." James began.

Amanda's phone began to vibrate and slide across the table top. Glancing down at the phone, she saw that a text had come in from Detective Morehead. After reading the text, she looked up and saw that the argument was once again flowing back and forth across the table.

"We've had a breakthrough," she said, but was ignored as the debate escalated.

Amanda reached down and dug her nails into Janet's arm. Her boss, deep into the argument, glared up at her.

"Director, we've had a breakthrough!"

"A serious one?" Janet asked, while removing Amanda's hand from her arm.

"Yes, ma'am. Detective Morehead found an eye witness who saw the truck after it left the storage facility."

Janet stood, then bellowed in a voice that had terrified Marine recruits for almost a decade, "All right people, listen up!"

The room, filled with self-important people who were not used to being shouted at, grew silent.

"We have had a breakthrough. Local police in Alexandria have been following leads in the hospital murders. We knew that the assailants escaped from the hospital in an ambulance and went to a nearby storage facility. We assumed it was to switch vehicles, but due to the early morning hours and the dense fog that blanketed the area, we had no idea what type of vehicle they were driving. Now we do. Agent Langford . . ." Janet said, and sat down.

"Young lady, this means nothing. The vehicle was in Virginia. The bomb was in Georgia. What does one have to do with the other?" James said.

"Sir, it means everything! Chinese agents from across the country have been detained. Based on the personnel list provided by their government, there is only a relative handful left at large . . . less than 20. My theory is that they are consolidating their remaining forces and continuing their mission. If we find them, we find the device," Amanda said, as Assistant Director Allen glared at her.

"So what was the vehicle?"

"A U-Haul moving van," Amanda said, then grew angry when Assistant Director Allen began laughing.

"Wonderful, that's a great lead. There are probably 50,000 U-Haul trucks in this country. Did the witness get a license plate number, at least a partial?"

Amanda bit her tongue as she picked up her phone, called Detective Morehead, set the phone on speaker, turned up the volume, and set it back on the table.

"Morehead here! I'm busy girl, what do you want?"

"Detective Morehead, I'm in a conference with high level personnel from other agencies in the Federal Government. I need some details about your text. Are you interviewing the witness who saw the U-Haul leave Public Storage?"

"Well, I was until you interrupted me?"

"Detective Morehead, my name is Clarisse Beaumont. I'm the National Security Advisor. Do us both a favor and cut the bullshit. Please answer Agent Langford's questions."

The cell phone was silent for a few seconds.

"I'm conducting an interview with Ms. Jennifer Stone. She was out running on the morning of April 20th when she saw a U-Haul van pull out from the driveway below the Public Storage facility located at 401 South Pickett Street in Alexandria, Virginia. The truck drove south and went right past her. She remembers seeing an Asian man in a ball cap sitting in the passenger seat."

"Did she get a license number?" Amanda asked.

"No, but she does remember the design on the side of the truck . . . or part of it."

"Great, no license and she saw 'U-Haul' on the side. That's helpful," James said.

"What did she see? What was the design?" Amanda asked.

"She remembers seeing a guy in a tube and it was yellow . . . if that makes any sense."

Amanda began laughing, and said, "Angelo, that's great! Email me if she remembers anything else."

"I'm glad you find this amusing, Agent Langford," James said.

"Actually, Assistant Director Allen, that partial ID was very helpful. When I first started with the Agency last year I drove up here in a U-Haul truck. Back in the 80's they started an advertising program called SuperGraphics. One of the things they did was place a large design on the side of their trucks for each state in the US," Amanda said, while reaching under the table and retrieving her IPad.

"All we have to do is find out which state has a man in a tube that's yellow," Amanda said, while keying in 'U-Haul SuperGraphics' on the IPad.

A minute later she looked up, smiled, and said, "South Carolina. Now we have something specific to look for. If they took any toll roads, stopped at gas stations. This is great! We have something to track . . . a U-Haul truck with the South Carolina logo and an Asian man in a ball cap sitting on the passenger side."

"Finding this truck will take a lot of resources. The assistance of the FBI would be very helpful. No one would need to know why this truck has to be found. They just need to find it," Clarisse said, while folding her hands and staring at Assistant Director Allen.

"I think we can help you with this," James said.

CHAPTER 16

The House
230 Harlless Bridge Road
Little Rock, South Carolina
May 10, 1930 hours EST

"Lingli, we're starting to run low on supplies," Jian said, while glancing around the nearly empty pantry behind the kitchen.

"I know. I'm going on a supply run tonight. With this many people in the house, we've run out more quickly than I expected," Lingli said, while displaying the long list of things they needed.

"There's a Food Lion in Dillon, a few miles away from here. They're open until 10PM. Since I buy in bulk, I had to have a cover story. I'm the crazy Asian 'Prepper' lady who lives out in the woods," Lingli said, while displaying her camo hunting attire and boonie hat.

"Prepper? I haven't heard that term before," Jian said.

"They think that the end of the world is coming. They hoard food, water, weapons, and live by themselves, or in tight-knit family groups," Lingli said.

"They might be right, but was that wise? You give them something to remember," Jian asked.

"An Asian in South Carolina is already noteworthy. The people here are rustic and individualistic. Now I blend in. Dressed like this, I'm one of them," Lingli said, while tucking her list into her pants pocket and walking out the pantry door.

"Do you need some help?" Jian asked, as he followed her out of the pantry.

"Chonglin already volunteered. He'll stay in the Suburban, but help me load after I buy everything we need," Lingli said.

The Suburban
2000 hours EST

As Lingli left the dirt driveway and pulled onto Harlless Bridge Road, she glanced down at the gas gauge on the 2007 Chevy Suburban.

"We'll have to stop for gas. It's nearly empty. There's an Exxon station just past the Food Lion. I always get $40 worth of gas, and always pay cash. That way there is no paper trail. I've read that that's the way preppers do things," Lingli said, as they turned left on Highway 57.

"Jian was telling me about 'Preppers'. I can't believe the American government allows such things. In China such practices would be considered subversive and reactionary. Such people would be sent to the new 'Professional Education Schools' along with the Muslims, Christians, and other deviants that threaten the stability of China," Chonglin said.

"The United States is based on individual freedom. Sometimes it works for them and sometimes it doesn't. They are as much an experiment as China. Neither form of government has been around very long," Lingli said, while glancing at the setting sun.

"A philosopher with a tolerance for American ways. Perhaps you should be the one sent to an Education School, Doctor Zhang," Chonglin said, while turning and staring at her.

"Perhaps, but Chairman Mao once said, ' Under Communism, the people enjoy extensive democracy and freedom, but at the same time they have to keep within the bounds of socialist discipline.' Do not doubt my loyalty to the cause, Chonglin!"

"Unlike you, I understand my place. I am a soldier, nothing more. If I'm told to kill, I kill. If I'm told to work, I work. You are just a doctor in service of the People. I am just a soldier in service of the People. Tonight, you fetch groceries."

"Yes, and tonight you work for me."

They did not talk again until they reached the Exxon gas station.

The Exxon Gas Station
2012 hours EST

The sun was on the edge of the horizon as they pulled into the gas station. One customer drove away as Lingli pulled up beside Pump No. 4.

"I will go pay for $40 worth of gas, and use the bathroom. Fill the tank and then get back in the Suburban," Lingli said, while walking toward the store.

Chonglin nodded, got out of the Chevy, and removed the gas cap. The night was warm. The sky was still lit by the setting sun. The orange clouds were being replaced with purple as the coming darkness loomed. He heard the gas pump click. The numbers on the gauge had returned to all zeros.

After inserting the nozzle and turning on the gas, Chonglin removed his combat knife from his belt and inspected the blade. He glanced around and, seeing that he was alone, walked over to one of the pillars that held up the rain shed above the pumps. Looking around once more, he then used his knife and carved the Chinese character for 'Tiger' (虎) into the painted surface. The character was not large, only two inches high.

Chonglin was not an intellectual, and his handwriting had always been crude, lacking any elegance; but this character was different. He had practiced this character a thousand times while growing up.

"*I always wanted to be a soldier like my father and grandfather,*" Chonglin thought, while inspecting the symbol he had carved into the heavy enamel paint.

"Grandfather fought the Americans in North Korea, and here I am invading the country of the imperialist aggressors," Chonglin said, while brushing a paint flake from his art work.

"Chonglin, are you day dreaming? It's through pumping. Put it up and get in the car. The Food Lion closes at ten," Lingli said, while walking around the Suburban and opening the door.

Chonglin nodded, glanced at the character once more while putting up the nozzle, and then got in the vehicle while thinking, "*Grandfather would be proud of me. We will strike down the aggressors once and for all.*"

CHAPTER 17

Alexandria City Police Department
Criminal Investigations Division
Office of Detective First Class Angelo Morehead
3600 Wheeler Avenue
Alexandria, Virginia
May 12, 1130 hours EST

Amanda knocked on Detective Morehead's office door and was greeted with a bellow to 'Enter'. She felt like she was entering the principal's office back in high school.

"You should try your inside voice, Detective," Amanda said, while opening the door and stepping into the room.

"That was my inside voice. Thanks for leaving your palace and paying us a visit. You remember the Jansons," Angelo said, his long legs draped over his battered wooden desk.

"*I'd almost forgotten how small his office is. Or is it, that he's so huge?*" Amanda thought, while greeting the father and daughter forensic team with a nod.

Doctor Wilton Janson sat at a small table jammed against the right wall. His daughter, Clair, sat with her legs hanging over an old wooden arm chair on the other side. Her hair was a pink Mohawk with black shaved sides. Her attire matched her hair.

They both ignored her.

The daughter was focused on her phone, the father on the contents of a folder spread across the small desk. There was no place for Amanda to sit, so she stood at the entrance to the room.

"Not exactly 48 hours, but what did you find?" Amanda asked, after taking a deep breath and ignoring the insults.

"Forty-eight hours? Who said this would take 48 hours?" Wilton asked, looking up from a particularly interesting spreadsheet.

His full head of white hair reminded Amanda of Doc Brown, in Back to the Future.

"I might have made that claim," Angelo said, while smacking on a large wad of Nicorette gum.

"Ridiculous! Things like this take precision. Precision takes time," Wilton said. Claire grunted in agreement, still focused on her phone.

"So . . . what did you find?"

"Make it concise, Doc. It's almost lunchtime and my stomach's growling."

"Concise? The man asks for the 'Cliffnote' version of a highly detailed analysis of a crime scene. Sometimes I don't know why I bother," Wilton mumbled, while glancing around the room over a pair of gold wire-rimmed spectacles.

"Doc!" Angelo said, as his size 18's hit the floor.

"All right! Concise! STR DNA testing revealed that seven adult males occupied the ambulance prior to its abandonment. This includes the man killed in the hospital and left behind. One of the six remaining men was wounded in the hospital. All seven were Han Chinese. Their actions were those of a trained assault team . . . with one exception."

"The calligrapher?" Amanda asked.

"Yes, Shūfǎ jiā, a calligrapher. I find the Mandarin language awkward, though I do love their visual language. But, 'calligrapher' . . . what a beautiful word. It just rolls off the tongue," Wilton said.

"Concise, Doc!"

"Yes . . . concise, how boring."

Once again, Claire grunted in agreement, still focused on her phone.

"All these men are from a PLA Special Forces unit renowned for its brutal training and discipline. This man is an outlier, a rebel. This calligraphy, this 'Tiger' character that he leaves behind, is his calling card. You will be able to follow these characters like bread crumbs. Everywhere this man goes he will leave behind this symbol. I guarantee it!"

"Was that 'concise' enough, Detective Morehead?" Wilton asked.

"Agent Langford, if you have any questions you'd like to ask him, now is the time. Tomorrow this case will be history, and he'll refuse to discuss it."

"Why did they come after their leader?"

"It's so obvious . . . they are loyal to a fault."

"Too simple, Father. Don't embarrass me," Claire said, still focused on the phone.

Wilton turned in Claire's direction and glared, before saying, "He's a symbol. He's all they have left of their connection to their nation. He's their Sun Tzu, their Washington and their Abraham Lincoln, all rolled into one."

"Close, Father, but you can do better," Claire said, glaring back at her father.

"He is their soul. He's the only reason they keep going. Kill him, and they'll crumble. Let him live, and there will be hell to pay," Wilton said, as he stood up, gathered all his papers back into the folder, and left the room, never acknowledging Amanda's presence.

Claire swung her legs over the chair arm and stood up. Amanda couldn't decide if the look was Goth, Steam Punk, or an amalgamation of both.

"He's right you know. He's the Dracula to their coven. If you don't put a stake through his heart, the peasants will pay dearly," Claire said, while walking past Amanda to follow her father.

"What the hell was that?" Amanda asked, while turning toward Antonio.

"I think I pissed him off with the concise bit. I should have known better, but I am getting hungry. How about some lunch, my treat? We could go down to The Torpedo Factory and eat at Vola's Dockside Bar & Grill for old times' sake," Antonio said, while slipping into his suit coat.

"Then we can go sit in the sun by the river and stare at that ridiculous diesel engine, slash sculpture. You know, the one that used to hold the nuclear bomb," Antonio said, while gesturing for Amanda to leave his office.

Amanda just stared up at him as he approached.

"Girl, your poker face still ain't for shit. You need to work on that if you're going to be a career spook. Now your boss, that woman is bad to the bone. I don't think she'd blink if she got shot," Antonio said, while nudging Amanda toward the door.

65

CHAPTER 18

Valero Gas Station
2599 New Market Road
Henrico, Virginia
May 14, 1015 hours EST

"Quit complaining, we're almost at the exit off 295," Amanda said, as she saw the sign for Exit 22B and cut into the right lane in her 2003 Honda CRV.

"I should have figured you would own a 'clown car'. Next time, I drive," Antonio said, while massaging his aching knees.

"Hey, this car lasted me through high school and college. It was used when my parents bought it for me. It's indestructible. So what do you own, an M1 tank?"

"Something sensible for a man who's 6'10" and 300 pounds."

"Three hundred pounds? Right! 350 pushing 400 would be more like it," Amanda said, while turning onto the 22B exit ramp.

"I thought women didn't like to talk about weight."

"They don't like to talk about their weight, because it's none of your business. A man's weight is fair game. Plus, most men don't care anyway after they're married," Amanda replied, while jerking to a stop at the bottom of the off ramp.

"That's stupid. Who told you that?"

"My mother," Amanda said, staring at Antonio as she turned right onto New Market Road.

"This place is where they stopped. I've watched the video from the station 20 times. The driver got out to fill the tank. The passenger went inside to pay with cash. Both men wore ball caps with loose hoodies to cover facial details. Then a third man slipped out of the back of the truck, and pissed on the right rear tire. Then he went out of camera view for 29 seconds. He was back inside before the other two men were through with their business," Amanda said, as she turned off New Market Road and pulled into the Valero Gas Station.

"Why would he piss on the tire?"

"You're a man. You tell me."

Amanda turned right, and then left, before parking at the same gas pump that the U-Haul truck had used. She got out and walked back to her right rear tire. Antonio groaned as he pried himself out of the compact CRV.

"I think I'll call a taxi for the ride back, a big one," Antonio said, while stretching his back.

"Where would he have gone for 29 seconds?" Amanda asked, as she turned to the right and began walking.

Antonio glanced around, and said, "Maybe he was hungry and went to the Subway?"

"For 29 seconds?"

She glanced to the right, at the edge of the paved area, and saw a trash can and a pay-for-use vacuum/air combo machine. She walked over and began circling the equipment. She found nothing.

"Crap! He stayed behind the truck. The camera never picked him up. Where else could he have gone?" she asked herself, while turning in a circle.

"Occam's Razor . . . keep it simple," she told herself, as she walked up to a small, gray square-sided light pole on the edge of the property, right beside the exit.

"Antonio! Good old Wilton was right. He left his calling card," she said, while staring at the Chinese character for 'Tiger' carved into the paint on the street side.

Antonio walked over, bent down, and stared at the strange script that was becoming far too familiar.

"This dumbass is going to lead us right to them."

"We knew they stopped here. I wanted to test Wilton's theory, and he's right. But where else do we look?" Amanda asked, as Antonio straightened up and groaned.

"Do those back seats fold down? Maybe I can lie in the back on the way back north."

She took a photo of the carving, and sent it to Antonio and Janet Davidson, along with the text, "We need to look everywhere for breadcrumbs".

CHAPTER 19

The White House
The Oval Office
Washington, DC
June 13, 0900 hours EST

"Damn it, Clarisse, it's been two months. Where the hell is this last weapon?' President Konrad Miller asked, while staring out the window of the Oval Office.

"Mr. President, we're doing everything that we can. Every appropriate federal agency has this as their top priority. It's just a needle in a haystack. We know the U-Haul went south down Interstate 95. We have a video of them stopping for gas near Richmond, on the 295 bypass. Agent Langford, with help from an Alexandria PD detective name Antonio Morehead, has discovered a marking that one of the individuals leaves behind everywhere they stop. But then, they haven't been able to find another one. I'm afraid the Chinese have disappeared. The range for that size truck is 400 miles. If they stopped again, it must have been off 95 at some place we haven't found," Clarisse Beaumont said.

"So, they could be anywhere in the Southeast?"

"Yes, Mr. President."

"Well, that just sucks. I am truly amazed that this whole thing hasn't leaked yet. If we can get hold of this last device, then I'll go public. I'll do it on national TV, and tell the people everything. I'll tell them why it was kept from them for so long. But I can't do it with one weapon unaccounted for."

"Mr. President, the only new lead is based on the personnel info that China provided. We have apprehended every one of Kung's agents on the list except for 11 individuals. We know that China has other agents located within the US, but that wasn't part of our agreement with them."

"So what do we know about the 11?"

"First, they're all from the same Special Forces Unit, the Siberian Tigers. In 2012, six of them were in a platoon commanded by 1st Lieutenant Gong Aiguo . . ."

"Damn, that's their connection with the hospital killer. They were rescuing their former officer."

"Correct, Mr. President. It seems they were all recruited from the Siberian Tigers by General Kung to be part of his organization in the United States. Our sources in the PRC tell us that there has been a serious culling of the leadership of the Siberian Tigers. Over 60 officers have been 'purged'."

"Well, the only difference is we'd court martial the group and send them off to Leavenworth. The Chinese take them out and shoot them. That sets an example for the rest of the military. They're just a little more blunt than we are. So what else do you have?"

"All these operators worked for Sergeant Major First Class Wang Jian. He was the lead for Kung's operation in the Southeast US. All of these men reported to him. The best theory is that he saw everything falling apart and consolidated what resources he had left. Then they went after their former Lieutenant. How they found out about him, we don't know."

"And the device?"

"They retrieved it from a location southwest of Fort Benning. Then they killed the family assigned to maintain the storage location. I suppose they were considered 'loose ends'."

"So what are they going to do with one bomb? What are the best theories?"

"Homeland thinks they'll go after a major military target. The FBI thinks they'll use the weapon as a bargaining chip to get passage out of the US, or go for a major city."

"How about the CIA? What was that young lady's name that worked for Janet Davidson?"

"Amanda Langford, Mr. President. Director Davidson says that Agent Langford has a theory that they're suicidal like mujahedeen or kamikaze. Janet's not so sure. It's just a theory. Another thing she found was a calling card being left everywhere they go."

"You mean something other than a stack of bodies?"

"Yes, Mr. President, a Chinese character for a Tiger. It's been found carved into different surfaces."

"How are we following up on this?"

"We're checking every gas station, bathroom and restaurant heading south on 95. So far . . . nothing."

"All of this points to the Southeast. That's the area they're familiar with. They're probably holed up somewhere planning their next move. We can't wait for that. I may have to go public now. Unless they're living in a cave, and eating grass, they have to come out in public for resources. That means that somebody has seen them. If we get the public involved . . . ," the President said.

"Sir, if we do that, then we risk the panic that we wanted to avoid in the first place. Plus, it will look like we're hunting Chinese. The ACLU and the Democrats will scream. They'll start saying you want internment camps. They'll want your head for allowing this whole thing to happen."

"Politics and PR, Clarisse. It's part of the job description. It just depends how you spin it. Arrange a meeting of the Homeland Security Council. I want opinions on going public. While you're working on that, I need to make a private call to my Chinese counterpart."

CHAPTER 20

Zhongnanhai Compound
Home of the General Secretary of the People's Republic of China
174 Chang'an Avenue
Xicheng District
Beijing, China
June 14, 1710 hours CT

"President Miller, an unexpected call. What do we have to discuss?" General Secretary Li Xibin said, to the image of the American President displayed on the large monitor in his private office.

"Interesting, the last time we talked you were in the Beijing Hall surrounded by comrades. Now you seem to be alone," President Konrad said.

"Do not gloat, Mr. President. You have a saying, 'What goes around comes around.' Perhaps our game is not yet finished. You have hidden the event from the media, your politicians, and the public. I wonder if you will survive their wrath once the information comes out."

"General Secretary, do you remember the four craters in Mongolia that pointed toward Beijing?"

"If you are referring to the unwarranted, naked aggression displayed by your country, then yes, I do. Thousands of innocent civilians . . ." the General Secretary began.

"Spare me the bullshit, General Secretary. We were very careful with the location of those impacts. We both know who the aggressors were. You cooperated because you had to. Trust me, you still have to cooperate, and I need some information."

Li Xibin paused, studying the face of the American president. He had a poker face, as the Americans called it, but the eyes . . .

"You didn't catch them all. You don't have possession of all the devices, do you?" the General Secretary asked, a faint smile crossing his face.

"Now who's gloating, General Secretary? Trust me; my problem is your problem. We have all the devices except one. If that device is detonated within the borders of the United States, or any of our allies, I will hold you and the People's Republic of China responsible. If we get to that point, your military facilities will disappear. I wonder how long you'll stay in power if that happens. Am I making myself perfectly clear, General Secretary?"

The General Secretary paused, looked away from the monitor, and considered his options. He had misjudged the American President before, and had been misinformed about their military capabilities. But the American President had a problem. A problem the Americans couldn't resolve by themselves.

"The People's Republic of China is always willing to cooperate with our friends in the United States, Mr. President. What information do you need?"

This time the President paused, studying his adversary.

"*Does the bastard think he can still win, or is he just playing me for concessions? He has to be under enormous pressure within his own party. His failure was too public. Too many people saw our planes and their display. Too many know about Manchuria. It would have been perceived as bending to the will of the United States He shut down the internet inside China, but that never works for long. How do I play this, hardball . . . softball, or something in between?*" the President thought, while studying the smiling face of the Chinese General Secretary.

"General Secretary, you gave us the name and location of every Siberian Tiger agent that General Kung had placed within the United States. Did he have any other agents, any support organizations located within our borders? Please don't lie. I already have a partial answer, but I need everything," the President said, bluffing, hoping for the information he needed.

"What exactly are you looking for, Mr. President?"

President Miller was out on a limb of his own making. He had made this call on a gut instinct without seeking advice from anyone else. He knew now that he should have waited, but he was beyond that point. He had to go on instinct, and the information that he already possessed.

"*How far can I push him? If I was him, I'd play my cards close. I'd give something, but not everything. If I ask for everything he'll stall and I don't have the time,*" the President thought, while the two men played a game of high stakes poker.

"General Secretary, I want to know the names and locations of every agent that you have in the southern United States. Remember, if they detonate this device inside our borders, there will be no turning back for either of us."

The General Secretary looked away once again, considering his position.

"*That bastard Kung has left me few options. We have infiltrated more places in their government, military, and business than they can imagine. How much can I discard before the whole thing falls apart? I'll give him something, and play the long game. In the end we'll still win. They are too flawed as a nation to last much longer,*" the General Secretary told himself.

"We might have a few personnel and facilities within that area. You probably already know about most of them, but I'll have a file delivered to your embassy in Beijing, Mr. President," the General Secretary said, while presenting his most humble and cooperative smile.

"*So that's what a snake looks like when it smiles,*" the President thought.

"I appreciate your cooperation, General Secretary. I hope for the sake of both of our countries that the information proves useful. I'd hate to have to make another call and inform you that the information was inadequate," the President said, paused while their eyes connected, then broke the link.

CHAPTER 21

The Medical Room
230 Harlless Bridge Road
Little Rock, South Carolina
July 15, 1130 hours EST

"So how does the leg feel?" Lingli asked Aiguo, as he sat with legs dangling from the examination table.

"The thigh is still stiff and aches after I exercise, but I'm getting stronger every week," Aiguo said, while pushing off from the table and doing a deep knee bend.

"Chonglin and Bingwen have developed workout programs for everyone. It has helped blend the two teams into one fighting unit. We will need the unity during our future struggles," Aiguo said.

"You sound like a political commissar," Lingli said with a smile, as she knelt down and examined the scar tissue on Aiguo's thigh.

"What we are going to do will take leadership and a great strength of will. To accomplish our mission we must be willing to sacrifice everything," Aiguo said, while grabbing the doctor by her shoulders and lifting her to her feet.

"And that includes you. We have begun to have planning discussions. Most think that you should be excluded. But I think that has been a mistake. You are part of the team, and the team is only as strong as it weakest member," Aiguo said, while staring into Lingli's eyes.

"No one has told me anything, Aiguo, but I'm not a fool. I have noticed the change in attitude amongst the men over the last few weeks. At first, I sensed that some of them were afraid. Then I sensed resignation. Now they seem unified, focused . . . more alive. What are you planning to do with these men?" Lingli said, while slipping out of Aiguo's grasp and taking a step away from him.

"We are going to complete our mission. We are going to destroy the United States of America," Aiguo said, and smiled.

Lingli stared up at him amused, then stunned when she saw that he was serious.

"But how? You have one weapon. It is a powerful thing, but it's nothing compared to the size of this country. Even if you blew up Washington, they would survive. Their military would survive. China would not survive."

"Chairman Mao once said, 'Don't make a fuss about a world war. At most, people die... Half the population wiped out - this happened quite a few times in Chinese history... It's best if half the population is left, next best one-third.' We will survive, Doctor. The American people are soft. Remove their electronic toys and their grocery stores, and they will tear each other apart. They are the nation that will cease to exist, not China. Our mission is to bring about that day."

"But how . . . you only have one bomb?"

"Like the story of Jesus . . . the loaves and the fishes . . . from one comes many. That is how, good doctor. It's quite simple," Aiguo said, while walking past her and toward the door.

"Planning session at 1400 in the upstairs barracks. Make sure that you are there," Aiguo said, as he opened the door and left the Medical Room.

The House
1400 hours EST

The second floor of the house was one long room with a bathroom at one end. The original owner had built it as an entertainment room. Beds now lined both sides. A pool table sat in the center. The table was now covered with plywood and served as a planning table for the Siberian Tigers.

"Over the past few weeks we have discussed the need for action. We were sent here by General Kung to accomplish a mission that would solidify China's position in the world. The so-called United States of America is a blight on this planet. Their perverse culture is a cancer that has spread across the globe. Their greed has enriched them and allowed their influence to spread. It is time for all that to end," Aiguo began, while pacing at the head of the table.

"You all know that we possess the sole remaining weapon that was part of General Kung's great plan. You also know that I intend to put this weapon to good use. Today, you will all find out our final target," Aiguo said, then paused to judge the impact of his words on each individual in the team.

"Due to our limited printing capabilities, a map has been cobbled together by Sergeant Heng from 8 ½ by 11 sheets of paper. But, as you can see, the detail is still impressive," Aiguo said, directing their attention to the mosaic mounted on the makeshift table.

"What we are looking at is a satellite view of the Shearon Harris Nuclear Power Plant located in central North Carolina. The plant sits adjacent to a lake that supplies cooling water for plant operations. It was originally designed to have four nuclear plants on the site, but they were only able to complete one unit because of cost overruns. Capitalists are always fighting over money. It leaves them incapable of building anything in an efficient manner. For our purposes, the operating plant is irrelevant. What we are interested in is this," Aiguo said, while pointing at a long rectangular building on one side of the facility.

"As I said, the site was designed to have four nuclear plants. To support that, they built a Fuel Handling Building with the capacity to store spent fuel from all four units for the operating life of each plant. After the other units were cancelled, the utility still had this huge building, but only one unit filling its spent fuel pools. Being crafty capitalists, they began storing spent fuel from other, older sites that the utility possessed. These other sites had run out of storage room due to the lack of support from their federal government. As a result, over the last 20 years, this building has become the largest spent fuel repository in the Southeast United States," Aiguo said, then waited for a reaction.

When it came, the source was unexpected.

"You want to put the weapon in there . . . and detonate it?" Lingli asked, as a shiver ran up her spine.

The others stared at her, then at Aiguo. Then they all began talking at once.

"Quiet! Are you clucking hens or Siberian Tigers?" Aiguo asked.

"The good doctor is quite perceptive . . . and correct. Our new mission is to insert our remaining weapon inside the Fuel Handling Building and detonate it. The spent fuel pools, and their connecting canals, contain over a million gallons of water. The two major pools contain over 3000 spent fuel assemblies. Each assembly contains 8 kg of U-235, 942 kg of U-238, 9 kg of Plutonium and a few kg of other assorted transuranic elements. Before Chonglin's head bursts trying to add up the numbers, that adds up to over 960 kg or 2100 pounds of deadly, long-lived radioactive isotopes in each assembly," Aiguo said.

"That's over 6,000,000 pounds," Lingli said.

"Correct, Doctor Zhang. When we detonate our nuclear device inside this building, a building filled with over a million gallons of water and 6 million pounds of radioactive material, there will be an explosion unlike any in history. The water in the pools will instantly turn to steam . . . and the building will explode. All of the radioactive material will be atomized and hurled high into the atmosphere. The prevailing winds in this area blow from southwest to northeast. This one little device will render the mid-Atlantic and the northeastern United States uninhabitable for centuries. This area is the heart of their economy and government. The United States of America will cease to exist," Aiguo said, pausing once again, to judge the impact of his words.

"If we do this . . . they will destroy China. Their rage will be unimaginable," Lingli said.

"Before we detonate the weapon, we will go public and absolve China of all blame. China has attacked no one. It will be the responsibility of a few rogue terrorists, not the People's Republic of China. China will then step forward and assist the world in recovering from this disaster. China might even forgive America its mountain of debt to aid in their recovery. China will emerge as the lone super power. In time, this will become a Chinese planet," Aiguo said.

"This is insane! We will be responsible for the deaths of millions of people," Lingli said.

"The plans and actions of The Great Helmsman resulted in the deaths of over 50 million Chinese. A birth is often a bloody event. It was the price of the re-birth of our nation. It resulted in the final unification of a culture that had existed for millennia . . . a culture that was responsible for many of the great discoveries that led to global civilization. Our division allowed the greedy capitalists to carve up our country like one of their Christmas turkeys. The Japanese were an extension of the West. Their culture was contaminated by capitalist ideals. Their warlike nature, combined with modern technology, created a beast that even the West could not tolerate. The Chinese Nationalists were no different. They wanted the United States of China. Mao knew that this was not what the Chinese people wanted. He wanted complete freedom from the West. This is the final step. After this, China will be truly free," Aiguo said, smiling as others around the table nodded in agreement.

"Fine words, Comrade Lieutenant, but what is your plan? I do not think that the Americans will allow us to walk into this nuclear power plant and drop our weapon in one of these pools," Guan Xing asked.

"Correct, Comrade Sergeant. As the Americans say, 'The devil is in the details,'" Aiguo said, as Heng placed a notebook on the table.

CHAPTER 22

3400 Avent Ferry Road
New Hill, North Carolina
July 21, 0630 hours EST

The sun was just starting to come up when Security Sergeant Jonathan Davies slipped in through the side door of his small, single-floor brick house. He knew that his wife would still be asleep. Dorothy would be in bed until the girls, 3-year-old Emily and 4-year-old Callie, made an entrance around 0730. A beer and a quick shower, and he'd be in a deep sleep before they tiptoed into the room and woke their mother. She would slip out of bed, close the door, and tend to their young daughters. That was their standard family routine when Dad was working night shift. If they got noisy and woke him up during the day, somebody was in big trouble.

Jonathan stepped inside and locked the door. Then he glanced to his left, noticing that the kitchen light was on.

"Like we don't pay Duke Power enough every month already," he said, then yawned, and began walking toward the brick stairs that led into the small kitchen off the carport.

He didn't even notice the black-clad man hidden in the shadows, until the 9mm was pointed at his face.

"If you move, I will kill you," the man said, in an odd accent.

Jonathan's right hand instinctively slid toward his own weapon at his hip.

"If you touch it, I will kill you. Then I will kill your family."

Jonathan stopped, and raised his hands into the air.

"Don't hurt them. I'll do whatever you want," Jonathan said, as he felt another weapon pressed against the back of his skull.

"Put your hands on top of your head. Interlock the fingers," the man behind him ordered.

Jonathan did as he was told. All he could think about was Dorothy and the girls. He barely noticed his own 9mm being removed from its holster.

"What do you want? I don't have a lot of money in the house, but I'll give you everything we've got, everything of value. Just don't hurt my family," Jonathan said, as the man began to push him toward the stairs.

"We don't want your money, Sergeant Davies. We just want your cooperation," the man behind him said, while the other man turned, climbed the stairs, and opened the door into the kitchen.

Jonathan entered the kitchen, turned left, and halted. On the other side of the kitchen was a small circular dinette. Dorothy sat in the shadows at the far end, facing him. His two girls had their arms wrapped around their mother. All three were shaking with fear. A third man stood behind his wife with a pistol pressed against her right temple. Tears were streaming down Dorothy's face.

"Whatever you want, I'll do it. Please, don't hurt them," Jonathan said, his heart pounding in his chest.

He was an Iraq vet and had been in the 'shit', as the saying went. He was more afraid now than he had ever been in combat.

"Well, I'm very glad to see that you're so cooperative. That will ensure that we all get what we want," Aiguo said, while lowering the pistol from Dorothy's head.

"I am not interested in your money. I am not interested in harming you or your beautiful family. What I want is information, Sergeant Davies. Information about where you work. If you provide that information, I give you my word that you and your family will be released unharmed. If you refuse to provide exactly what I want, then I will slit your daughters' throats, while you and your wife watch. Then I will slit your wife's throat, while you watch. Then I will kill you very slowly," Aiguo said, while ruffling the hair on the youngest child.

His wife began to sob as Jonathan dropped to his knees.

"Please, whatever you want to know, I'll tell you. Please don't hurt them."

"Good! We have an understanding. Your wife and your children will be escorted into your bedroom while we start our conversation. Bǎohù tā bìng ràng tā zuò zài yǐzi shàng (Secure him and sit him in a chair)," Aiguo said, while Chonglin lifted the wife by the arm, and pointed toward an open bedroom door.

"Get up," Aiguo said, while stepping forward and pointing his weapon at Jonathan's head.

Jonathan stood up and placed his arms behind his back.

As he felt the tye wrap being secured around his wrists, he thought, "*Holy crap! Was that Chinese? What the hell is going on?*"

Aiguo sat in the far chair as Jonathan was dropped into the chair opposite him. Bingwen stood behind Jonathan with his left hand resting at the nape of the security guard's neck.

"Sergeant Jonathan Paul Davies, age 32, formerly of the 3rd US Infantry Division. You are an Iraq veteran with a Silver Star for gallantry. Your father was a Vietnam veteran. But then he came home and drank himself to death. Perhaps it was guilt for the atrocities committed by him and other US forces. Your grandfather was also a veteran of the 3rd Infantry Division during the Korean War. We call it the War to Resist US Aggression. Your family has a history of invading other countries and murdering the civilians there," Aiguo said.

"Fuck you! We all served honorably," Jonathan said, then choked back other words as Aiguo raised his pistol and pointed it at Jonathan's head.

"Sergeant Davies, is your wife right handed or left handed? Answer the question, please," Aiguo asked.

"Right handed . . ." Jonathan said, as tears began to well up in his eyes.

"Please, don't hurt her. Please! I'm sorry about what I said. I didn't mean it," he pleaded.

"Chonglin, break the pinkie finger on her left hand," Aiguo said, pistol still leveled at Jonathan's forehead.

Jonathan heard a thud, then his girls screamed as their mother pleaded with her captor. Then she screamed in agony.

"That was a lesson, Sergeant Davies. I am a kind man. I will treat you and your family well . . . as long as you cooperate. If you resist me, or don't provide the information that I request of you, then your family will suffer. This is the last time I will ask this question. Do we have an understanding?"

Jonathan could hear his children and wife crying in the bedroom.

"I'll do whatever you want. I'll keep my mouth shut. Just don't hurt them again," Jonathan said, his voice shaking with rage and fear.

"Excellent! I know all about you and your family history. I have selected you to assist me in a project that I have. This project will go on for some time. This means that you will continue to go to work, and then come home. Your family will be under my . . . protection, during this entire time. If you tell anyone about our arrangement, your family will die," Aiguo said, lowering the pistol and returning it to his holster.

"What do you want to know?" Jonathan asked, knowing that he was in a trap with no way out.

"Many things, Sergeant Davies, many things. So let's get started."

CHAPTER 23

Central Intelligence Agency
Mission Center for Weapons and Counterproliferation
Office of Director Janet Davidson
Manassas, Virginia
July 21, 1000 hours EST

"Yes, Director, I understand your frustration. I'm feeling the same thing. When I was a little girl, my parents used to hide small chocolate Easter eggs inside the house. They would give me an empty basket, and I would have to find all the eggs. There were always 33 eggs because that's how old Jesus was when he was crucified. There were years when I would find an egg months later. It was extremely frustrating," Amanda said, as she paced in front of Janet's desk.

Janet sighed while shaking her head, and then said, "Agent Langford, it's not my frustration, it's the President's. It's been over eight weeks since you and Detective Morehead made that find at the Virginia gas station. Since then, we have nothing."

"I know, I really thought that we had a verified breakthrough. We just needed to throw enough people at the problem and we'd find more . . . eggs."

"It's also been three weeks since we received the file from the Chinese. We've unearthed more Chinese agents and safe houses, but no weapon, and none of the personnel inserted by General Kung," Janet said.

"I know. A combined task force of CIA, Homeland and FBI personnel have made over two dozen raids in the Southeast and found nothing related to this case."

"Amanda, the President is becoming desperate. Rumors of this whole thing are running wild in certain offices in Congress. There are hints on different networks that something dangerous is going on inside the country. Just like us, some reporters are starting to pick up all the pieces. This whole thing is set to explode, no pun intended. If we don't find something this week, the President told Clarisse that he's going public," Janet said, while standing up and walking to the window behind her desk.

"Director, I hate to say this, but that might be for the best. We're stuck. For some reason, this list that the Chinese provided isn't panning out. Either they're holding back, or Kung had assets that they don't know about. At least if the President goes public, then we'll have 300 million additional sets of eyes helping us."

"And riots, a stock market plunge, and calls for the President's head."

"I know, ever since the 'hanging chad' election back in 2000, both parties have been at each other's throats. They don't even pretend to cooperate anymore. They can't see how much it hurts the country."

"True, but our mission hasn't changed. We still have a duty to protect the nation and the American people," Janet said, her back turned, still staring out the window.

"Amanda . . . I feel it in my bones. They've had so long to plan. We've heard nothing from them, no threats, no demands . . . nothing. You have a nuclear background. What can they do with one weapon, and a small one at that? What would you do if you were in their position? In the Marines we called a situation like this a 'Force Multiplier'. How do you make something big out of something small?" Janet said, as she turned and stared at Amanda.

"My background isn't in weapons. My degree is in nuclear power, civilian use of . . ." Amanda said, and then stopped, staring at nothing as her mind began to spin a horrifying scenario.

"You said, 'force multiplier'. I'd blow up a nuke plant with a nuclear bomb. That would be a big increase in lethality. You'd add the plant's radioactive material to the fallout," Amanda said, as she raised her eyes and stared at Janet.

"How many nuke plants are there in the Southeast?" Janet asked, as her heart began to pound in her chest.

"Over 20 different sites, as I remember," Amanda said, while pulling her phone out of her satchel.

"Some of the sites have one unit. Some have as many as three, but all of them are heavily guarded. They have been since 9/11," Amanda said, while keying in a search.

"There are 31 units at 18 sites. That's south of Alexandria and east of the Mississippi. As I said, all of these locations are heavily guarded. The security of these places is tested periodically by US Special Forces. They do mock assaults to test the validity of the security at each site," Amanda said.

"We're still just guessing. This is just another theory, but it makes sense. Blow up a nuclear power plant with a nuclear weapon. If it was me, I'd go after the biggest site . . . the one with the most units. Clarisse is coordinating all the various agencies in this hunt. I'll give her a call and see what she thinks," Janet said.

Amanda's mind was already in overdrive. Different possibilities were flowing through her faster than she could evaluate each one. Then a face appeared, unbidden, Major Anthony Thompson's face. She had a strange feeling as she remembered him, then cast the feeling aside.

"*No, not now! What's wrong with you? He's still mourning his wife. Focus!*" she told herself, as she turned, and headed back toward her office.

"Amanda, flesh out your hunch. Look at every site as a potential target. If you need help, contact the Nuclear Regulatory Commission, the Pentagon, whatever you need," Janet said, as Amanda nodded, and left the Director's office.

CHAPTER 24

3400 Avent Ferry Road
New Hill, North Carolina
July 21, 1815 hours EST

Security Sergeant Jonathan Davies put his 2010 Nissan Frontier truck in gear and backed away from the house. He could see the leader of the men who had taken over his life standing in the shadows under the carport. Jonathan had managed only two hours sleep, and knew that the lack of sleep would haunt him ten hours from now. But he didn't care about sleep. He didn't care about his job. He turned the truck around, and stopped at the end of his driveway. He stared at Shadow Ridge Baptist Church across the street. He had been raised as a Southern Baptist. One of the reasons he had bought this house was the church across the street. He found great comfort inside its wooden, white-painted walls. Every Sunday they would all get dressed up, walk down the driveway together, cross the street, and attend church. The congregation was small, only 80 members, but all were involved. The building had been built in 1870 and had always been a house of the Lord.

"God, please help us. We are surrounded by evil, Lord," Jonathan prayed, knowing that the man was still standing in the shadows behind him, staring at his truck.

Ephesians 6: 12-13 popped into Jonathan's mind.

"For our struggle is not against flesh and blood, but against the rulers, against the authorities, against the powers of this dark world and against the spiritual forces of evil in the heavenly realms. Therefore, put on the full armor of God, so that when the day of evil comes, you may be able to stand your ground, and after you have done everything, to stand," he whispered.

As he turned left onto Avent Ferry Road, he felt his heart lighten a little, but the dilemma was still there.

"What do I do now? My mind says go directly to the Shift Lieutenant and tell him what happened. A SWAT Team will appear around my house within hours. Those bastards will be killed or captured," Jonathan said, while stopping at the intersection, turning right and heading down New Hill-Holleman Road.

"Maybe they won't hurt my family. They'll just use them as bargaining chips to get away. They'd have to be crazy to hurt them if they had a chance to get away," he said, while wiping away tears.

"Oh dear God, help me . . . they are crazy. They're fanatics, like mujahedeen. This is all about the plant. They want to do something to Harris. If I turn them in, I'll never see my family again," he said, and began pounding the steering wheel in frustration.

"I can't risk it. I'd go insane if I lost them all. This must be how Job felt as his life fell apart. I have to give them what they want. I'll play along until I get a chance. When the time comes, I will be ruthless and strike them down," Jonathan said, while his truck was crossing the bridge over Harris Lake.

Small fishing boats were on either side. A man held up his beer as if in mocking tribute . . . to a traitor.

His mind was torn by conflicting emotions. The soldier in him felt duty bound to protect the plant, the father duty bound to protect his family. One of them had to lose.

. . . .

Aiguo watched Sergeant Davies drive away, confident that the 'understanding' they had would keep him silent.

"Now it's time to move the others," Aiguo said, while sending a text to Heng in South Carolina.

'Move all to location 2, including item. Leave the present'.

Harris Nuclear Plant
1830 hours

Jonathan turned left onto Shearon Harris Road, the access road that led to the plant. The cooling tower, over 500 feet tall, loomed above the trees on the right. A thick plume of steam billowed from the top. Turkey vultures were visible high in the sky, riding the heated air in looping spirals 1000 feet high.

As he headed down the road toward the boxy, gray security shack, he felt his hands begin to shake. His photo ID security badge hung from his neck on a lanyard. A Thermoluminescent Dosimeter (TLD) was clipped to a plastic band above the ID. As he approached the guard shack, he lowered the driver side window and held out his ID badge.

"Jonathan, you're running a little late tonight. You know how JB is about his turnover meeting," said Security Officer Omar Tines, standing outside the guard shack.

"Yeah, I know. 'If you can't show up on time, don't bother to show up at all'," Jonathan said, as Omar started laughing.

Another guard appeared from the other side of the shack and began rolling a vehicle inspection mirror under Jonathan's truck.

Jonathan popped the hood on his truck, knowing this was a standard part of incoming vehicle inspections. A third guard stayed inside the shack, part of the security protocol for this duty station. The two guards outside the shack were considered expendable. The 'shack' was built like a Brinks Truck, and anchored to a huge concrete pad. If a vehicle tried to ram the shack, the vehicle would take a worse beating. The windows were bullet resistant up to .50 cal. The walls would stop even that large caliber round. Firing ports were built into every side of the shack, allowing the third guard to duck down and safely return fire.

The shack was a trip wire. Cameras were mounted inside and outside and were linked to Command Central, nicknamed "Overwatch". Under attack, the third guard would activate the vehicle barrier at the top of the hill a quarter mile past the guard shack. If the shack was somehow taken out, the vehicle barrier could be activated from Overwatch. The access road leading to the plant led past two concrete barriers. The ground on either side had been sculpted to prevent any vehicle from getting around the barriers. The slope was too steep for even a four-wheel drive vehicle. Even a tracked vehicle would have difficulty getting over the rise. The barrier was a steel wall that would rise from the ground between the two barriers. A tank could get past the barriers, but that was it. This system, the shack and the vehicle barrier, were only two of the many layers of protection that had been built into the overall Security Plan of the Harris Nuclear Plant. Jonathan knew every detail, every schedule, the crisscrossing fields of fire, the armored fallback positions, the cameras, the dozens of security doors within the plant that could be remotely locked. He knew the strengths and weaknesses of the Security Plan. It was this knowledge that his attackers wanted. He knew that eventually he would have to give it to them to protect his family.

The front hood of his truck slamming down woke Jonathan from his stupor.

"Get your focus, Jonathan, or JB will be reaming your ass during the turnover briefing," Omar said, while waving Jonathan through the entrance.

Jonathan smiled while raising his window, then drove up the hill past the two concrete barriers. The switchyard appeared on the left, the huge cooling tower on his right. Parking lots stretched from the cooling tower all the way to the Security Building, over two hundred yards, then around to the left past the Administration Building. The lot there was even bigger. There were over 3000 parking spaces, but during a refueling outage that was never enough. There had been an outage in April. There wouldn't be another scheduled outage for 15 months. Things had settled back down to normal, routine online operations. All the outage contractors were gone, and the parking lots were nearly empty.

Jonathan kept driving down the access road as far as possible. No one wanted to park near the cooling tower. The huge basin at its base gave off a mist that would ruin the finish of a vehicle if left on for too long. During an outage, the parking lot would be jammed with vehicles from day shift. Surrounding fields would be opened up and roped off for the oncoming night shift personnel. Some of the spots were over a quarter mile away. Today, Jonathan got a great spot, only 30 yards from the Security Building entrance.

After parking his truck and turning off the engine, Jonathan paused, staring at the entrance to the Security Building.

"Get your shit together or they'll know something's wrong. You'll wind up in the Lieutenant's office. He'll send you for a 'For Cause' piss test and have you evaluated by a shrink. They'll pull your security access and you'll no longer be useful. Your family will be dead," Jonathan told himself.

He took a deep breath, exhaled, opened the door of his truck, and went to work.

CHAPTER 25

447 Weldon Lane
Sanford, North Carolina
July 25, 2315 hours EST

Lingli sat in the swing on the front porch of the small, wooden farm house. The heat of the day had finally abated. She longed for sleep, but it eluded her. Eighteen hours of non-stop work had left her exhausted. The new medical clinic was almost ready, though she wasn't sure why she had bothered.

They had spent the previous day moving everything from South Carolina. This property was the last remaining safe house that Jian had purchased many years ago. Men were scattered in every room. Being soldiers, they were able to sleep anywhere. They also filled the house with their snores.

She glanced over at the barn. The lights on the second floor were still on. While Aiguo and two others were away, Jian was still planning. As information was provided by the captive security guard, Jian was modifying the assault plan. She rose from the swing, yawned, and started walking toward the barn.

The moon had not yet risen. Only a few clouds danced across the starlit sky. Out here, so far from any sizeable city, the stars were bright. Jian had all the exterior lights extinguished. Shan Li, one of the new team members, sat in a tree stand on the edge of the woods a hundred yards down the road. His silenced rifle would remove any unwanted visitors that disobeyed the 'Do Not Trespass' sign that they had installed at the entrance.

A slight breeze swept across her face. The sound of the cicadas, tree frogs and crickets reminded her of home. Her parents were farmers, and she had wanted to become a veterinarian, but the Party thought otherwise. Her parents had been told that she was far too intelligent to be wasted on animals. That led her to medical school, which led her to the army, and now to this farm in North Carolina.

She stopped halfway to the barn, and breathed deeply.

"That scent, what is that?" she asked herself, as she closed her eyes and focused on the scent.

She relaxed her mind, wanting desperately to be anywhere else.

"It's honeysuckle. It grows here as a vine. The fence line on the west side of the property is covered with it. The wind direction just changed," Jian said, while walking closer to Lingli in the dark.

"How did you know . . ." she began, startled that she had not heard him approach.

"I saw you leave the porch. You were backlit by the light in the kitchen. You left it on. You've been out here for over five minutes. I was wondering if you had fallen asleep standing up," Jian said, as he walked closer, stood beside Lingli, and stared up at the stars.

"I was lost in the scent. I couldn't sleep, too noisy in the house."

"Most of it is Yunru. If Chonglin was here it would be worse, like two competing male bullfrogs. You might try sleeping in your clinic."

"That's where I was headed. Where do we stand with the planning? I've been so busy with the clinic that I haven't asked about it."

"The security guard was reluctant to cooperate at first, but with his wife and children as leverage, he had little choice. What man would willingly sacrifice his family?"

Lingli said nothing, but turned away, taking in the sweet scent once more.

"I have read that the locals make a sweet wine from the flower petals," Jian said.

"If it's as sweet as the scent, then it must be very sweet indeed," Lingli said.

"Doctor, sometimes I sense that you don't approve of what we're doing here."

The tone in his voice registered as a warning in Lingli's mind. She knew that the friendly conversation had the potential for an unfortunate ending.

"Sergeant Major First Class Wang, I am here as support cadre for this mission. Neither my opinion, nor my feelings, have any relevance in these matters," Lingli said, while snapping to attention.

"Relax Doctor, you aren't a trainee in the Female Special Operations Company anymore. I'm just asking your opinion."

"Sergeant Major, my duty is to obey the orders of my superiors, not to question them or have an opinion about their decisions," Lingli said, still standing at attention, her eyes straight ahead.

"Is that all you are, Doctor, just another automaton produced by the PLA to run into machine gun fire while faithfully singing 'The Sword March'? I'm disappointed. Good night, Doctor," Jian said, while turning away and heading back to the barn.

Lingli stood at attention until she heard the barn door slam shut.

"*Jian, I wanted to tell you how I really felt, but I was too afraid. China nurtures obedience, not freedom of expression. Tiananmen Square taught us that opinions, spoken openly, are dangerous. You would not have asked my opinion unless others had questioned my loyalty. I'll have to be very careful in the future,*" Lingli thought, while remembering other moments of carelessness.

She turned back toward the porch, having decided that the swing looked more comfortable than the clinic in the barn.

The Barn
2nd Floor
2340 hours EST

Jian stood staring at the mosaic of the satellite photos of the Harris Nuclear Plant. The loft in this barn didn't have a pool table, so the map was pinned to one of the side walls. Notes had been written in Chinese on the map and in the margins. Each bit of information that the security guard provided was forwarded to Jian for analysis. The plan was slowly evolving as more questions were answered, but for every question answered, two more arose.

"Damn, before 9/11 this would have been easy. According to Sergeant Davies, the guards were old and fat. They only carried a revolver and had no body armor. If they were veterans, it was from Vietnam or Korea. The fences were thin, no guard towers, most of the cameras were broken or pointed the wrong way. They couldn't have protected a shopping mall. Now it's different, very different. All of the guards are military veterans, most are combat veterans. They are motivated to protect the plant. The defense of the plant is in great depth. Assets from outside organizations can be there in an hour. A battalion from Fort Bragg can be there in four," Jian said, while sitting in a wooden chair five feet from the map.

"Aiguo wants to assault the place, but that's impossible. There are cameras and motion sensors all over the perimeter. Double fences, 12 feet high, topped with razor wire. The area between the fences filled with more razor wire. Guard towers on the perimeter would have to be taken out with rockets or their fields of fire would shatter any perimeter assault. If the perimeter towers are destroyed, then internal guard towers still cover the main avenues of approach to the main power block. That's what they're really protecting. A dozen guards patrol the plant site with loaded automatic weapons. They carry an additional four magazines. Weapons lockers are stored throughout the plant, so additional ammunition and weapons are available during an attack on the site. Armored shields with firing ports are placed all over the plant site. A single guard could hold off a dozen men for an hour. It would take a thousand men to take this place, and by the time you did, the 82nd Airborne would be all over you," Jian said, while closing his eyes and rubbing his hands together.

"No, a direct assault is impossible. We don't even have enough men for a diversionary attack. Somehow we must appear amongst them. They can never see us coming, until it's too late. As Sun Tzu said, 'Let your plans be dark and impenetrable as night, and when you move, fall like a thunderbolt.'" Jian said, as a different plan began to form in his mind.

CHAPTER 26

3400 Avent Ferry Road
New Hill, North Carolina
July 26, 1015 hours EST

Dorothy Davies sat alone at the small, round table beside her kitchen. The girls were playing quietly in their room. Her husband was asleep in their bedroom. One guard, the one who had broken her finger, sat in a chair outside the bedroom, his automatic weapon draped across his lap. He watched her, and her sleeping husband.

"I need to go to the grocery store. We're running out of food," she said, startled at her raspy voice.

The man turned his head and stared at her, saying nothing.

"I said, we're running out of food," she repeated, in a louder voice.

The man yelled something in Chinese, and their leader appeared. Aiguo walked in from the living room where he had been reviewing the previous day's information provided by Sergeant Davies.

"Mrs. Davies, what do you want?" Aiguo asked, while walking over to the kitchen counter where he refilled his coffee mug.

"I told your man that we're running out of food. I need to go to the store."

Aiguo stared at her, then walked over to the small pantry and opened the folding wooden doors. He turned and took a seat beside her at the table.

"*She reeks of fear. If I let her go alone, would she tell someone?*" Aiguo asked himself, while staring at the woman. She would not look him in the eyes.

"Mrs. Davies, we have the same agreement with you that we have with your husband. If you cooperate with us, then you will survive this. We will leave you alone, and you will restart your lives together after we leave. Your daughters will grow up and go to school. One day you will see them happily married. They will bless you with grandchildren. You and your husband will grow old together. But if I let you go shopping, and you tell anyone, or you drop a note, or just burst into tears and someone becomes suspicious, then none of this will happen. Your daughters will not grow up and go to school, get married, or have children of their own. They will be dead, and you will be responsible for their deaths. Do you understand?" Aiguo said in a soft voice, as if they were conspiring together.

Dorothy turned to face him. Aiguo could see the hatred and the fear on her face. Her eyes were bloodshot from crying. Her hair was disheveled, no makeup on her face.

"Good! You understand. First, you must become more presentable. No sane woman in China or the United States wants to be seen in public without looking her best. You need to make a shopping list, shower, get dressed, and say goodbye to your daughters. This is your test, Mrs. Davies, like the first time your husband went back to work. I'm sure you will pass this first test, and please, buy some green tea . . . in bags, not in a bottle," Aiguo said, and smiled.

Dorothy stared at him, grasping both hands together to keep from shaking. The she nodded, stood up, and headed for the pantry. She had a list to make.

CHAPTER 27

Harris Teeter
324 Village Walk Drive
Holly Springs, North Carolina
July 26, 1158 hours EST

Dorothy had left the house in a daze. She had hugged her children goodbye, knowing that if she made a mistake she might never see them alive again. They had burst into tears, run to their father, and woken him from a deep sleep. She had explained to him what was going on. He had only nodded, comforting his weeping children. Both girls climbed into bed with him.

Now she sat in the parking lot at the Harris Teeter. She glanced around at other people going about their normal lives, shopping, talking, and yelling at their children to watch for cars in the crowded parking lot. She longed for that normalcy.

She lowered the visor and looked at herself in the mirror. Her eyes were still red and puffy from crying. She removed a pair of dark sunglasses from her purse, put them on, and checked herself in the mirror again. Glancing at the bandage on her left pinkie, she opened the door of her car and stepped outside. The summer heat and humidity were stifling. She glanced up at the sky.

"There will be thunderstorms this afternoon," she said, while closing and locking the car door.

"*Calm down, you can do this. Just follow the list, pay for everything, and go back home*," she thought, as she crossed onto the sidewalk and headed for the entrance.

"Dorothy, hello, I thought Tuesday was your shopping day, and where are the girls?" said Camila Ortiz, as she walked up to Dorothy and hugged her.

"Oh, hi Camila . . . I was delayed a day. The girls are both sick," Dorothy replied. The last thing she wanted to do was meet someone from church.

"Oh, I hope it's nothing serious," Camila said, as both women headed into the store and pulled shopping carts from the stack.

"No, nothing serious, just colds and a mild fever. They're at home with Jonathan. I got out to do some shopping."

"Then we can shop together. We missed church service the last two weeks. We were out of town at the beach. You can tell me everything that's been going on," Camila said, as the women headed into the vegetable section of the store.

"Not much, just routine stuff, you know. Jonathan has been on night shift for a while. So we keep it quiet during the day while he's asleep.".

"Don't you get scared living so close to that place? We live on the other side of Holly Springs and that's still too close for me. What if the place blew up?"

"Nuclear plants can't blow up. It's not like a nuclear bomb. It's perfectly safe," Dorothy said, repeating the same answer that Jonathan had given her when they had first moved into the area.

"Well, I don't know. I think they need to tear the place down and put up those big wind mills," Camila said, while sampling a green grape.

"Wind turbines, they're called wind turbines," Dorothy mumbled, wishing the chatty woman would just leave her alone.

"I think I'm going to head over to the pharmacy. I need to ask them some questions," Dorothy said, while turning away from Camila.

"Well, okay, I'll see you in a while."

Camila was one of her best friends, and Dorothy was afraid that she would start to weep if she stayed and talked to her. She knew that once she started crying again she wouldn't be able to stop. It would all come out, and she would be responsible for the death of her daughters.

As she neared the pharmacy, she saw an ad posted by the front counter. It was an old sign from March saying, "National Poison Prevention Week". She could feel her heart begin pounding in her chest as a plan began to form in her mind.

"What if I poisoned them?" she asked herself, then blushed and looked around when she realized that she had said it out loud.

CHAPTER 28

The White House
The Oval Office
Washington, DC, USA
July 30, 2000 hours EST

President Miller sat behind the massive, ornate Resolute Desk, a gift to President Rutherford B. Hayes from Queen Victoria. Created in 1880, the gift had been made from English oak timbers from the Artic exploration vessel, the HMS Resolute. The President was feeling older than the desk.

"I know, Clarisse, you still think that this is a mistake, but the decision is mine. All the decisions have been mine. That's the way this job works. As the saying goes, 'The buck stops here'," the President said, while rapping the desk top with his knuckles.

"Mr. President, my concerns are not about the reactions of the American people, the media, or the world. I'm afraid we'll drive these men into action."

"Well, they've had the upper hand so far. They have the weapon, and we can't find them. We've been fighting with one hand tied behind our back. That ends now. The American people have a vested interest in this situation. The American people can't disappear into a secure bunker if this weapon is detonated. We have to find these men. We have to find this weapon," the President said, while being cued with a hand wave.

"It's time, Mr. President. We go live in 10 seconds," the White House Communications Director said, while verifying the starting point of the teleprompter.

"Mr. President! 5 . . . 4 . . . 3 . . . 2 . . . 1 . . .

"My fellow Americans, I am addressing you tonight from the Oval Office with information that will shock most of you. In 1992, a general in the People's Liberation Army of the People's Republic of China initiated a plan to smuggle nuclear weapons into the United States of America. He continued in this endeavor over many administrations, both Democratic and Republican. As of this year, 50 nuclear warheads had been placed within our nation in an attempt to blackmail us into surrendering any influence in the western Pacific and Asia. If we refused, the presence of these weapons was going to be leaked to the global media in an effort to create panic and chaos within the borders of the United States of America," President Konrad said, pausing to allow the impact of his words to sink in.

"This heinous attempt at blackmail and intimidation was thwarted due to the gallant efforts of various Federal agencies that discovered this plot and were able to determine the location of these devices. Of the 50 devices smuggled into our country, only one remains undiscovered. I have reluctantly withheld the information of this plot from you, and most of your elected officials, for security reasons. The panic and dismay that you are feeling at this moment would have been magnified many times over if I had gone public with this information when it first became known. The reason I am going public now . . . is that your country needs your help. I need the help of every American citizen in finding this last threat to our Homeland," the President said, pausing once again.

"This last nuclear device is believed to be located somewhere within the southeastern United States. The device is approximately three times the size of the weapon detonated above Hiroshima during World War 2. The individuals who control this device are agents of the late General Kung Yusheng. This plot was enacted without the permission or backing of the People's Republic of China. Their leadership has cooperated with the United States in bringing to an end this great threat to world peace. They are to be commended for this effort. But I need your help, the help of every citizen of this great nation, in bringing this threat to an end. We are looking for a dozen men, members of the Siberian Tigers Special Forces Unit (a dozen images appeared, provided by the Chinese government). They all have a distinctive tattoo on their upper right arm," the President said, as the Siberian Tigers logo appeared on a screen behind him, above the images of the men.

"These men are present in our country, and are assumed to be in possession of this last nuclear device. Their leader is Gong Aiguo (one picture was highlighted). He is responsible for multiple murders in Alexandria, Virginia. All of these men are highly trained, heavily armed, and extremely dangerous. One of these men has left a 'calling card' everywhere that we have been able to track him. He carves this Chinese character onto a surface," the President said, as the character for 'Tiger' was displayed on the screen for all to see.

"This is not intended to be a witch hunt of loyal Chinese-Americans. The last thing we need is indiscriminant persecution of innocent individuals. This is a nation of acceptance and inclusion. Look for this symbol. Look for suspicious actions by individuals fitting the descriptions given. Take no actions on your own. If you see something, if you suspect something, notify your local law enforcement agencies," the President said, pausing one final time.

"My fellow Americans, we have stood together in the past against threats to our national survival. I ask you to stand together once more. Together, we will survive this trial and emerge a stronger nation, a stronger people, unified in our belief that all people have the right to life, liberty and the pursuit of happiness, free from the intimidation of outside forces. May God Bless you and may God bless these United States of America."

Across the world, including China, the reaction from the media and the public was immediate. Servers all across the globe tripped, as social media use exploded. Talking heads raged or praised, based on their own agendas.

At two locations in North Carolina, the reaction was no less.

CHAPTER 29

3400 Avent Ferry Road
New Hill, North Carolina
July 31, 2020 hours EST

The Kitchen

"Your President has brass balls, I'll give him that," Aiguo said, while sitting at the round dining table beside the kitchen.

Jonathan Davies sat across from him, saying nothing. He had rotated off night shift two days ago, and wasn't scheduled to return to work for another five days. It had been two days of constant grilling. He knew from experience that these men were in the final stages of planning their attack on the plant.

Unless they have a tank or a hundred men, they're wasting their time. They would have to take out the whole security force in their initial assault. Even at night, we have 25 people on duty. I've given him everything he asked for, but it won't do him any good. Local SWAT teams will be at the plant in less than an hour. The initial Bragg personnel will be there in less than two hours. By plan, they won't hesitate. They'll head straight for the Main Control Room and kill any hostiles they encounter. That's the heart of the plant, the Control Room," Jonathan thought, careful to keep his face subdued.

"Your President is either trying to force us into action or cow us into submission. Neither tactic will work. The only potential problem will be at the plant," Aiguo said, while sipping on a mug of green tea.

"So what will happen at the plant, Sergeant Davies? What changes will the Security Force make?"

Jonathan paused. He wanted nothing more than to lay his head on the table and find blessed sleep. He forced himself to focus.

"During normal online operations we're in a Level 3 security. Because of the President's speech, we'll go to a Level 2, maybe even a Level 1, but I doubt it. We only go Level 1 if an attack on the plant is imminent or in progress. At Level 1, all unnecessary personnel are evacuated from the plant site. We go into lockdown. No personnel remaining on site are allowed to move outside their immediate area without being escorted by armed security personnel. The on-shift Operators, Mechanics, Electricians, Radiation Protection and Chemistry personnel will stay for the duration until relieved. We've never even practiced it with site personnel. Operations would go berserk. It would slow down their routine activities inside and outside the plant. They push back hard against anything that restricts their ability to move freely on plant site. They're prima donnas, and almost always get what they want. I might even get called back in early," Jonathan said, without thinking, as his fatigue became overwhelming.

"Excellent, I certainly hope that they do call you back. I need you inside the plant," Aiguo said, while flipping back through the pages of a notepad.

"You are due for a duty rotation back to Command Central, are you not?"

"Yeah, unless they change the schedule, which they might at a Level 1."

Jonathan had been trying to carefully weigh everything that he told this man, but a lack of sleep, the fear for his family, and the time change of shifting his body from nights to days, was affecting his thinking, and he knew it. He was exhausted, getting careless and chatty.

"So let's talk some more about Command Central, the place you call Overwatch. Let's go over the details once again," Aiguo said, while turning a fresh page on the notepad.

Jonathan rested his head in his hands, his elbows on the table. He knew that the fate of his family rested in those same hands.

"Command Central is located inside the security fence, in one of the unused diesel generator buildings. The original plant design called for four Emergency Diesel Generators, one for each of the reactor units they were supposed to build. By the time the plan was cut back to two units, the concrete building had already been built, one bay for each diesel generator. The diesels are huge monsters, over two stories tall. Each one can generate over 10 megawatts of power, enough to operate all the essential electrical needs of the plant. Being inside one of the bays when one of them is running is unbelievable. Hearing protection is mandatory," Jonathan said, feeling his mind begin to wander.

Jonathan had been trained in the Army to resist interrogation, and knew that one of the primary weapons of the interrogator was fatigue. The more tired you became, the less rational you were. It became more difficult to pick your words carefully. Things began to just spill out. He sensed that he was at that point.

"When the construction plan was changed again, and the second reactor was cancelled, the second diesel generator had already been installed. So we have two diesels. That left two of these huge concrete bays empty. After 9/11, security improvements were mandated by the NRC. Instead of being the 'red-headed stepchild' on site, Security became necessary for plant operations. If the NRC wasn't satisfied with the security at the plant, then the plant was shut down and forced to make improvements. We got plenty of money from CP&L. The last thing they wanted was for this plant to sit idle. They would lose over $1,000,000 a day when it wasn't running at 100% power, and that was 10 or 15 years ago."

"Command Central, Sergeant Davies, how many personnel work inside? How is access controlled? How are the personnel armed?"

"Like I said, two empty bays, security moved into the fourth one, the one furthest from the operating diesels. It's on the north side. A second floor with an elevator was installed in the main bay, where the diesel would have been. The lower floor is filled with servers, cooling units, storage lockers, spare parts, even spare servers. The second floor is accessed by an elevator or a single stairwell in the front of the building. It takes a key card to access the building. Each person on site has a key card. Different people are allowed access to different areas. It's based on need. Plant Operators have access to everything except Command Central. Only about half of security personnel have access. It's far more restricted than the Main Control Room," Jonathan said, as his head dipped toward the surface of the table.

"Does your key card allow you access to Command Central?" Aiguo asked, looking up from his note pad.

"Yeah, I can get in there. I've been trained at every station, so I have access," Jonathan said, as his mind drifted into blessed sleep and his head slid to the table.

"Do you want me to wake him?" Chonglin said, as he rose from his chair in the hallway and approached the table.

"No, let him sleep for half an hour. He's still providing useful information. As long as he cooperates, he and his family will stay alive."

The Bedroom

The door to the master bedroom was shut. Her husband was outside, being interrogated once again. Dorothy knew the big Chinese guard was sitting outside her door, always just outside her door. He had the look of a pit bull; that barely restrained aggression just waiting to be unleashed. You could see it in his eyes. She was terrified of him. She hated him. Callie and Emily were buried in the sheets and covers of their parents' bed, sound asleep. They were too afraid to sleep in their own beds. Dorothy, wrapped in a blanket, sat in the old NC State rocker, a present from Jonathan's late mother.

"She was so happy when she found out I was pregnant with Callie. She was finally going to be a grandmother," Dorothy said, while caressing the rocker's worn arms and staring at the lumps in the bed, her life's work.

"*Three generations of Davies women have used this rocker while nursing their young, but Nana never got to see Callie. Life was too cruel, too short*," Dorothy thought, hoping that the back and forth motion of the rocker would ease her mind, but it didn't.

"They let me tend my garden out back. That was a mistake. But I'm just a woman. They have my children. But they don't know about the wild hemlock growing down by the creek. I've got enough now. When I mix it with the green tea, they'll never taste it. There will be enough toxins in the drink to take down a bull. When the leader leaves, he always leaves this one behind, the one who broke my finger, his pit bull. He doesn't sip. He gulps down cup after cup. By the time he starts to feel something, it will be too late. His hands will get numb. He won't be able to walk or talk. He'll drop like a stone. I'll call the police, the Marine's, the damn President. Maybe I'll just take his gun and shoot him. Jonathan said that he'd protect us, but he's trapped. I'm all alone, all alone with the girls. I'm going to do the protecting. I'm going to kill that bastard," Dorothy said, her voice as quiet as a mouse, as the rocker's back and forth motion lulled her into sleep.

CHAPTER 30

447 Weldon Lane
Sanford, North Carolina
July 31, 2030 hours EST

The Barn
2nd Floor

"Jian, come back to the house. You have to see this," Heng said, while standing at the top of the stairwell on the second floor of the barn.

"What do I have to see, Heng? I'm in the middle of planning. I'm expecting a call from Lieutenant Gong at any moment," Jian said, while turning toward the stairs.

"The American President . . . he has made a speech about us. Our pictures are all over the TV. That idiot Chonglin has doomed us. We are being hunted by all of them," Heng said.

"All of them? All of whom? Who is hunting us, Heng?" Jian asked, turning away from the map of the plant.

"They know all about us. The Americans . . . they are all hunting us . . . all 300 million of them," Heng said, while gesturing for Jian to follow him back to the house.

Jian stood, and stared at the map of the Harris Nuclear Plant, knowing that they would attack the nuclear plant within the next 48 hours, or they wouldn't attack at all.

CHAPTER 31

Central Intelligence Agency
Mission Center for Weapons and Counterproliferation
Office of Director Janet Davidson
Manassas, Virginia
August 1, 1100 hours EST

"I'm glad the President went public, but every law enforcement agency in the Southeast is getting calls from people claiming to have seen the Chinese boogeymen. Some asshole is already advertising 'Siberian Tiger Special Forces' t-shirts with the Chinese character for 'tiger' included for an additional fee," Janet Davidson said, while staring out the window.

"That doesn't surprise me, Director. If World War 3 started, some entrepreneur would try to sell t-shirts and bumper stickers to make a buck off the event," Amanda said, while scrolling through texts and e-mails on her phone.

"Director, it looks like DHS got two good leads last night from the same place in South Carolina. An Exxon gas station owner sent in a pic of the tiger character carved into one of the pillars at his station. The second lead was from the same town. A woman called in about an Asian female in camo who always comes to the grocery store late at night, and buys large amounts of food and supplies. She said the woman claimed to be a 'Prepper' who lives in the area. The last time she came in, the woman said she saw an Asian man waiting for her in the passenger seat of a Suburban. She said she stared out the window of the store, and the man glared at her. Scared her half to death," Amanda said, as Janet walked toward her.

"What's the name of the town, and what action is DHS taking?"

"Dillon, South Carolina, and they've sent a team down there from Columbia. I'd like to check this one out personally. I can hit the road now and be there in eight hours."

"It looks like the best lead so far. We've been playing catchup for months. It's about time we had some luck. But screw the road. I have a personal jet. Be at Manassas Regional Airport in an hour. I'll have the crew waiting for you. You'll be on site in two hours," Janet said, while picking up her cell phone.

CHAPTER 32

Exxon Gas Station
Dillon, South Carolina
August 1, 1430 hours EST

"Nice to meet you, Agent Langford. I got a call a few hours ago that you might be showing up. I was told you were the one who broke this whole Chinese conspiracy wide open. That makes you a national hero," DHS Senior Agent Jack Honer said, while shaking her hand.

Amanda was shocked. It was the first time anyone outside her office had recognized her work. She had never even considered the possibility of her actions being heroic.

"Nothing heroic from me. I was just doing my job, and following the leads. I'm here to see what you've found so far, Agent Honer," Amanda said, feeling herself blush at the man's words, and hoping he didn't notice.

"Here's what we've got," Jack said, while pointing at the second gas pump on the outside row.

"Look at the pillar beside this pump. You can see the symbol on the right side," Jack said, as he walked over to the pillar.

Amanda followed him, and stared at the Chinese character. She then removed her phone from her suit coat, and began looking for previous pictures of the character left behind in the ambulance and in the storage building. She held her phone beside the new character, comparing all the images.

"So what do you think, Agent Honer?" Amanda asked, having already reached her own conclusion.

"Can't say as I'm an expert on Chinese writing, but I am a member of the American Society of Questioned Document Examiners," he said, and laughed.

"I guess you would call me a handwriting expert, among other things. That's why DHS sent me down here as lead on this case. But in answer to your question . . . let me see your phone for a second," Jack said, as Amanda handed him the phone.

He held it beside the pillar, comparing her pictures with the new sample. After a moment he handed the phone back to Amanda and turned away.

"So what do you think? Did the same man make both characters?"

"I have a basic familiarity with Chinese characters. They consider their written language an artistic expression of human language in written form. There's an emphasis on motion charged with dynamic life. Western culture is far more practical . . . utilitarian. We're function before form. That's why most schools in the United States are doing away with teaching script. It's outdated, a relic . . . an art," Jack said, paused as if considering another subject, and then continued.

"The man who carved all three of these characters is not an artist, but he is consistent. He has practiced this character hundreds of times. The lines aren't graceful, they're brutal. He didn't just scratch the surfaces where he left his sign, he carved them in. The way he writes reflects his personality. The man is a killer, and a bit of a loner. Only a man with that personality type would do something like this. If he was an American, I'd say he was giving us the middle finger," Jack said, while running the tip of his right index finger gently across the character on the pillar, tracing each line.

"I've heard a similar analysis from another individual involved with this case. He had many of the same conclusions about this man's personality type. I've thought for a while that this Tiger character that he keeps leaving behind would be the clue that broke open this case," Amanda said, while taking a picture of the character to add to her collection.

"So what else has DHS discovered in this area? What about the witness at Food Lion?" Amanda asked, while sending the image to her boss, along with a summary of agent Honer's opinions.

"Mrs. Jennifer Parkins . . . she's been the manager of the Food Lion in Dillon for the last seven years. She gave us a description of the Chevy Suburban and a partial South Carolina plate. I got the feeling that she's in everybody's business, as the saying goes in the South. The partial had 18 South Carolina matches. There were only five that belonged to Suburbans or vehicles of that type. So far, we've cleared four. Unfortunately, there's a Chevy dealer in this area, so Suburbans aren't that rare."

"And the last one?" Amanda asked, as they both turned away from the pumps.

"Feel like taking a ride? I'll drive. It's not far from here, a town called Little Rock," Jack said, pointing toward his own black Chevy Suburban.

Two other large vans had pulled into the station after Amanda had arrived. They seemed to be waiting.

Jack noticed Amanda staring at the vans and said, "Reinforcements. One of our assault teams is in each van. Local law enforcement and the Highway Patrol have already isolated the farm where the vehicle is registered."

"You can ride shotgun. The boys can pile in the back," Jack said, and smiled, while opening the passenger side door.

CHAPTER 33

Farm House
230 Harlless Bridge Road
Little Rock, South Carolina
August 1, 1550 hours EST

"It seems we're finally ready, Agent Langford. This farm house is buried in the woods. That's unusual for this area. Most old farm houses in South Carolina are surrounded by . . . farmland, not woods," Jack said, as he and Amanda stood at the back of his Suburban.

"Maybe that's why they chose this place. It's isolated and hidden in the woods," Amanda said, while adjusting the Velcro on her bullet-proof vest.

"All right, get the drone up. Let's see what we're dealing with," Jack said to the operator standing beside him.

"On the way, Sir," the operator said, and the RMUS Multi-mount drone lifted off from an open space ten yards behind them.

Jack and Amanda stood beside the man, staring at the split screen mounted on a stand in the back of the Suburban.

"The screen on the upper right is forward visual. Upper left are split screens of peripheral left and right. Lower right is thermal and audio. If the ambient air temperature is close to body temperature, thermal isn't very effective. Lower left is a map overlay. It shows the position of the drone," Jack said, as they watched the drone slip just below the dense foliage of the trees.

"I've seen drones on the news, but I've never been involved with the use of one," Amanda said.

"They've saved a lot of cops and agents in the last few years. We don't get many runners anymore. They know they aren't going to outrun the drone. That also means we have less physical confrontations by having officers chase them down. Some officers get

'Hunting Dog Syndrome'. They get pumped up and involved in the physical chase. The adrenalin high can make them less than objective when they finally catch the suspect. The same thing happens to the suspect. So you get two jacked-up individuals confronting each other. That usually ends with somebody getting messed up. With a drone, it doesn't become as personal," Jack said, as the drone stopped on the edge of the tree line.

"It's too open. Get the drone above the tree line and swing around to the south. The trees are closer to the house from there," Jack said.

The drone reversed course, and then began rising through the trees. When it rose above the trees, it skimmed above the green field of branches and headed west, then south.

"We've got over 30 officers and agents surrounding the house, but I don't want to just charge in. If the Chinese Special Forces guys are there, then they'll have someone on guard duty. They might even have their own sensors deployed to warn them of anyone approaching the farm. Either way, I don't want a shootout if I can help it."

"Everyone stay in position, stay silent and stay hidden, until I give the order to move in," Jack said over his comm link. Multiple clicks answered in response.

"Sir, I'm south of the buildings," the drone operator said.

Amanda could see that the drone was hovering just above the trees. It looked like the house was only 30 yards away.

"Okay, no vehicles present, but they could be parked inside the barn. No personnel visible, but thermal is iffy," Jack said, wondering where a guard would be placed.

"Let's start with the barn. Start at the south end, and then swing around the east side. If there are any windows, pause and look inside."

The operator nodded. They could follow the flight path as it dropped down past the trees and approached the south side of the barn. The window on that side was covered on the inside, so the vehicle slid to the right, and flew to the east side. A second window was also covered.

"Who would cover the windows in a barn? They almost look like curtains," Jack said.

"A woman would. I know that's sexist, but a woman would put curtains in a room. That room must be different from the rest of the barn for some reason," Amanda said, while pointing at the ruffles visible through the window.

"But there aren't any women on this team. They're all Siberian Tigers," Jack said.

"That we know of. Remember the report about the Prepper. They may have safe house all over the country. Somebody has to maintain them," Amanda responded.

"There's a window at the far end. I'll check that one," the operator said, as the drone drifted sideways, stopping outside the last window on the east side of the barn.

"No vehicles or personnel visible inside the barn," the operator said, while the drone shifted to the far side of the window.

"Swing around the end of the building. See if there's a window on the north end of the barn."

The view showed an empty barn. An inside door at the south end led to a closed room.

"That door leads to the room with the curtains," Amanda said.

"Turn and check the house. If you don't see any movement, then swing around to the west side and enter the barn," Jack told the operator.

"No movement at the house, entering the barn," the operator said.

The drone drifted to the edge of the open barn doors and paused. The concrete floor had been swept clean, but oil spots from a leaking vehicle's oil pan showed that at least one vehicle had been parked inside.

As the drone flew inside the barn, Amanda said, "Wait! The wooden beam on the left . . . the vertical support. Go toward that and zoom in about five feet up."

As the drone shifted and zoomed in, they could see that the beam had been carved. The Chinese character for 'Tiger' was clearly visible.

"Holy shit! This is the place," Amanda said, while turning toward Jack.

"All personnel, we have visual indication that this site has been used by Siberian Tigers. Prepare to move on the house, but wait for my signal to begin the approach," Jack said over the comm link.

"Get in the vehicle. Maintain contact with the drone while we move in. I want an eyes-on look before we go in," Jack said, as the drone operator slid into the back, and Amanda rushed to the passenger side.

All the other agents from the vehicle were on the assault team. Thirty armed officers and agents began to slip through the trees until they were at the edge of the woodline on all sides.

"Move the drone to the back of the house, southeast corner. We'll start from there," Jack said, as he guided the Suburban down the long unpaved driveway.

The drone drifted from window to window until the entire outside had been inspected. No sounds were heard or movement detected. The Suburban had reached the edge of the treeline. Jack and Amanda jumped out as the drone operator reestablished his control position at the back of the vehicle.

"All personnel, no indications of movement. Begin the assault. Proceed with caution," Jack said, as he and Amanda joined a group of heavily armed agents at the edge of the woods.

"I hate this part. You never know what you're going to run into. There are two EOD personnel on the assault team. If anyone finds anything suspicious, they won't touch it. They'll leave it for the EOD personnel," Jack said, while he and Amanda began jogging toward the house. All the teams were closing in from every direction.

Jack and Amanda ran down the driveway, as other groups breached the woods to their left and right. The farm house had a long porch that ran the length of the front. Wooden steps in the center led to a bright red door.

Amanda and Jack were at the rear of the second group. As the first man placed his foot on the lowest step, a pressure switch triggered the IED. The explosion ripped off the front of the house. The 55-gallon drum, hidden under the front porch, was filled with ammonium nitrate fertilizer, nitromethane, and diesel fuel. Just for good measure, 1000 nails had been added to the lethal mixture.

Five men and women were killed in the initial blast. Eleven more suffered the effects of shrapnel and concussion from the explosion.

Amanda later remembered a flash and flying through the air. When she recovered consciousness, it was to the sounds of a battlefield. The screams of the wounded mixed with the wail of sirens and the sound of helicopters. Medical personnel were rushing the most severely wounded onto medivacs. Others were placed in ambulances.

She found herself standing by the woodline, beside the same Suburban that had driven them to the house. She had no memory of walking there. Her ears were ringing, as she stared at her hands. They were filthy and shaking. She raised her eyes toward the house. It was a burning ruin. Firefighters were setting up to extinguish the blaze before it spread to the nearby woods. Dozens of law enforcement personnel were scouring the area, and searching the barn for suspects.

Amanda touched her face. It felt raw, like a bad sunburn. Her clothes were torn and filthy. She moved her arms and legs, examining herself for any wounds. Other than a few scrapes, and a raging headache, she had escaped serious harm.

As her mind began to clear, she thought of Agent Honer, and began walking back toward the house. The dead were still lying where they fell. Priority was given to the many wounded, and securing the area. She found him under a sheet. A breeze had blown the white linen off his face. The sheet was soaked with his blood. She could see a nail imbedded in his forehead; another had torn open his throat as it spun through the air. She remembered that he had cut in front of her as they were running toward the house. He had shielded her from the shrapnel of the explosion with his body.

The cell phone in her coat pocket began chiming. It was the sound of the doorbell on the house where she had grown up. A memory flashed through her mind of the previous Christmas. Her two brothers had arrived from the West Coast. One lived in LA, the other in San Diego. They were all sitting at the dining room table that her father had built 40 years earlier.

"It was a great Christmas. It even snowed," she said, as tears began flowing down her dirty face. She wanted desperately to be sitting at that table, surrounded by her family.

The phone had stopped. Then it rang again. She pulled the phone out of her coat pocket, noticed that it was almost 6 PM, and answered. The assault on the house had started at 5 PM.

"Agent Langford," Amanda answered, and cleared her throat, shocked at how raspy her voice sounded.

"Amanda . . . it's Janet, are you all right? The explosion at the farm is all over the networks. I'm watching video from a helicopter circling over the scene. What happened?"

Amanda began coughing, stopped, and then replied, "IED. They set a booby trap. My mind is still a little foggy. A lot of people are dead, a lot more wounded. The farm house is gone. They were definitely here. The 'Tiger' was carved into a wooden post in the barn. We saw it with a drone. I think the barn is still standing. I'll head there now," Amanda said, while kneeling down and placing the bloody sheet over Agent Honer's face.

"Amanda, are you injured? How close were you to the blast? Have medical personnel examined you? You probably have a concussion," Janet said, while remembering her own experience with being in an IED explosion in Iraq.

"I'm fine. I'll call you back when I get to the barn," Amanda said, then terminated the call.

CHAPTER 34

The 2nd Farm
447 Weldon Lane
Sanford, North Carolina
August 2, 1530 hours EST

Aiguo stood in front of the map of the Harris Nuclear Plant. The map was now covered with details provided by Security Sergeant Davies. Each guard tower was highlighted in red, security patrol patterns in blue. Notes filled the margins of the map, color-coded to the subject. A hand-drawn map of the floor plan of the Security Building was attached to one edge of the plant map. It had almost as many notes in the margin as the large map.

Ten men stood at attention in the middle of the room, facing the maps. All were dressed in the gray uniforms of the Harris Security Force. Each man was wearing covert body armor under his uniform. Aiguo inspected each man from head to foot. The ball cap properly perched and of the correct size, the insignia on each shoulder, the name tags above the right shirt pocket, the positioning of the web gear and the standard issue 9mm Glock, the highly polished black combat boots. Each item was critical to the effectiveness of the deception. Most importantly, each man had a photo ID, key card and TLD procured by Sergeant Davies.

"Remember, for the purposes of this mission, you are additional personnel assigned to the plant because of the upgrade to Security Level 1. You have been sent by the Duke Energy Corporate Security Manager. Sergeant Davies will secure Command Central. From there, he can control all security doors and gates within the facility, including the small building at the entrance to the plant site that they refer to as the 'Shack'. We will approach the shack in the black van that Bingwen has modified for this mission. There are three guards at the entrance. After they are removed, we will proceed to the Security Building. The device will be transported in the brown truck. The truck will wait at the top of the access road until I call for it. Security turnover takes place in the back of the Security Building at 1930. We will proceed to the main entrance; eliminate all personnel in the search area, and anyone else we come across. At the end of the search area is a series of personnel entrances. They call them turnstiles. Sergeant Davies will unlock these barriers as we enter the building," Aiguo said.

"Comrade Lieutenant, everything seems to depend on Davies. If he fails to cooperate, we will fail," Heng said.

"If he fails to cooperate, he believes that his family will die a gruesome death. He is weak. He will betray his country and his comrades, before he will allow that to happen," Aiguo said.

"As I was saying, after we penetrate the barriers, Team Fang will dispose of all the security personnel located in the Security Building," Aiguo said, as the team stepped forward, snapped to attention and clicked their heels.

"Guards who are assigned to patrol the Power Block and the plant grounds will be at the turnover meeting. The only personnel absent will be in the six guard towers located across the plant site. Sergeant Guan and Team Claw will 'relieve' the security personnel at those locations," Aiguo said, addressing the group.

He paused as Sergeant Guan's team began to laugh.

"Correct, Lieutenant . . . we will relieve them . . . of their pitiful lives," Sergeant Guan said, as his team stepped forward and snapped to attention.

"But . . . my comrades . . . remember who you really are, and the true purpose of your mission. We represent the Chinese people. The Chinese created an advanced civilization when the Europeans were still living in caves. The Europeans, and their bastard progeny, the Americans, have conquered, raped, and ravaged whole civilizations into extinction. They have stolen advanced knowledge from other cultures and used it to advance their militaries. Today the West is represented by the so-called United States, whose culture is so contaminated that they can't tell a woman from a man. China has risen from the ashes of history, and is ready to take its rightful place as the dominate power on this planet. Only one thing stands in our way. General Kung understood this. Our national leadership still does not.

They have become contaminated with financial success. They are no better than their Western counterparts. They have forgotten the words of Chairman Mao. 'Power grows out of the barrel of a gun.' Comrades . . . we are the gun, and tonight we will place that gun on the forehead of the bastard child of Europe . . . and pull the trigger," Aiguo said, his voice filled with fury.

All of the men before him still stood at attention. Several were shaking with the righteous anger that Aiguo had hoped to instill in them. Others had the grim visage of the warrior preparing for his final battle. Two wept, not in fear, but in rage.

"I can see that you are ready for battle. The fire is lit and burning bright. Now you must tamp down the fire. Keep a smoldering cinder in the center of your chest. On the outside you will appear calm, but on the inside sits the tiger waiting to be unleashed . . . the Siberian Tiger," Aiguo said, as he stepped back from the line of men and saluted.

Nine pair of boots clicked as one, as the men snapped to attention once more, and saluted their commanding officer.

"At ease! You have the zeal for this mission. Now, each one of you will approach the map, and show me your knowledge of your particular assignment," Aiguo commanded, knowing that his men were willing to sacrifice themselves for victory.

Farm House
1630 hours EST

Aiguo sat in a rocker on the front porch of the farm house. He found the heat and humidity of the afternoon relaxing. The men were inside eating what would probably be their last meal. The door opened and Lingli stepped out onto the porch.

"Good, I have a mission for you, Doctor. I want you to go relieve Chonglin at the Davies' house. It's a 30-minute drive. Here are the directions," Aiguo said, as he handed her a slip of paper.

"You will stay with them as the mission unfolds. Tell Chonglin to return here. You will not allow the family to leave the house or contact anyone. After the device detonates, I would suggest that you flee to the south. The woman has her own car. What you do after that, or what you do with the family, is up to you."

"I thought you were going to kill them," Lingli said, while reading the directions on the paper.

"I was. Chonglin was disappointed when I told him my decision. He's a brutal bastard, and has almost ruined the mission with his damn carvings. But he's a killer, and I can't afford to lose him now. It's funny, I'm prepared to destroy a country, to kill millions of people, but I don't want to kill that woman and her two young girls. It is a weakness in me that I can't explain. I suppose it's a character flaw. A tiger has no mercy when it hunts . . . prey is prey, whatever its age or sex. I have made that mistake before on this long mission. Never get to know your enemy as a person. That was part of my training. I took it as just another lesson. Instead, it was a warning," Aiguo said, while rising from the rocker, and resting his hands on the front porch railing.

"Take your old Suburban. Leave now; and thank you for your help on this mission. Thank you for healing me. Without you, this mission would have failed," Aiguo said, never looking at her.

"You don't have to go through with this," Lingli said, knowing that the words might cost her life.

"I'm afraid that I do. General Kung was right. The Americans have to go. Do not force me to kill you, Doctor. Leave, and do as I ask."

Lingli turned away, walked into the house, grabbed the keys and left. She didn't say goodbye to any of the men she had lived with for the last few months. Tears rolled down her face as she stepped off the porch and walked toward the Suburban. She hated the path that her life had taken. Instead of being a healer, she had turned into a killer.

"I'm no better than he is. I could stop this with one phone call, but I won't. I can't betray the mission. I can save one woman and two children. That will have to be enough," she said, as she started the vehicle and pulled away from the farm house.

CHAPTER 35

The Davies House
3400 Avent Ferry Road
New Hill, North Carolina
August 2, 1700 hours EST

Lingli turned into the driveway and drove around to the back of the Davies' house. The small brick home stood 50 yards off the road. The nearest house was a quarter of a mile away. The house was surrounded by woods on three sides. Chonglin was standing outside the back door as she got out of the Suburban.

"Greetings, comrade Doctor. The Lieutenant told me that you were coming. I still think it's a mistake to leave them alive," Chonglin said, as Lingli approached the large wooden deck attached to the back of the house.

"Our duty is to obey, especially on this auspicious day," Lingli said, while climbing the stairs and crossing the deck.

"Aiguo wanted you back at the other house as soon as possible. I'm here to make sure they stay secure until the plan unfolds," Lingli said, while walking up to Chonglin.

"They're in here," Chonglin said, as he turned and entered the house.

Lingli found the mother sitting at a round table beside the kitchen. The two young children were sitting beside her on the floor, playing a board game.

"What have you been told to do with them after I leave?"

"To keep them secure until the mission succeeds. After that it doesn't matter," Lingli said, while studying the woman and her children.

"*I can't imagine what this poor woman has gone through. She's exhausted and afraid. The children seem distracted, which is good. I'm sure that she's doing everything she can to protect them,"* Lingli thought, while handing the keys for the Suburban to Chonglin.

"She makes a passable green tea, but your cooking is far better. She only cooks American. It's either boiled or burnt," Chonglin said, and then laughed at his own humor.

"Remember, Doctor, Zhège nǚrén hé tā de háizi shì dírén (this woman and her children are the enemy). Never forget that," Chonglin said, as he stared at Dorothy, grabbed a handful of her hair, and pulled her face upward.

"Do as my comrade tells you. If you disobey, I'll return and punish your children. Do you understand?" Chonglin askedd, while twisting her hair tighter.

"Yes . . . yes, I understand," Dorothy said, trying not to cry out and scare her girls.

Chonglin released her, nodded to Lingli, and left through the back door. When the Suburban drove away, Lingli sat at the table across from Dorothy.

"I'm sorry about that. He can be an animal. I know this has been very hard on you."

Dorothy looked up, studying this new guard.

"Please don't try anything. I won't hurt your children, but I will restrain you if I have to. I am trained to fight, but that would only upset the children and cause you pain."

"I just want this to be over. I want us to have our lives back. I want my husband to be free of this. He's a good man and a kind father. Why are you people doing this?" Dorothy asked, her voice quiet and subdued from constant pressure to comply.

"It doesn't matter why we are doing this. That's not important to you. It will be over soon. When it's over, you will have to leave here. You need to pack a suitcase for you and your children. You will be leaving today or tomorrow at the latest," Lingli said, knowing that it was a mistake to have said anything at all.

"What are you going to do? It's the plant isn't it?"

"It doesn't matter. That's not your concern. The future of your children is all that matters. To protect them you will have to leave here, and head south," Lingli said, as she felt her eyes begin to well up with tears.

124

"You don't want to do this. You're as much a victim as I am. Just let us go. We can all be free of this nightmare," Dorothy said, rising from her chair.

"Sit down, Mrs. Davies. Don't make this any worse. I am a Doctor, but I am also a soldier. I have a duty to perform. I don't have to like the duty, but I have to obey. That is our way."

"A doctor? You're supposed to protect people. How can you be involved in this?" Dorothy asked, while sliding back into her chair.

"In our culture, duty and honor are very important. Sometimes bad things have to be done to accomplish great things. This is one of those moments. I don't expect you to understand. All we have to do is stay here until it's time to leave," Lingli said.

"How will we know? Will they call you?" Dorothy asked, afraid at what the answer might be.

"They won't need to call. We'll just know . . ."

CHAPTER 36

Harris Nuclear Plant
5421 Shearon Harris Rd
New Hill, North Carolina
August 2, 1850 hours EST

Kay Snaps entered the Radiation Protection Office prepared for a quiet night shift. Her shift partner, Cornell Waines, sat at his desk, his face buried in his PC. He was the Lead Technician for the shift. She knew he'd be on the internet for most of the night.

"Anything interesting at the Operations turnover meeting?" Cornell asked, not bothering to look up from the screen.

"Plant's at 100%. There are a couple of problems in the Turbine Building, but nothing that involves us. Looks like a snoozer. Day shift won't be so lucky. Have you ever heard of Security Level 1?" Kay asked, as she sat in front of the Radiation Monitoring System console and began the shiftly routine of checking the hundreds of radiation monitors scattered throughout the plant.

"I vaguely remember something about security levels during initial plant training, but that's about it. You know they don't like us asking about security stuff. 'Need to Know' and all that crap. So what did they say about security?" Cornell asked, still focused on his PC.

"Between the President's speech, and some explosion in South Carolina, Security is in a tizzy. I think the site is going to Security Level 1 starting day shift tomorrow. I got the impression that it's going to be a lot harder to get around on plant site. I think a lot of people are going to be told to stay home and get paid for sitting on their butts. It's kind of like preps for a hurricane, cutting back to essential personnel only," Kay said, her focus on the RMS console.

"I should be so lucky," Cornell said.

"Hey, it's our last night. We'll be off for all the crap. I'm looking forward to a week off. Hopefully, things will be back to normal when we rotate back to day shift," Kay said.

"That explosion in South Carolina is all over the internet. They think it was the Chinese agents the President talked about. I bet Security is going berserk down at Robinson. They're close to the area of the explosion," Cornell said, referring to another Duke nuclear plant in Hartsville, South Carolina.

"Yeah, I heard about the explosion in Dillon on the way in tonight. Robinson's only about 50 miles from Dillon. So when are you going to do your Daily Surveys?" Kay asked.

"I'll head into the plant after the mid-shift briefing, after midnight."

"I'll probably go out early. I've got the Fuel Handling Building tonight, plus some Monthlys at the north end," Kay said, while scrolling through the various screens, checking the radiation levels, and checking each one off on a list.

"So what's up, girlfriend?" Chris Baardsen said, as he strolled into the office.

"What are you doing here tonight?" Kay asked, as Chris walked over to the console, leaned on the side, and smiled down at her.

Kay and Chris had been friends for over 20 years. Chris was flirty, and Kay liked it. She also wouldn't hesitate to jerk a knot in him if he got too 'flirty'.

"Barker changed the due date on a project that he has me and Tommy working on. It was due three days from now. But now it's due tomorrow morning. Tommy and I are doing an all-nighter," Chris said, while scanning the RMS screen that Kay was monitoring.

"Oh, so Tommy's here, too? I know he hates that," Kay said.

"Yeah, but he focuses on the overtime. 'If you're going to screw me, pay me.' That's his motto," Chris said, as they both began laughing.

"If you need any help tonight, we'll be next door in ALARA," Chris said, as he winked and walked away.

"Hey, Tommy, need a refill? I'm going for coffee," Chris yelled, as he entered the ALARA office. There were four cubicles in the office. He and Tommy had the back two . . . more privacy.

He and Tommy Borders were ALARA Technicians. As Low As Reasonably Achievable was their job function at the plant. They helped keep radiation exposure to site personnel as low as possible by getting involved in day-to-day operations and long-range planning. It was a tough job, but beat doing the same routine surveys over and over like the shift techs.

"No, I'm good. If I have any more coffee, I'll have to delay my trip up to 286'. I need to take a look at a few things up there before I finalize my part of the report," Tommy replied.

"Kay's got 286' tonight. You two can make it a date . . . go up at the same time," Chris said and laughed.

"That's your line. I'm happily married, thank you very much."

"Hey, I love my wife. I don't fool around. I just like to talk, that's all," Chris said, while walking out of the office.

Ground level at the plant was 261' above sea level. The 286' level of the Fuel Handling Building was where the Spent Fuel Pools were located. The three pools used for storing spent fuel were each over 40 feet deep. The two main pools held almost 2500 spent fuel bundles. They were connected by a series of transfer canals that allowed the movement of the highly radioactive spent fuel bundles from one pool to the next.

Tommy Borders had been working with Chris in ALARA for almost 15 years. They were both Navy nukes from back in the day, and were as close as two friends could be. They were part of a solid cadre of Radiation Protection technicians that had been working together at Harris since the plant started up.

"Crap, I might as well get this over with. I'll take the camera with me," Tommy said, as he stood up, stretched and yawned.

He and Chris had been on site since 0600. It was going to be a long night, a very long night . . .

Command Central
Overwatch
1900 hours EST

Like Lingli, Security Sergeant Jonathan Davies had his assignment for the assault on Harris. If she felt reluctant, he felt like a traitor as he exited the Security Building, and began walking toward Command Central. His mission was to take over control of the facility. He wasn't scheduled to work there. But he was one of the Training Sergeants. His plan involved another ploy.

Command Central was inside the fourth bay of the huge Emergency Diesel Generator Building, 50 yards east of the Turbine Building. As he walked past the Turbine Building, Jonathan could hear the high pitched whine of the Low Pressure and High Pressure Turbines as secondary side steam drove their blades at 3000 rpm. The turbines spun the generator that provided electrical power for 500,000 homes and businesses.

"It's a political statement, like hijacking a plane. That's what he told me, but he's lying. There are so few of them. They aren't nuclear workers, they're soldiers. If they break something, even blow something up, the plant will go on automatic recirculation. The core will be protected. That's what they tell us in training. In the end, they'll all be dead. The plant will recover. I'll go to jail for the rest of my life, but Dorothy and the girls will be safe," Jonathan told himself, while approaching the far end of the massive concrete block that contained Command Central.

"This will work. I know it will," Jonathan said, while sliding his key card into the reader.

The light on the reader turned green. He heard an audible click as the lock on the Security Door released. He pulled the six-inch thick steel door open, stepped inside, and pulled it shut. If it didn't shut within ten seconds after opening, an alarm would sound upstairs in Command Central, and a security guard would be sent to investigate. All the security doors on site worked the same way.

"Okay, it's shut. I didn't need any more complications. Now I have to put on my game face," Jonathan said, setting down the briefcase that he had been carrying.

He removed a yellow armband with black printing and fastened it around his right arm with Velcro. The armband said 'Drill Controller'. Next he removed a clipboard, closed the briefcase, and pressed the UP button on the elevator located on the right side of the entrance vestibule.

The elevator door opened on the 2nd floor of Command Central. This level was referred to as 'Overwatch'. The stairwell from below exited opposite the elevator on the far side of the room.

Jonathan turned right and began walking past the southern bank of servers. The control position for the on-shift Security Lieutenant was located in the center of the room, just past the servers. This raised platform was jokingly referred to as the 'Iron Throne', due to the metallic black texture of the metal furniture. The Overwatch Lieutenant was gone, attending shift turnover at the Security Building. The three active duty positions in Overwatch would be relieved on station after the turnover meeting was complete.

Jonathan walked up the stairs to the Lieutenant's position and announced in a loud voice, "My name is Sergeant Jonathan Davies. I will be the Drill Controller and Evaluator for this unannounced drill."

The two men and one woman turned around and stared at him. One of them groaned aloud.

"You're kidding me, a damn drill at turnover? What asshole came up with that idea?" asked Sergeant Daniella Barnes.

The two men began laughing.

"Corporate Security believes that our drills are too predictable. I would suggest that you cooperate to the fullest extent unless you want to be placed on outside patrols for the foreseeable future," Jonathan said.

No one wanted outside patrols in the summer or winter, for obvious reasons. Outside patrol meant helmets, tactical body armor and 30 pounds of equipment. You walked from one inspection station to the next, while being timed. It was considered a 'shit job' suitable for newbies. It was also used for punishment.

"For the purposes of this drill, I am also the lead terrorist. I have gained access to Overwatch, and have secured all the personnel present. At this time you will secure each other to your duty chairs with these tye wraps," Jonathan said, while walking forward, and handing four sets of tye wraps to each security officer.

"You have got to be shitting me!" Daniella said, while staring at the tye wraps in her hand.

"Do I have to document your lack of cooperation in an assigned duty assignment, Security Sergeant Barnes?" Jonathan asked, while motioning the other two officers to start securing themselves.

"Secure your legs to the chairs at the ankles. Then secure one wrist to the arm of the chair. I'll get the other arm," Jonathan said.

"Why all four?" Daniella asked.

"Is a terrorist going to secure three?" Jonathan asked.

"He ain't gonna secure shit, cause I'm gonna kick his ass!" Daniella said, as the other two officers hooted in approval.

"Come on, Jonathan, what's the purpose of this?" Will Matthews asked.

"You guys go offline. How long before Security notices that your gone? How long before they send an armed mission to find out? The Security Plan gives them 15 minutes. It's never been tested off-hours or at turnover. Now, we'll find out. Daniella, tighten the tye-wraps, or I will," Jonathan said, observing the barely connected tye wraps around her ankles.

"Whatever!" she said, as she pulled the thick tye wraps tight.

"Okay, that looks good. Put your second arm on the arm rest," Jonathan said, then secured the officers to their chairs and verified the tightness of the other tye wraps.

"Good, drill's over. I'm sorry guys. I'm really sorry," Jonathan said, while walking over to one Overwatch console and calling an outside number.

"Overwatch is secure. All personnel terminated," Jonathan said, and hung up the phone.

"What the hell? Is this still part of the drill or what?" Daniella asked, while squirming in her binds.

"I'm sorry. They have my family. They wanted me to kill all of you. I won't do that, but I can't let you go," Jonathan said, while wheeling Daniella over to one of the railings by the entrance and securing her chair to the rail with additional tye wraps.

"Jesus, Dani, I think this is for real. Jonathan is a terrorist!" Will said, as he was placed ten feet away from Daniella, and secured to the railing.

"Jonathan, tell me this isn't real. You're just getting in our heads, right? This is just a spoof, right?" Wayne Douglas said, as he joined the other two secured at the rail.

"Wayne, I'm sorry . . . they have Dorothy and the girls. I don't have a choice. I have to do what they say," Jonathan said, as he walked up to the 'Iron Throne' and sat down.

All three guards began shouting and struggling at the same time. Jonathan ignored them, and got to work. Each of the other six stations at Command Central focused on a particular portion of the plant, but from the 'Iron Throne' he could see everything, and control every door, including the sealed door at the armored Guard Shack.

The Guard Shack
1910 hours EST

The black van, with Duke Energy Security markings, pulled up to the right side of the Guard Shack. One guard began smiling as Aiguo lowered the driver side window. A second guard began the standard check of the bottom of the vehicle. Aiguo shot them both in the head with a silenced 9mm.

Chonglin burst from the rear of the van as the guard inside the Shack, secure in a locked and armored box, began to call Command Central for help. No one answered. He had a shocked look on his face when the locked access door popped open. Chonglin smiled, and shot him in the throat while the man was fumbling for his handgun. A few seconds later, after watching the man choke as he bled to death, Chonglin added three shots to the man's head. Sliding his knife from its sheath, he carved his mark on the inside of the door. Then he installed a surprise, and partly closed the door.

"Chonglin, back in the van!" Aiguo shouted.

"Bring up the second vehicle," Aiguo said, over the assault team's comm link.

An unmarked brown delivery truck appeared at the top of the access road, and began heading for the Guard Shack.

"Sergeant Davies, are you listening?" Aiguo asked, over the comm link.

"I'm still here," Jonathan said.

"When we get past the top of the hill, raise the steel barrier."

"Understood," Jonathan said, knowing that three guards were dead, and more would follow.

"Remember, Sergeant Davies, I can call your house at any second. You don't want me to have to do that."

"I understand," Jonathan whispered, turning away from the image of the guard shack on his screen.

Jonathan's hands were shaking. He had to fight the urge to throw up. The three guards secured behind him could see what had happened on the large monitors at the front of the room. They all

132

began yelling and cursing. All Jonathan could see were the faces of his wife and two daughters.

"I'm a murderer. There's no going back," Jonathan said, while turning back to his screen.

The tripwire for the Harris Security Plan had been activated, but no one was listening.

CHAPTER 37

The Davies House
3400 Avent Ferry Road
New Hill, North Carolina
August 2, 1900 hours EST

"I have some leftover spaghetti from last night, if you'd like some. I have to give the girls their supper, and spaghetti is one of the few foods they'll eat without fussing," Dorothy said, while pulling a large pot out of the fridge.

"No, I'm not hungry, but I'd like some green tea. Chonglin said you made a good pot of tea," Lingli said.

"Sure, I'd be glad to," Dorothy said, as her heart began pounding in her chest.

"I don't hate this woman, but she's with them. That makes her as bad as they are. This is my chance," Dorothy thought, as she removed the canister of modified green tea from the pantry.

"I'll put the water on to boil, while I warm up their food in the microwave."

A few minutes later, the girls were both making a mess of the spaghetti. Emily was still learning to use a fork, so more sauce went on her face than in her mouth. Lingli smiled as she watched them eat.

"I always hoped for children someday. Now I don't think I want to bring a helpless child into this barbaric world," she thought, while sipping on her hot tea.

"This green tea has an odd aftertaste, earthy, like parsnips," Lingli said, while Dorothy sat opposite her drinking coffee.

"I don't drink it. Your friends asked for it when they let me go shopping."

"She's had almost a full mug. It has to start taking effect soon," Dorothy thought, while getting up to get more coffee.

Lingli drained the mug, went to set the mug on the table, but tipped it over. She stared at her hands, and then began rubbing her fingertips together. Then she looked up at Dorothy, standing at the kitchen counter, sipping on her coffee.

"You poisoned me," Lingli said, and tried to push away from the table, but felt her knees buckle and fell to the floor.

"Yes, I would have enjoyed watching that big bastard suffer more than you, but you'll have to do," Dorothy said, as she put down her coffee, walked over to the table, and knelt down beside Lingli.

"It's called conium maculatum, poison Hemlock. It grows in our backyard, down by the creek. I found it a month ago, right before your friends showed up and took over our lives. Jonathan was going to get some Roundup and kill it, but he didn't want to do it while he was on night shift. I kept the girls away from the area. I understand that it takes a while to die from this poison. I read once that they gave this to Aristotle. I don't think it's painful. First you lose control of your limbs. Then you will lose control of your bowels, and then other organs will shut down. Eventually, your heart will stop. I had to guess at the dosage. My estimate was for that big bastard. He's twice your size, so you should go quicker. I'd like to say I'm sorry, or that I feel guilty about doing this, but I'm not, and I don't. You brought this on yourself," Dorothy said, while slipping the 9mm from Lingli's holster, and setting it on top of the table.

Lingli couldn't control her limbs anymore, but her mind was fully alert. She knew that Chonglin would laugh at her and call her stupid. Then he would make fun of the other women who had become China's first female Special Forces soldiers.

She could feel her heartbeat become irregular. Her lungs seemed to stiffen, as if they were filling up with water or becoming paralyzed. Then she remembered Aiguo's last words to her, "*A tiger has no mercy when it hunts . . . prey is prey, whatever its age or sex. I have made this mistake before on this long mission. Never get to know your enemy as a person. That was part of my training. I took it as just another lesson. Instead, it was a warning.*"

"But still . . . I would not kill them . . ." Lingli whispered, as she closed her eyes, her last breath gurgling in her lungs, and died.

Dorothy stared at the dead woman, her mind filled with elation and horror. She had saved her girls, but she knew that this woman's dead face would haunt her forever.

She glanced at the clock on the kitchen wall. It was 7:20 PM.

"Jonathan, I have to call Jonathan and tell him we're free."

Her cell phone still sat in the charger on the kitchen counter. She had been warned by Chonglin not to touch it without permission.

"Jonathan, baby, please pick up!" she said, while autodialing his cell phone.

There was no answer. It was as if his phone was dead or turned off. Then she remembered . . .

"Oh God, he's some place the signal won't reach. The plant . . . the damn concrete . . . the walls are too thick," Dorothy said, as she stared at the girls.

Callie had slid from her seat, and was standing over Lingli, staring at her. Emily was finished eating and was busy spreading the remaining spaghetti across the surface of her high chair.

"Come on girls, I have to get you cleaned up. Then we're going for a car ride," Dorothy said, while scooping Emily out of the high chair, and taking Callie by the hand.

Ten minutes later, Dorothy, Callie and Emily Davies left their home on Avent Ferry Road for the last time. As they headed away from the house, Dorothy dialed 911.

CHAPTER 38

Security Building
Harris Nuclear Plant
5421 Shearon Harris Rd
New Hill, North Carolina
August 2, 1910 hours EST

The black van pulled up in front of the Security Building. Twelve men exploded from the van like fire ants from a mound. Two plant workers were exiting the Security Building, having worked over from day shift. Both were shot down by silenced weapons.

Team Claw remained behind at the entrance to cover their rear. Team Fang formed a stick and entered the Security Building. They turned right, crouching behind a glass-topped wall, walked 30 feet, then turned left, and left again. Two guards sat behind consoles on the other side of a row of metal/explosive detectors and x-ray machines. They looked up. Both were taken down with single shots to the head.

A third guard sat in an armored cubicle called The Box, elevated to the right of the entrance area. This location was the second tripwire of the Security Plan. If the entrance area was attacked, the guard in The Box would lock the turnstiles and call for help.

Sergeant Carlos Vance was the last of the 'Old Guard'. He had been working at the plant since 1987. He was a Vietnam veteran, and was scheduled to retire on December 1st. He thought it was an unannounced drill until his men began dropping. He knew what men looked like when they were shot in the head from close range. Skull fragments and brain matter were splattered on the wall behind them. Blood went everywhere.

"Holy shit! We're under attack," Carlos said, as an assault team swarmed into the inspection area, through the turnstiles and into the Protected Area of the plant.

"No, no, no . . . the turnstile gates are key card access only. That's impossible," Carlos said, as he pressed the alarm button on his console.

A warbling alarm should have sounded all across the plant site, but nothing happened. He picked up the Hot Line that connected to the 'Iron Throne' in Command Central. It was turnover, but one of the duty officers would pick up the line.

"Command Central . . . we're under attack," Carlos yelled, as the phone on the other end was picked up.

. . . .

Jonathan Davies had unlocked the door to The Box. He could hear the sound of silenced gunfire over the Hot Line, as Sergeant Carlos Vance cursed, and then died. He looked down at the phone and gently set it back on the cradle.

. . . .

The two assault teams formed up on the other side of the turnstiles. Sergeant Guan and Team Fang stood aside, as Aiguo formed up Team Claw for the attack on the remainder of the security force left in the building. Aiguo glanced at his watch.

"1913 . . . the meeting will be over in two minutes. We have to go now," Aiguo thought, while placing his key card in the reader that isolated the security offices from the open hallway.

He stepped aside as the door opened. Team Claw passed him and began proceeding down the hallway. There were three rooms on each side. They peeled off one by one and cleared each room as they came to it. They were all empty. Each man joined the end of the stick after clearing a room. The last room on the right was the largest. It served as a training, briefing and turnover room.

Aiguo glanced at his watch once more, thinking, *"All of the remaining personnel should be in that room for another 90 seconds."*

With a gesture from Aiguo, Team Claw reformed, weapons forward, and proceeded down the hall. Aiguo was third in position, crouched behind Chonglin and Bingwen. Heng walked backwards, covering their rear.

The door to the last room was open. From the sounds, turnover was still in progress. Aiguo glanced around, verifying that each man in Team Claw was ready. He held up three fingers, then two, then one. When his fist closed, he, Chonglin, and Bingwen stepped into the room and began firing. The remainder of the team spread out beside them. Only two guards managed to remove their weapons from their holsters before they were killed.

In less than ten seconds, 25 officers were shot down. Chonglin was stepping over and through the piles of bodies, using his knife to dispatch anyone who moved or made a sound.

Thirty seconds later, Team Claw had reformed back in the hallway, and headed back to the main hall, and Team Fang.

"1916 . . . back on schedule," Aiguo said, as his team exited the security area.

Team Fang was still in position covering both ends of the main hall. Three more bodies were piled up to one side, employees who were exiting the plant after working over their scheduled hours.

"Sergeant Guan, have your team proceed to their next assigned targets," Aiguo ordered, while changing the clip in his pistol.

"Yes, Comrade Lieutenant! Team Fang, sling your weapons. You know the drill. You must control your emotions and your actions. Walk slowly, be casual. The guard in each tower will be ready to go home. They will probably be looking at you as you approach the stairway leading to their position. Once you get inside, terminate the target. Make sure that the door is closed before you shoot," Sergeant Guan ordered.

Each man nodded, slung his weapon, and started breathing deeply, trying to come down off the adrenalin high of the assault.

"Comrades, this part is critical. We must secure these positions. Once this is over, the plant is ours. Then we proceed to Phase 2," Aiguo said, as the six men began to walk for the main exit leading outside, and to the remainder of the plant.

Security Tower #3
1921 hours EST

"Jeez, who is this clown? Look at him strolling across the yard. Ten minutes and I'm off the clock. It must be some new guy. We'll see

139

how he likes it tomorrow morning when I show up late for turnover," said Security Officer Maurice Jones, while standing at the guard rail atop Tower #3.

"What an asshole. This is going to be one of those 'I had it, you got it' turnovers. My bowling league starts at 8 PM. I'll look pretty damn stupid bowling in combat boots," Maurice said, while reentering his armored guard tower.

"Damn, that idiot even brought his own weapon. Now I can't turn my weapon over to him in the log. I'll have to stop at the damn armory and sign the weapon back in before I leave," Maurice said, as he flipped open his log book and began writing the turnover entry.

He had just finished writing the entry, and signing it, when the door opened.

"*That's odd I didn't hear a click as the door lock deactivated,*" Maurice thought, while turning around.

The last thing that Maurice ever thought was, "*Why does this asshole have a silencer on his weapon?*"

At 1937 hours EST, First Lieutenant Gong Aiguo, of the Siberian Tigers, received the notification that the last Security Tower had fallen. The Shearon Harris Nuclear Power Plant now belonged to him.

CHAPTER 39

Harris Nuclear Plant
5421 Shearon Harris Rd
New Hill, North Carolina
August 2, 1940 hours EST

The Security Building

Aiguo stood at the western end of the Security Building. His sense of accomplishment was almost overwhelming. He had destroyed the security force without having one casualty.

"*If this was combat, I'd receive an Order of Republic. I would be a hero of the people of China for this accomplishment, but that doesn't matter now. The mission isn't finished,*" Aiguo thought, as his team assumed defensive positions at the end of the building.

"Jian, Chonglin, take these buildings on the left. Clear every floor. They are all common plant workers. Kill anyone you find. I don't want anyone working against us. Remember, our mission is not to capture this plant. It is to use this plant to destroy America. We don't need any of these people."

The two men nodded, and began running toward different doors into the first big building on the left. The Service Building held the Maintenance shops and offices, the cafeteria, and most of the offices for Plant Management.

"Renshu, Bingwen, as per our plan, proceed to the Main Control Room. Kill any personnel that you come across on the way. Once you reach the Main Control Room, order them to trip the plant. It will remain stable for at least 24 hours with no further actions. After that has been performed . . . kill them all. We don't need them. Return here when you have completed your mission," Aiguo ordered.

Renshu and Bingwen both nodded, and began trotting toward the Turbine Building. At the northwest end of the Turbine Building, on the 305' elevation, was a massive, steel security door. It was the first of three barriers between the Main Control Room and the rest of the plant. Jonathan had unlocked them all.

"Sergeant Davies, lock the turnstiles inside the Security Building. Open Security Gate No. 1. I have a vehicle that I need inside the fence," Aiguo ordered, over the comm link.

"Understood. When will you free my wife and family?" Jonathan asked.

"When the mission is complete. I need your continued cooperation. As long as you provide that, your family will be safe. When this is over I will free them. That was our agreement. Now do as I requested," Aiguo said, while walking back into the Security Building to verify his other orders were being carried out.

Moments later, the brown truck pulled inside Gate No. 1 and parked on the right side of the Security Building.

Across the plant site, day shift holdovers and night shift staff were slowly finding out that this was not a normal day at work.

The Service Building

Site Vice President Gail Jacobs was working late. She always worked late. She had been married twice and divorced twice. Husbands and children had never fit into her schedule. Two husbands and three children now lived apart from her. Now she sat in her corner office, alone, staring out the window at her nuclear plant. Security was having another drill. They were always having drills.

"Now what are they doing?" she asked herself, while rising out of her custom leather chair, and staring at the west end of the plant.

"It looks like he just threw a body over the rail of the guard tower. What the hell are they doing? That looks like a safety hazard. What if someone was standing down below? I don't even see a spotter down there to keep people away. The Security Director is going to hear about this," she said, as two armed men came running toward the Service Building.

Gail began to reach for her phone. She paused, as two shift workers walked out of the Waste Processing Building and began walking toward the Service Building. They were supposed to stay clear of the area when security was playing, but they didn't seem to be concerned. She noticed one of the guards point at the two workers. Then one of the guards seemed to shoot at them. They both spun to the ground. One of them was still crawling back toward the Waste Processing Building. The door to the building stood open. A man was standing there, staring at the carnage. Then he turned and went back into the building.

"Oh my God! Is she bleeding? These drills are getting pretty realistic."

When the shooter ran over to the worker and shot her again, Gail saw skull fragments and more blood. The President's warning flashed into her mind.

"Oh my God! This isn't a drill," she told herself, sat back at her desk, and picked up the phone.

"Who do I call?" she asked, and stared at her phone.

She speed dialed the Security Director, but there was no answer. Then she tried the Shift Lieutenant at Command Central, again no answer.

"That's impossible. That place is always staffed, just like the Main Control Room."

She could feel her heart pounding as she selected an outside line and dialed 911.

"911, what is the emergency?" the operator asked.

"My name is Gail Jacobs. I'm the Site Vice President at the Harris Nuclear Plant. We have security guards killing people on site. At least, they're dressed like security guards. I can't get in touch with anyone in Security," she said, knowing that she was rambling.

"Ma'am, I hope this isn't a joke. We've had a lot of these calls since the President's speech. We prosecute people for making false reports on 911," the operator said.

"Hold on, I'm leaving my office," Gail yelled.

Gail put her phone on speaker, ran to her door, and opened it. She heard people begin screaming in the building. The sound of slamming doors, pounding feet, and furniture being tipped over was spreading throughout the building.

"They're killing people. Please send help," Gail screamed, as she ran back to her phone.

She heard a sound behind her and looked back. A large man was standing in her doorway. He was dressed like a security guard, but he was Asian. She didn't remember seeing any Asians when she attended the monthly Security Safety meetings. She had been encouraging them to become a more diverse organization for the last two years.

"Who are you? What do you want? If this is a damn drill, then you've gone too far," Gail said, as Chonglin pulled his knife, entered the room, and shut the door.

"Ma'am, are you still on the line? What's happening?" the operator asked, as the sound of screaming came over the open line.

Waste Processing Building
Radiation Protection Office
1945 hours EST

"Everybody, get the hell out. The guards are killing people!" Cornell yelled, as he ran through the ALARA Office and into the Radiation Protection office.

"What? Have you gone crazy, Cornell. I'm not going anywhere. I've got to finish my RMS checks. Then I'm starting my Dailys," Kay said, while ignoring Cornell's pleading.

Tommy and Chris both walked in from the ALARA Office.

"Damn, Cornell, you've got to get back on Valium. I know you're a Vietnam vet, but that was a long time ago. You having flashbacks, or what?" Chris asked, as both he and Tommy began laughing.

"Deever and Betty Miller just left here. They signed out of the RCA and were headed back to I&C. I followed them out. I wanted some chocolate from the vending machines across the street. I opened the door, and they got shot dead by a guard. They were right in front of me, not ten feet away," Cornell yelled, as he began walking for the exit in the office that headed into the power block.

"I always said that if something bad happened at the plant, it would be some damn guard," Chris said, as he turned and stared at Tommy.

"Dude, is this for real? Cornell, you better not be bullshitting us!" Tommy said.

144

"I don't believe a word of it. You boys are just plain stupid. I can't believe you're falling for Cornell's bullshit," Kay said, as she stood up and began walking toward the building exit that led outside.

"Don't do it, Kay. You'll die out there! I'm not kidding!" Cornell said, from the doorway.

Kay pushed Cornell out of the way and walked out of the office. Cornell had come into the building from the double doors on her left. She walked to the doors on her right, 50 feet from the other set of doors, and pushed one open. Off to her left, two bodies lay on the pavement in pools of spreading blood. A guard was at the other door, with his hand on the knob. They stared at each other from 50 feet. He raised his weapon and fired as Kay ducked back into the building. The bullet struck the steel door, and ricocheted away, grazing Kay's cheek.

Kay ran back to the office with blood streaming from her face. She stuck her head into the door and yelled, "Run! Cornell's right. The guards are killing people!"

At the sight of her bloody face, all four technicians turned, and began running deeper into the Waste Processing Building.

The Turbine Building
1945 hours EST

Auxiliary Operator Tony Bostic and I&C Technician Bob Moore were on the 286' level of the Turbine Building. One of the High Pressure Governor valves was sticking at 80 percent open. This was limiting the amount of high pressure steam entering the High Pressure Turbine and decreasing plant output. Output was money from the customers, and maximizing that made Duke Energy management in Charlotte very happy.

"Quit bitching, Bob. We could be doing this on day shift. It would be a lot hotter," yelled Tony Bostic, as he and Bob Moore were carrying a 30' extension ladder across the 286' level of the Turbine building.

"Yeah, like 140 degrees instead of 120. It's still frikin' hot," Bob yelled over the intense noise of the operating plant.

In the South, Turbine Buildings were open on the sides. They had no outer walls. If they did, the inside temperatures would surpass 200 degrees Fahrenheit during the long, hot and humid summer months in the South. As is, it was over 100 degrees as they headed for the faulty governor valve.

They never noticed the two guards who were walking by on their right. But Renshu and Bingwen noticed them. Neither man made it home to their families the next morning.

Renshu and Bingwen walked to the end of the building, and then up an open stairwell to reach the 305' level of the Turbine Building. Another Operator lay at the base of the stairs on 286'. He had started his shiftly round of inspections a little early.

They came to a 'T' as they entered the Auxiliary Building, which was connected to the Turbine Building. The Main Control Room entrance was through a key card door on the left. The door on the right led to an office area called the AO Corral, where Auxiliary Operators, not assigned to the Main Control Room, had cubicles, offices, and a group eating area. Renshu entered the Main Control Room. Bingwen entered the AO Corral.

Main Control Room
1952 hours

The Main Control Room was considered the inner sanctum by Operations. This was their cathedral. All other personnel on site were subservient to them. From here they controlled the multi-billion dollar marvel that was the Harris Nuclear Power Plant. Almost all of the operators were veterans of the US Navy nuclear power program. As such, they were a highly trained, highly motivated group of very select individuals. The Navy had trained them that way. They had ruled the seas in the name of the United States of America. Now they ruled commercial nuclear power. Each individual was licensed by the Nuclear Regulatory Commission as a Reactor Operator or Senior Reactor Operator. Almost all of them were men. The Shift Superintendent was their leader. It was his plant. Site and corporate management were irrelevant. If the plant ran, it was his call. If the plant shut down, it was his call . . . until now.

Shift turnover had concluded at 1900. All the day shift operators had left site.

Renshu was a bit stunned when he walked into the Main Control Room. It reminded him of an American science fiction movie that he had seen years ago. An older man stood to the left on an elevated platform. Two others were constantly scanning the curved array of indicators, gauges and lights, known as the Main Control Board. A sign at the entrance to the area said, "Access Restricted. Request Permission to Enter.'

A row of glass-fronted cubicles lined the wall on the left. A man stepped out and asked, "What are you doing in here? Security drills are restricted in this area," the man said, staring at Renshu's raised weapon.

Renshu shot him in the chest from a range of two feet, and then entered the restricted area without asking permission.

All three operators turned and stared. Renshu shot the older man and the closest operator, and then yelled, "Do not move or you die!"

Barton James was a Senior Reactor Operator. He had been at Harris for 11 years. Another year and he would have qualified for Shift Superintendent. He froze and raised his hands.

"Trip the reactor!" Renshu ordered.

Renshu wasn't sure what that meant, but those were the words he had been told to use.

"What? Why do you want . . ." Barton asked, trying to understand what had just happened.

"Trip the reactor, or I will kill you and find someone who can."

Barton turned and stared at the center of the Main Control Board. A large red button stood on an angled panel. It was covered with a plastic case to prevent inadvertent actuation. The SCRAM button was for emergency shutdown of the nuclear reactor.

The term was from the original reactor built by Enrico Fermi under the spectator seating at the University of Chicago's Stagg Field. It stood for "Safety Control Rod Ax Man." A man with a fire ax had been assigned to cut a manila rope and drop a wooden board covered with cadmium into the core if the neutron flux became too high. The antiquated term was a tradition in the nuclear reactor business.

Barton pointed at the red button and lowered his arms. To press it without express orders from the on-shift Operations Shift

Superintendent was career suicide, but so was disobeying this man. He walked over to the Main Control Board and used an attached key to unlock the cover. He looked back once, then stared at the button. Then he placed his right index finger on the button and pressed. It clicked, and a hundred alarms began blaring on the Main Control Board.

Barton stared at the alarms, wanting to take the actions drilled into him by years of training. The blare of the alarms and the flashing lights were the last thing he saw as a bullet entered the back of his head.

. . . .

Renshu and Bingwen met in the hall outside the Main Control Room.

"Good hunting?" Renshu asked.

"I went through two magazines in there. They were all sitting down to eat when I walked in. When I started shooting, they were running around like chickens," Bingwen said, while handing Renshu a fried chicken leg.

Renshu laughed at the joke, and then took the chicken leg and took a bite. He was getting hungry.

As of 2000 hours, only a handful of Harris personnel were still alive, and they were in hiding within the vast plant.

Rad Waste Control Room
2000 hours EST

The four Radiation Protection techs, burst into the Rad Waste Control Room, and all began yelling at once.

Steve Kroder, the on-shift operator for the processing of radioactive waste, was sitting at his desk and thinking about the next home improvement project that he and his wife Judy were planning.

"What is wrong with you people? This may not be the Main Control Room, but you still require permission, my permission, to enter this area. Damn Kay, what happened to your face? Did you run into something?" Steve asked, while discarding a magazine on in-ground swimming pools.

Steve was an aberration in the Operations organization. He wasn't ex-Navy. He was an ex-Army nuke and he refused to kiss anyone's ass. That's why, after 15 years as an operator, he was still buried below ground in the Rad Waste Control Room, processing all the liquid radioactive waste that the plant generated.

"Where's your First Aid Kit? She got shot!" Tommy asked, as he began looking for a kit.

"Damn it, Steve, call the Main Control Room! We were in our office upstairs when a guard starting shooting people outside the building. Cornell saw two get shot dead. When Kay didn't believe him, she went to look for herself. The guy shot at her and she got hit with a ricochet," Chris said, as Steve tossed Tommy the First Aid Kit from one of his desk drawers.

"You guys better not be messing with me. Is that real blood or ketchup?" Steve asked.

Kay gave him the finger.

Steve looked at Kay's cheek, and then picked up his phone and hit the autodial for the Main Control Room. No one answered. He tried four other Operations numbers, but no one was answering. Then he called Security Command Central. No one answered.

"What the hell is going on? The Control Room didn't answer. Security didn't answer," Steve said, while staring at the four RPs.

Cornell was pacing back and forth. Tommy and Chris were taking care of Kay's injury. Kay was shaking, and holding onto Chris's arm, while Tommy cleaned her wound.

"We've been overrun. This is just like 'Nam. My last day in country and the fire base I was on got hit that night. They blew through the mines, the wire and the phougas, just like it was nothing. We fought for two days. Two full companies; and only ten of us got out unhurt," Cornell said, as the pacing continued.

"Look, exactly what did you see? How many guards were shooting?" Steve asked.

"I only saw one, but there were more of them out by the Security Building," Cornell said.

Kay nodded in agreement, as Tommy applied a bandage to her cheek.

"Who got shot?" Steve asked.

"Deever and Betty Miller were both on the ground, and it was real, Steve. Their brains and blood were scattered everywhere. Trust me it was real. I know what the real shit looks like," Cornell said.

Steve tried the Main Control Room again. The phone rang and rang, but no one answered. He hung up the phone and stared at the four RPs.

"Did you guys see the President's speech last night?" Steve asked.

They all said that they had seen it or read about it.

"Could either one of you see what the guy looked like who was doing the shooting?" Steve asked.

"Are you shittin' me? All I saw was bodies and some asshole shooting at me," Kay said, as she stood up and then sat back down.

"Tommy, I feel dizzy," Kay said.

"Lay on the floor. Put your knees up. The wound wasn't bad, but you may be going into shock. Just breathe deep and try to relax," Tommy said.

"He was dressed like a security guard. He was Asian, and the weapon . . . the weapon had a suppressor," Cornell said, as the scene he observed began playing back in his mind.

Steve tried the Main Control Room and Security Command Central. Again, there was no answer.

"If I'm wrong they'll have my ass for this, but I'm calling 911," Steve said, as he dialed an outside line, and then dialed 911.

The line clicked dead, as if the call was automatically terminated. He tried it again and again, with the same response. Then he tried calling his wife at home. The line clicked dead. Then he tried the internet. It was blocked.

"I can't get an outside line and no access to the internet. That means that this is real. Something bad is going on. Either the guards have gone nuts, or we've been attacked by these Chinese dudes the President was talking about," Steve said.

"The President talked about a missing bomb. These guys had a missing bomb, a friking nuke," Chris said.

"They want to blow up the plant," Tommy said, while staring at Chris.

"You boys are all crazy! It has to be something else," Kay said, while lying on her back with her knees up.

"Yeah, and the last time you said that, your ass got shot," Chris said.

"Screw you, Chris!" Kay replied.

"We need some guns," Cornell said, as he began pacing again.

"The guards have lockers in all the buildings. I had a guard tell me a few years ago that they keep backup weapons and ammo in those lockers," Chris said.

"Yeah, I've seen those lockers. They have the mother-of-all padlocks on them, and the lockers are steel and bolted to the floor," Steve said.

"Yeah, and the Tool Room one floor up has the mother-of-all bolt cutters. There's one in there that's four feet tall. The cutting heads are the size of my hands," Tommy said.

"If we cut one of those open and this is bullshit, they won't just fire us. The FBI will put us behind bars for 20 years. They'll call us the terrorists. Just saying . . ." Tommy said.

"We should just wait this out and do nothing," Kay said.

"The Main Control Room is down. Security is down. Comm with the outside has been cut. This is serious shit. If it's these Chinese guys, why would they attack a nuclear plant? Why this one?" Cornell asked.

"Like Tommy said, the plant's the target," Chris said.

"Back in the 90's I worked on a project to convert the Spent Fuel Pools to hold more spent fuel racks. When Jimmy Carter screwed the pooch, and forbid spent fuel recycling in the US, the utilities were caught with no place to put their spent fuel. We had to reinforce the floors on the bottom of the pools to hold more than their original design load. The problem was that the pools were already in use. That project was a bitch. We contaminated the whole floor more than once. But in the end we made enough room for Robinson and Brunswick to start sending us all their old fuel," Tommy said.

"So what's that got to do with anything?" Kay asked.

"I don't know how many spent fuel bundles we've got in our pools, but it must be thousands," Tommy said.

"If it is the Chinese and if they've got the missing nuke . . ." Steve began.

"Then we're a big ass target. If you want to mess this country up, then pop a nuke inside that building," Tommy said.

"That would be crazy," Kay said.

"Yeah, that would be crazy," Tommy replied, and stared at her.

CHAPTER 40

The Langford Home
106 East Whitaker Mill Road
Raleigh, North Carolina
August 2, 2000 hours EST

Amanda had finished searching through the barn in South Carolina, and what remained of the house. Then she forwarded her findings to Director Davidson. Janet told her to take a few days off to recover from the effects of the IED before reporting back to work. Amanda didn't argue. She had a blistering headache that wouldn't go away, and she couldn't get the sight of DHS agent Honer's torn face out of her mind.

Not wanting to spend a few days in some motel in South Carolina, she decided to rent a car, drive up to Raleigh, and visit her parents in their new house.

The sun was heading down, and the shadows were growing, as Amanda pulled up to the front of the house. She turned into the driveway, her engine still running, and verified the address from an e-mail that her mother had sent. Texting was still a little too advanced for her parents.

The lot was small, but well kept. It was a two-story brick house painted tan with white trim. A covered porch ran the length of the house. The steps were on the left. A wooden swing, painted white, hung on the right side of the porch. She saw her father pass by a window and she began to cry.

"Great, I walk in crying like a little girl who had her feelings hurt at school. That'll make a great impression. I haven't seen them since Christmas, and in that time they sold the farm and moved here. They're getting old, and I've been too busy to even pay them a visit," Amanda said, while wiping tears from her eyes.

"Okay, girl, get your act together," she said, while lowering the visor and checking her face in the mirror.

"Great . . . red, baggy eyes from no sleep. I'm exhausted. Momma will go into full mother hen mode, and Daddy will start lecturing me about taking better care of myself. Maybe that's what I need right now," she said, while wiping her eyes and blowing her nose.

The front door opened, and her mother appeared with a broom. As she began sweeping the porch, she glanced up at the car in the driveway and stopped.

Amanda turned off the car and stepped out. As she slammed the car door, her mother dropped the broom, and rushed off the porch. As Amanda stepped onto the sidewalk, her mother wrapped her arms around her and hugged her. Amanda began to cry and hugged her back.

"Amanda, are you all right? You don't look well, and it's not like you to cry like this. What's wrong?" Selma asked, while guiding Amanda toward the house.

"I'm okay. It's just work has been really hard lately, that's all," Amanda said, holding her mother's hand as they walked onto the porch.

Her father appeared in the doorway, a cold beer in hand. Amanda began crying again as he hugged her. He set the beer down on the porch rail as they walked toward the swing. A tissue appeared from her mother's apron, and Amanda wiped her eyes as they sat down.

"I like the swing. It's big enough for all of us," Amanda said, tears welling up unbidden, as the swing began to sway.

"It's the first thing your father made after we moved in. He was going to set up his workshop in the basement, but I wouldn't have it. Too much dust would get in the house. So he set up his workshop behind the house, in an old garage," her mother said.

"So what's going on, baby girl? Why are you so upset?" Will asked.

"Daddy, you know that I work for the CIA. There are just things that I can't talk about. The last few days have been stressful. I'm taking some time off, and I just thought that I'd pay you both a visit. I'm sorry I haven't come down here before," Amanda said, relishing the physical contact of sitting between her parents.

154

"We're glad to have you for as long as you can stay. You don't have to apologize for anything," Selma said, while patting her daughter on the knee.

Amanda winced, and both her parents noticed. They glanced at each other.

"Amanda, are you hurting?" Selma asked.

"Yeah, maybe a little bit. Did you hear about the explosion in South Carolina?" Amanda asked.

"Yes, it was all over the TV. After the President's speech, I was in a tizzy. Then the explosion happened, and the people on the news said that it might be connected to the horrible things that the President was telling us. Does that have anything to do with you?" Selma asked.

"I was there, Momma. I kind of got caught up in the blast. The man in front of me was killed," Amanda said, and began crying again.

She knew that she wasn't supposed to talk about it, but things just started to spill out. Before she knew it, she had told them almost everything.

"Amanda, you need to find another job, and I mean right now. You need to call up your boss and quit. That stuff is too dangerous for a woman," Will said.

"Will, just hush. This isn't 1950. A woman can have any job she wants," Selma said.

"Daddy, I know you both care, and that you're worried about me. But I'm the one who found out about these weapons that the President talked about. Me . . . your little girl, figured it out. You both raised me to be strong and independent. You raised me to be proud to be an American. I want to help my country, and my country needs me. I can't just quit and walk away," Amanda said.

All three began crying as Amanda put her arms around both her parents. No words were exchanged. They all just sat, and rocked, and hugged each other as the sun set, and the coming darkness loomed.

CHAPTER 41

Harris Nuclear Plant
5421 Shearon Harris Rd
New Hill, North Carolina
August 2, 2000 hours EST

West of the Security Building

"Comrade Lieutenant, we searched all the buildings. We found less than a dozen people. There are so many places to hide that I can't guarantee that we got everyone," Jian said, as he and Chonglin ran up to the rear of the Security Building.

"Our friend, Sergeant Davies, has blocked all outside calls from land lines and internet service. Cell phones will work, but it won't make any difference if any people are left. It's time for Phase 2. I want you two to escort the device to the north end of the Fuel Handling Building. Heng, you bring the truck up. When you get to the door, it should already be unlocked. You know the rest of the plan. If you have any problems, call me," Aiguo said.

As the truck drove off with the three men and the device aboard, Renshu and Bingwen could be seen exiting the Turbine Building. Bingwen discarded a chicken leg, and wiped his hands on his pants, as they walked up to Aiguo.

Aiguo said nothing, as he stared at Bingwen.

"What? I was hungry. They were sitting down to eat. After taking care of business, I figured . . . why waste the food? There's plenty left," Bingwen said.

"The Main Control Room and all the operators are dead. I had one of them trip the reactor before I killed him," Renshu said.

"Good, the device is on the way to the Fuel Handling Building. Sergeant Guan and Team Claw have the towers. They will maintain security on the perimeter and the open areas inside the fence. If anyone moves in the open other than us, they're dead. I have another mission for you two," Aiguo said, as he turned and began walking back into the Security Building.

Tool Room
Waste Process Building 236'
2015 hours EST

"Damn boy, you weren't kidding. These things are huge. I bet they weigh 30 pounds," Chris said, as he lifted the huge bolt cutters from their storage stand and put them back down.

"So where's the nearest security locker? I hate walking around this place unarmed. Sooner or later those bastards are going to start searching this building to find us," Tommy said.

"There's one locker on this level, just inside the key card door going into the Reactor Auxiliary Building (RAB). It's on the wall opposite the Personnel Air Lock (PAL)," Steve said.

"Damn, you're right. The guard sits beside it during every outage when we have to set up access to the Reactor Containment Building (RCB)," Tommy said.

"So then what, we go all A-Team and start hunting these guys down?" Kay asked.

"A-Team? How old are you, Kay?" Chris asked.

"Screw you, Chris!" Kay replied, and added a gesture, along with her comment.

"Kay, we have to get outside. We've got our cell phones, but they won't work in here . . . too much concrete. We have to make sure that the outside world knows what's going on in here," Tommy said, as he picked up the bolt cutters and began walking down the hall toward the RAB.

"I'll feel better when we're armed. I don't like being shot at and not being able to shoot back," Cornell said.

"Remember what the President said about these guys. They're the Chinese equivalent of Delta Force. These guys are trained killers, not rent-a-cops. We don't hunt anybody. We don't want to get in a shootout either," Steve said.

"I still know how to shoot," Cornell said.

"So do I," Tommy said.

"Yeah, you ever had a deer shoot back?" Steve asked.

They were silent until they approached the massive security door leading into the RAB.

Steve was reaching for his key card when Chris said, "Wait, the light's already green. See if it's unlocked."

Steve pulled on the heavy door and it opened. They all ducked inside, and Steve shut the door as quietly as possible.

"Hey, there's the cabinet, and that is a big padlock," Kay said.

"Shit, that's nothing. Watch this," Tommy said, as he walked over with the bolt cutters.

"Damn, that's hard steel. Chris, give me a hand," Tommy said, as he began squeezing the long handles of the bolt cutter together.

Soon, all four men were on the handles and trying to cut through the padlock.

"Let me help," Kay said, as she grabbed an open space on the handle and began pushing.

A few seconds later the hasp on the padlock snapped. The padlock spun and fell to the floor. The four men stared at Kay.

"Girl power, boys!" Kay said, while crossing her arms.

"Holy crap! Look at all this stuff," Chris said, as he opened the door to the cabinet.

"Four M16A2s and four 9mm Berettas. What are those, some kind of grenades?" Tommy asked.

"Flash bangs . . . stun grenades. Security wouldn't want anything that would tear up equipment, like a fragmentation grenade. But a flash bang would definitely knock somebody down for a while," Cornell said, while picking up one of the M16A2s and two 30-round magazines.

"Kay, have you ever shot a weapon?" Tommy asked.

"Point and pull the trigger . . . it can't be that hard," Kay said, as she picked up one of the M16s and placed the butt of the stock in her shoulder.

Cornell lifted the barrel after she pointed the weapon at him.

"Rule number one; don't ever point a weapon at someone unless you're gonna shoot them," Cornell said.

"Does Chris count?" Kay asked.

"Kay, watch me, and I'll show you how it's loaded," Cornell said, then demonstrated.

"I'll take a handgun. They're easier to use," Steve said, while strapping on a holster.

"Long gun for me. I haven't touched one of these since Boot Camp, but I do own a Ruger Model 44. This will do just fine," Tommy said, as he took the third M16A2.

After they were all armed, Chris asked, "Now what?"

"I say the Main Control Room. If we try to go outside, they'll find us for sure. We'll stay in the RCA to get there. We don't want to get in a gun fight with these guys. Then we check the Main Control Room and then try for the roof. We can get a cell connection there," Steve said.

The others nodded in agreement, and began walking through the 236' level of the RAB toward the north stairs that lead up to the Main Control Room on 305'.

CHAPTER 42

Troop C Headquarters
North Carolina Highway Patrol
1831 Blue Ridge Road
Raleigh, North Carolina
August 2, 2000 hours EST

"Hey, Sarge, you're going to love this one. 911 got a call from some woman claiming that the guards at the Harris Nuclear Plant were killing everyone on site," Master Trooper Mac Williams said to Sergeant Louise Baker, Shift Supervisor on nights.

"Why does this always happen on night shift when I'm in charge? Is it a full moon tonight? I swear all the crazies come out during a full moon," Sergeant Baker said, while staring at Trooper Williams.

"The 911 operator thought it was legit. That's why she called us."

"See who we've got on US 1. Have Dispatch vector them to Harris and have them check in with the guards at the entrance. If this was real, we should have gotten more calls from the plant by now. I've toured out there. The place is a fortress, and the security force is first class. This is bullshit, but we'll check anyway," Sergeant Baker said.

"That's not the only one from that area. Another woman called and said that Chinese soldiers had taken over her house and terrorized her family. She claimed that she had just killed one of them and was fleeing for her life with her two little girls. It was some place on Avent Ferry Road, a few miles from Harris. The Sheriff's Department is looking into that one."

"Like I said, full moon and all the crazies come out."

. . . .

160

Harris Nuclear Plant
2020 hours

Three North Carolina Highway Patrol cruisers turned onto the Harris Nuclear Plant access road and stopped at the top of the hill. The sun was starting to set, and the clouds above the plant were violent shades of swirling red and orange.

"You guys wait up here. I'll go talk to the guards and verify that everything is sat," Senior Trooper Destiny Jones said, over her radio.

"Roger that," replied the other two troopers over the comm net.

Destiny Jones was cautious by nature, having grown up in southeast Raleigh. The neighborhoods there were rough, and she never took any situation for granted.

"*Something doesn't seem right. I've only been out here twice, but I remember the guards were always visible,*" she thought, while approaching the guard shack.

She stopped 50 feet from the shack, and waited.

"They should come out when a vehicle approaches . . . always," Destiny said, as she picked up her mike.

"Both of you, get down here. Fan out on either side of this guard building. Exit your vehicles and cover the building. When you're in position, I'll go check the area," Destiny said.

She waited for a confirmation, then parked her vehicle facing the shack, and turned on the dash cam.

When the other two cruisers were in position, the officers left their vehicles, using them for cover as they drew their weapons.

"Okay, girl, let's go see what's going on," she said, while exiting her vehicle and drawing her service pistol.

At 20 feet from the guard building, she could see the blood trails leading around the shack. From the pattern, she could see that two people were shot outside the building and dragged to an entrance on the left side.

"I see indications of a shooting . . . two victims. I'm going for the entrance," Destiny said, over her comms to the other two troopers covering her approach.

She crouched, her weapon forward, and approached the closed door. She could see that the building was designed to be a fighting position for the guards if attacked. The walls were steel, and firing ports were built into the sides. After checking the rear of the building, she looked through the glass, and saw three men piled up on top of each other. All had been shot at close range. She turned, and ran back to her cruiser.

"Dispatch, this is Senior Trooper Destiny Jones, over!"

"Dispatch, over!"

"I'm located at the guard shack at the entrance to the Harris Nuclear Plant. Three guards have been shot and killed. I repeat, three security personnel have been shot and killed, over!"

"Understand three dead at the security entrance to Harris? Is that correct? Over!"

"Correct . . . Dispatch, this looks serious. We're going to drive up to the plant. We need backup and an ambulance, over!"

"Roger that, backup and medical, over!"

As Destiny talked on the radio, another trooper approached the guard shack. He had intended to verify that the victims were deceased. As he opened the door, the explosive that Chonglin had left behind detonated. The trooper was hurled 30 feet through the air. He was dead before he hit the ground. As the smoke cleared, Destiny stared at the shack. The bulletproof glass had resisted the explosion. She could no longer see inside. All she could see was blood coating the inside of the windows of the guard shack.

CHAPTER 43

Harris Nuclear Plant
5421 Shearon Harris Rd
New Hill, North Carolina
August 2, 2010 hours EST

Behind the Main Control Room

"Chris, if you walk through that radiation portal monitor and make it alarm, I'll shoot you myself," Kay said, as the five night shift workers prepared to exit the Radiation Controlled Area and enter the Main Control Room complex.

"Sorry, hard to break the habit," Chris said, as they all slipped past the portals and walked up to the door leading into the rear section of the Main Control Room.

"I'll go first. It should be empty, but if I yell, run back into the RCA," Steve said, while sliding the 9mm out of its holster.

They all nodded. Steve cracked the door, and slid inside the server room located behind the Main Control Room. A minute later, the door opened. Steve signaled for them to enter. After they were all in the room, Steve pointed at the exit that led to the Main Control Room.

"We'll do it the same way. I'll go first," Steve said, as he approached the door and walked through.

A minute later he ran back in and threw up in a trash can beside a desk.

"Jesus, Steve! What did you see?" Chris asked.

"Bodies . . . they're all dead, all shot up. Everything was in alarm. I think the plant tripped. But where are the rest of them? We need to check the AO Corral. The Operators were having a big meal tonight," Steve said, while wiping off his mouth.

"We'll go around back. I don't want to go in there again," Steve said, as he holstered his pistol, bent over the trash can, and threw up for the second time.

"Steve, you and Kay wait here. We'll go check the AO Corral. Cornell, you cover our backs," Tommy said.

The light on the key card door was green as the trio approached the side entrance to the AO Corral. Tommy pushed the massive door open as Chris and Cornell covered him. After closing the door, they began to search the various offices and bathrooms. The last room on the right was the AO Corral. It was filled with operators' cubicles with a large open area in the middle. The long table in the middle was used for briefings, and once a week for a shift dinner.

Tommy went in first, then froze in the doorway. Chris stood ten feet behind him, waiting for Tommy to enter the room.

"What is it? Move in. Let's get out of the hall," Chris said.

Tommy backed out of the room, leaned against a wall and slumped to the floor. Cornell bypassed them both, and walked into the room.

"Holy Jesus, they're all dead!" Cornell said, while stepping into the room with the M16A2 braced into his shoulder.

The room was silent, but the smell of death was overwhelming. Chris ducked past Tommy and entered the room. The sight of bodies piled on top of each other struck him first, then the smell of so much blood. His mind went numb as he recognized the faces of so many friends, people that he had known and worked with for years.

"Yeah, it smells just like this. You never forget the smell of death once it gets into your nose. Give it a couple of days and it's ten times worse," Cornell said.

Chris walked out of the room and looked down at Tommy.

"Come on, brother, we've got to get out of here. We'll go back and tell the others . . . then figure out what to do next," Chris said, as he reached down and helped Tommy get up.

"Chris, I've killed my share of deer, and gutted them too. But this . . . all those people," Tommy said, while leaning against the wall.

"I tried a couple of the phones . . . no signal," Cornell said, as he walked out of the room.

"We have to remember why we came up here. We were going to go outside and try to get a cell connection," Tommy said, while taking a few deep breaths to clear his head.

"Not here. It's too open. They could be waiting outside," Chris said.

"Let's go get the others, and then go back down the stairwell to 286'. There's an exit in the ventilation room. We can get out on the roof by the Containment Building. It's pretty secluded, and we might get a signal," Tommy said.

286' Roof
2030 hours EST

As they exited the RAB onto the roof, they were greeted by the howling roar of the Main Steam Dumps. The Reactor may have tripped and stopped the fission process in the core, but an enormous amount of heat energy was still being released. Tripping the Reactor tripped the Main Turbine, leaving nowhere for the secondary side steam from the three Steam Generators to go, but up.

"They won't stay around here. It's too damn noisy," Chris yelled, as he reached into his pants pocket and removed his cell phone.

"Are you getting a signal?" Kay asked, while looking at her own phone.

"There's still too much interference. We need to get out in the open," Cornell said.

"Cover me. I'm going to go out on the open section of the roof," Steve said, as he pointed toward an open area past the steam dumps.

Steve ran through the maze of steam piping. The heat and the sound combined to shake his bones as he ran through the cloud of secondary steam. As he broke into the open, he stopped and looked at his phone.

"Three bars!" he said, as he entered 911 on the key pad.

He never felt the three bullets that entered his chest. One penetrated his heart. He died before his body slumped to the roof. Cornell had followed Steve through the steam, but had stopped at the last row of piping. When he saw Steve fall, he turned and ran back to the others.

"Get back in the building . . . now! Steve's dead," Cornell yelled, and began pushing his stunned friends back toward the exit door.

Aiguo stood beside Sergeant Davies and watched the plant worker drop to the roof.

"Good shooting, Renshu. Did you see any others with him?" Aiguo asked over the comm link.

"I don't think so, but there is so much steam in the area, I can't be sure," Renshu said, from his sniper position on the adjacent Tank Area Building roof.

"Go down there and check the area. If you find anything, call me!"

"Understood!"

"I've seen Chonglin on the cameras. Who did you leave with my family, or have you already killed them?" Jonathan asked.

"I have another individual with them. It was someone who I didn't really need here. Your family will remain safe as long as you continue to cooperate," Aiguo said.

"Yeah, I can see how much you trust me," Jonathan said, as he pulled against the tye wraps securing his feet to his chair.

"Just a precaution. What is the American saying . . . 'trust, but verify' . . . something like that," Aiguo said, while checking the various camera views across the plant site.

"What will they do? How will they react? By now they will have found the guards in the shack and Chonglin's surprise. They know that we have the plant. All ground communications in or out have been shut off. I thought we had killed all of the plant staff, but I suppose a few stragglers were to be expected," Aiguo said, and patted Jonathan on the shoulder.

"What do you think, Sergeant Davies? How will your government react?"

"They'll come in here and kill every one of you," Jonathan said, as he glanced to his left at the three day shift guards still secured to the railing.

Aiguo had shot each one in the head when he had entered the area and saw that they were still alive.

"I was touched that you tried to save a few of your former comrades, instead of killing them like I told you. But to me, they were just loose ends and potential problems. I am a man of my word, Sergeant Davies. We have a deal. You cooperate, your family lives. I didn't make a deal with them."

"Will you really let my family go when this is done?"

"Despite what you think, I'm not a murderer. Your wife and your children are not a threat to the accomplishment of this mission. I don't need to kill them. They are leverage to keep you obedient, nothing more. You keep monitoring the cameras. Call me if you see anything. I have some other things to do. They may try to probe the perimeter or send in drones to look around. Your continued cooperation ensures the safety of your family, Sergeant Davies. Remember that," Aiguo said, while turning away to leave.

Reactor Auxiliary Building 261'
2035 hours EST

The four RP techs were sitting behind an air handling unit. Kay was softly crying, her head on Chris's shoulder.

"Are you sure he was dead?" Tommy asked.

"Yeah, he was hit in the chest at least twice. There was a lot of blood. I don't think he got off a call. I don't know where the shooter was. There was too much noise. I never heard a shot, Steve just dropped. His face turned when he fell. His eyes were still open, just staring . . . blank. He was gone," Cornell said.

"So now what?' Chris asked.

"We know these bastards have a bomb with them. That's what the President said. They'll put the bomb in the Fuel Handing Building, up on 286'. We have to stop them," Tommy said.

"You're crazy, Tommy Borders. I'm not going anywhere near there. We need to go deep in the plant and hide. We're not soldiers; we're technicians, and Steve's dead because we tried to do something that's none of our business. Let Security take care of them," Kay said, and began crying again.

"Kay, we're dead either way. If they set off a nuke, there aren't any safe places on site. Tommy's right. We have to try to stop them. I think they've already taken care of the security guards," Chris said, while hugging her with one arm.

"The only way up to 286' is through the Waste Processing Building. That means we have to stay on this elevation and go all the way back through the RAB. Then we take the stairs up to the south end of 286' Fuel Handing Building," Tommy said.

"I'm not doing it. You boys are being stupid . . . again," Kay said.

"Cornell, why don't you take her back to the Radwaste Control Room? Chris and I will go look around up on 286'," Tommy said.

"We should all stay together. You'll just get yourselves killed . . . just like Steve," Kay said.

"Why don't we all go back to Radwaste? There's a fridge. We could all use some rest and something to drink. Then we'll decide what to do," Cornell said.

"Cornell Waines, you're not as stupid as I thought," Kay said, while patting Cornell on the knee.

"That's the plan, then. We'll go back to Radwaste. Let's get going," Tommy said, while standing up.

Fuel Handling Building 261'
North End Railcar Bay
2035 hours EST

"I told you. I've looked everywhere. I can't find the damn keys," Heng said, while continuing to search the forklift parked at the south end of the Railcar Bay.

"They probably have some rule about leaving keys in a parked vehicle. There has to be an office here somewhere. Chonglin, put your knife up and search for an office. Without the keys, we can't unload the bomb," Jian said.

"Who cares? It's a nuclear bomb. We back the truck in here and leave it. What difference does it make?" Chonglin said, while carving his trademark 'Tiger' character into the green paint of the massive outer steel door that sealed the Railcar Bay.

"Would you like to tell the Lieutenant that you think his plan is stupid?" Jian asked.

Chonglin began mumbling in Chinese, and then placed his knife in the sheath on the front of his chest.

"I'll go look for the keys," Chonglin said, while walking deeper into the building.

He returned a few minutes later, and tossed a set of keys in Heng's direction.

"They had a locked key box on the wall in a small office. I pried it open with my knife," Chonglin said.

"Heng, start up the forklift. I'll open the back of the truck," Jian said, as he ran outside to the brown truck.

"Chonglin, go check the elevator. We'll use that to move the weapon to the top floor," Jian yelled from outside.

Chonglin nodded, then climbed the three stairs from the railcar bay floor to the office level and went through another set of doors looking for the elevator.

When he returned, Heng was backing the forklift into the railcar bay. The nuclear device was strapped to a large steel pallet.

"Jian, this will never work. The hallways are too small and the elevator is for people, not equipment," Chonglin said.

"How do they get things up there?" Jian asked.

Heng looked around; then up. He pointed at the ceiling high above them.

"That's a hatch cover. They must bring things in here and then offload them with a crane. There has to be a crane up there to remove the hatch, or it just slides to the side, or maybe it's hinged," Heng said, while staring at the red plate in the ceiling.

"You two go look upstairs. I'm going to go outside and call the Lieutenant. This is going to delay us for hours," Jian said.

Security Building Armory
2050 hours EST

"How long a delay?" Aiguo asked.

"I'm not sure. Chonglin and Heng are upstairs looking for a crane. There has to be a way to remove this hatch. Are you sure you want us to move the weapon up there? It may take hours," Jian said.

"The map shows a large open area between the two main pools. I want the weapon between the two pools. Call me back when you have a time estimate," Aiguo said.

Aiguo placed his phone back inside a pocket on the outside of his body armor, then resumed his inspection of the armory.

"Impressive, very impressive for a plant security force," he said, while opening a crate marked 'Raytheon Missile Systems, FIM-92D, 1ea'.

"Eight Stingers, not the latest model, but still effective," Aiguo said, as he continued to search the armory.

He began laughing, as he removed three weapons crates to verify what was beneath them.

"Raytheon Missile Systems, FGM-148 Javelin. . . . an anti-tank missile launcher. Were they expecting an assault by tanks? Why would a security force have one of these? And why only one?" Aiguo asked, while opening the case.

"Bingwen, come into the armory. You have some deliveries to make," Aiguo said over the comm link.

CHAPTER 44

The White House
The Oval Office
Washington, DC
August 2, 2100 hours EST

"Mr. President, I'm sorry to interrupt, but I have some information that you need to be made aware of," Roger Yost, White House Chief of Staff said, having just opened the door to the Oval Office.

"Come on in and close the door, Roger. I'm on the line with the FBI Director. It's probably the same information from North Carolina," President Miller said.

Roger nodded in agreement and closed the door.

"Director Campbell, if you don't mind, I'm going to put you on speaker phone. My Chief of Staff in now in the room," President Miller said.

"As I was saying, Mr. President, we have received confirmation of an incident at the Harris Nuclear Plant located in New Hill, North Carolina. We think it pertains to the missing Chinese terrorists, and possibly the missing nuclear device. Local 911 personnel received a call from a woman at the site claiming to be the Site Vice President. My understanding is that Duke Energy has a vice president assigned to every one of their nuclear sites . . . in this case, a Ms. Gail Jacobs. In the middle of the call the woman began screaming, and the call was terminated. North Carolina Highway Patrol personnel were dispatched to the plant to investigate. They found three dead security personnel in the security building at the plant boundary. When one of the highway patrol troopers opened the door to the building to verify the status of the three guards, a bomb detonated, and the trooper was killed."

"I'm not seeing the connection, Director Campbell. This is a possible threat to a nuclear plant, but . . ." the President began.

"Mr. President, another Tiger mark . . . another Chinese character . . . was found carved into the inside of the door where the dead security guards were found. An image was forwarded to a police forensic analyst familiar with this case. This analyst, Doctor Wilton Janson, verified that the character was made by the same man as the ones involved in a previous case in Alexandria, Virginia."

"Jesus, Bill . . . are you trying to tell me that these rogue Chinese Special Forces operators, in possession of a nuclear weapon, have taken over one of our nuclear plants?" the President asked.

"Yes, Mr. President . . . that is our worst case scenario, and the most likely one. We have been unable to contact any personnel inside the plant. The NRC tried to contact the Main Control Room on a dedicated emergency line. There was no response."

"What does the NRC have to say about this?"

"Mr. President, since they can't contact the Main Control Room or anyone else on site, they are going to declare a General Emergency at the Harris Nuclear Plant in an hour or so. When they do that, the whole world will know."

"Do we know for a fact that they've taken over the plant? Don't these places have a large armed security force?" the President asked.

"Yes, Mr. President, they do. But the fact that there were casualties at the gate, no word has been heard from any more personnel on site, and the Main Control Room is out of contact, lead us to believe that hostile personnel have control of the plant. Mr. President, there was one other item. A local 911 operator also received a call from a woman near the plant who said her house had been taken over by Chinese soldiers. She claimed to have killed one of them. The sheriff's department responded and found a dead Asian woman inside the house. At first, they thought it was a simple murder. Then one of the deputies noticed a symbol carved into the handle of a chair sitting in the hall. He remembered your speech, and took a picture of it and forwarded it to his boss. It was the 'Tiger' character. That same guy was at this house. The house is only three miles from the Harris plant," Director Campbell said.

"First, the farm in South Carolina . . . now this place . . . they were moving closer to Harris," the President said.

"Mr. President, I was just handed a note. This second woman, the one who made the 911 call, her husband is a security guard at the plant. My guess is that the Chinese used the family as leverage, and forced this man to provide information and access to the plant," Director Campbell said.

"Damn, we shouldn't be surprised. These men are trained Special Forces operatives. This whole thing has been well planned and thought out from the beginning. It all started when they snatched their former leader from the hospital in Alexandria. Keep me informed of any changes, and I mean anything. Is that understood?"

"Understood, Mr. President. If anything changes, I'll let you know."

The President hung up the phone, closed his eyes, and began rubbing his temples with both thumbs.

"Damn it! These bastards are always one step ahead of us. Holy crap . . . a nuclear plant. Roger, arrange a meeting of the Homeland Security Council. Have them here in one hour. Make sure the NRC sends a representative. One hour, Roger, and no damn excuses from anyone, or I'll have their heads," the President said, while rising from behind the Resolute Desk.

"Yes, Mr. President . . . one hour," the Chief of Staff said, as he hurried from the Oval Office.

CHAPTER 45

The White House
The Situation Room
Washington, DC, USA
August 2, 2200 hours EST

The President sat at the end of the long mahogany table. The Great Seal of the President of the United States was mounted on the wall behind him. The mood of the Homeland Security Council was grim.

"Roger, if you would, please brief all the attendees on the latest information available," President Miller said.

"Yes, Mr. President," Chief of Staff Yost said.

"Ladies, Gentlemen, the briefing package in front of you contains the latest information on the ongoing incident at the Harris Nuclear Plant in New Hill, North Carolina," Roger said, and proceeded to present the timeline and all available information.

After each individual had read through the package, the President said, "All right, I need opinions and analysis. We'll start with Vice President O'Quinn."

"Mr. President, when this goes public, people will panic. If we don't get ahead of this it will make Katrina look like a picnic," Vice President O'Quinn said.

"Agreed, and your advice?" the President asked.

"We have to evacuate the area now. We can't wait like the administration did before Katrina. We can't worry about the inconvenience to people. Their lives are at stake," the Vice President said.

"Chairman Wisnicki, I know that the NRC is required by law to publically announce the declaration of an emergency at the Harris

Nuclear Plant. When is this going to occur and what steps is the NRC taking to ensure the safety of the public?" the President asked.

Doctor Carol Wisnicki was a nuclear engineer and had been Chairman of the Nuclear Regulatory Commission for almost ten years.

"Mr. President, the Harris plant went off line at 1954 hours today. We have been unable to contact any personnel in the Main Control Room or anywhere on site. The plant's Reactor Coolant System is designed to go into automatic recirculation if the reactor trips and no further actions are taken by the plant staff. The reactor core will remain stable for at least 48 hours with no further action. After that, there will be a series of escalating problems. The NRC will be making a public statement reference Harris sometime in the next few minutes. Since the plant staff is deemed no longer capable of ensuring public safety, we have no choice but to declare a General Emergency. This will activate the State and County Emergency Operations Centers, and a variety of federal agencies. Harris personnel who are part of the Harris Emergency Plan and located off site will be contacted to start staffing a backup emergency facility located in downtown Raleigh," Chairman Wisnicki said.

"What about evacuations?" the President asked.

"Mr. President, I agree with the Vice President. We should initiate a mandatory evacuation of the 10-mile Emergency Preparedness Zone as soon as we declare the General Emergency. In addition, I would recommend that we evacuate all people in the 50-mile Ingestion Preparedness Zone upwind of the plant site," Chairman Wisnicki said.

"How many people are we talking about?" the President asked.

"Approximately 500,000, Mr. President, with the current and projected wind vectors."

"Chairman Wisnicki, please coordinate with your staff and start those evacuations as soon as you declare the General Emergency," the President said.

"Yes, Mr. President," she said, and began texting instructions to her staff.

"Now, what is the objective of these terrorists? Director Davidson, I'm glad to see that you were invited to represent the CIA at this meeting. You have been involved in this mess since the beginning. What do these people want?" the President asked.

"Mr. President, I hate to say this, but we have reached the conclusion that these men don't want anything. What they intend to do is take everything from us . . . from the United States of America. They intend to destroy us," Janet Davidson said.

The outburst in the room didn't stop until the President began pounding on the table.

"Please explain, Director Davidson," the President said, while straightening his tie.

"One of my agents, Amanda Langford, was the one who developed the theory of a Chinese plot to smuggle nuclear devices into the United States. She was also involved in the tracking of these individuals in the Southeast, and was present during the recent explosion in South Carolina at one of their safe houses. As most of you are aware, several DHS personnel lost their lives. Agent Langford received a concussion, and minor scrapes and bruises due to the blast. She's recovering at her parents' home in Raleigh, North Carolina," Janet began.

"Over the last few weeks, as we were all searching for these terrorists and the missing device, Agent Langford asked me this question, 'What would you do if you were in their place? What would you do with this weapon?'" Janet continued.

"I'm a retired Marine . . . a combat veteran. She and I had a discussion about force multipliers. At the end of the discussion, she looked at me and said, 'I know what I'd do. I'd blow up a nuclear plant'. At first I thought that was a stretch. But the more we talked about it, the more sense it made. After we looked at all the plants in the Southeast, Agent Langford told me that she would choose the Harris plant. I asked her why and she said, ' . . . because of the spent fuel stored there. I'd blow up the spent fuel.' Janet said, as several gasps were heard in the room.

"I thought reactor fuel couldn't blow up," said Attorney General Delores Bull.

"It can't Attorney General; the U-235 enrichment is far too low. Nuclear weapons are enriched to at least 95%. Commercial reactor fuel is only enriched to around 4-7%. After the fuel has been used for three reactor cycles, with each cycle around 12-18 months, depending on the reactor, the fuel is removed and stored deep underwater in pools," Chairman Wisnicki said.

"Then what happens to it?" the Attorney General asked.

176

"Then it just sits there. Some plants are going to Dry Cask storage after the fuel is ten years old or so, but Harris isn't one of those plants. Their Fuel Handling Building was designed to support four reactors, so it has a huge capacity for spent fuel storage," Chairman Wisnicki said.

"Chairman, what would happen if a nuclear weapon was detonated inside this fuel handling building?" the President asked.

"Mr. President, we have exact data on what is in the pools at Harris. I'd rather not speculate. Let me have some of my staff run some models. That would be far more accurate than my guess," Chairman Wisnicki said.

"Chairman, it's my understanding that you have a degree in Nuclear Engineering. Is that correct?" the President said.

"Yes, Mr. President, that's correct," she replied.

"So guess! I won't hold you to the exact numbers, but I want an idea of what the impact would be of this weapon being detonated inside that damn building," the President said.

"If you will give me a few minutes, I can give you an approximation, Mr. President" she said.

"Proceed, Chairman," the President said.

Chairman Wisnicki reached under her chair and removed her laptop. Three minutes later, she closed it, but said nothing. She just stared at her hands resting on the closed laptop.

"Chairman?" the President asked, but she didn't respond.

"Chairman Wisnicki!" the President said.

She looked up and stared at him, unblinking.

"Mr. President, when I was a young girl, I watched an old movie with my dad. He loved old black and white films. I remember this one film that scared me to death. I had nightmares for a week," she began.

"What the hell does this have to do with . . ." Vice President O'Quinn interrupted.

"Quiet! Please continue, Chairman, the President said.

"The movie was 'On the Beach' starring Gregory Peck. World War 3 had started. Fallout was circling the globe and killing all life on the planet," she began, and then paused to carefully select her next words.

"Mr. President, if my primary calculations are correct, a 30 kt device detonated inside the Harris Fuel Handling Building will have close to the same effect. After about two weeks, the Northern Hemisphere would be uninhabitable. These idiots won't just destroy the United States . . . they'll destroy Europe, Russia and even China. It would poison the Northern Hemisphere. The Southern Hemisphere . . . I'm not sure. It all depends on the dispersal rate. Does it stay in the Stratosphere or are the particles too heavy? That would require further analysis," she said.

Once again the room erupted into turmoil and disbelief. Chairman Wisnicki opened up her laptop, and began going over the calculations once again, while the President tried to silence the room.

"I don't buy it. Chernobyl was a terrible disaster. The Russians screwed up and had a steam explosion that blew their core into the upper atmosphere. It was scary, and may have caused a few additional cancer deaths, but that's it. Other than the area around the plant, the long term impact on Russia and Europe was next to nothing," said Clarisse Beaumont, the National Security Advisor, after the room had calmed down.

"At the time of the Chernobyl accident, the RMBK-1000 reactor vessel contained approximately 180 tons of uranium. The Harris spent fuel pools contain over 3,000 tons of Uranium and other long-lived radioactive material. What makes it even worse is the amount of water in the building. If you add up all the water in the various pools and canals, it's over 1,000,000 gallons of water. If a 30kt device is detonated in that building, all the water will turn instantly to steam. The building will be blown apart. I'm talking about a building that has walls four feet thick and a ceiling two feet thick. No one has ever modeled a steam explosion combined with a 30kt fission device. The vast majority of the spent fuel would be atomized and carried upward with the plume. The height of the plume would exceed that of the largest volcanic explosion in human history, in excess of 50 kilometers," Chairman Wisnicki said, while finishing the repeat of her calculations.

"The calculations are correct. I had to make a few assumptions about meteorology, but they're accurate within 5-10 % . . . higher or lower," she said, then closed the laptop again.

The Situation Room was silent. The majority seemed to be in shock at the information they had just received.

"General Munford, military options?" the President asked.

"I know that Special Forces teams from Ft. Bragg have used the Harris site for practice. It was very useful for the spec ops people, and helped the plant security folks identify some of their weaknesses," said General Munford, the Chairman of the Joint Chiefs of Staff.

"Evidently not enough," said Vice President O'Quinn.

"We have detailed information about the plant, Mr. President. We can try something subtle or we can pound the place into dust, your choice," General Munford said.

"Mr. President, if we bomb Harris, we'll damage the reactor and probably the cooling system for the spent fuel pools. Neither one of those situations is desirable. We might even trigger the nuclear device," Chairman Wisnicki said.

"Mr. President, what we need is for these terrorists to be dead without destroying ourselves in the process," the Vice President said.

"Then we have to hunt them down and secure the weapon, Mr. President," General Munford said.

"Can you do that, General?" the President asked.

"Mr. President, hunting down assholes that our government wants removed is one of our specialties," General Munford said.

"General Mumford, I don't want any of them getting away. I don't want that device getting away. This whole thing has to end," the President said.

"Mr. President, we'll secure the area around the site to ensure that no one gets out. Then we'll terminate these people and secure the weapon," General Munford said.

"How, General? We don't have much time," the President said.

"Everything we need is at Ft. Bragg, 50 miles south of the plant. The 82nd Airborne, Special Forces Ops Command, more than enough, Mr. President," General Munford said.

"When can you start?" the President asked.

"Mr. President, I'll have troops on the road from Ft. Bragg before midnight. They'll secure the perimeter. Then I'll unleash the dogs. Delta will hit them some time tonight. With any luck, this will be over tomorrow," General Munford said.

"Any opinions on this aggressive course of action?" the President asked.

"What if we spur them into detonating the weapon?" the Vice President asked.

"Mr. Vice President, they're going to detonate the weapon even if we don't do anything," Janet said.

"Mr. President, the TV . . ." the Chief of Staff said.

One wall of the Situation Room was covered with video monitors. A representative of the NRC was on screen declaring a General Emergency at the Harris Nuclear Plant.

"All right, we've talked enough. General Munford, proceed with your plan. By tomorrow night, I want this done with," the President said.

"Yes, Mr. President," General Munford said.

CHAPTER 46

The Langford Home
106 East Whitaker Mill Road
Raleigh, North Carolina
August 2, 2230 hours EST

"Daddy, I still can't believe you and Momma sold the farm, and moved into the city," Amanda said, as she sat on the front porch swing of her parent's new home in Raleigh.

She and her father rocked back and forth, enjoying the cool night air. The sun had set hours ago. The stifling heat and humidity of the day had finally departed.

"Well, your brothers had no interest in farming, and you certainly weren't moving back in. So your mother and I decided it was time for a change. I'll admit . . . the farm was getting to be too much. We're both getting too old for that much work. The only problem now is that she still feeds me like I'm working from sunup to sundown. I've already put on ten pounds, and now I can smell fresh apple pie," Will said, as he began sniffing the cool night air.

"Kind of late for Momma to be cooking a pie, but it sure does smell good," Amanda said, as she felt her cell phone buzzing in her back pocket.

"We got an offer we couldn't refuse for the farm. You know, developers are always looking to expand. The county population has more than tripled since 1970, and it doesn't look like it's going to slow down anytime soon."

"What do you know about the house?"

"Evidently, it used to belong to a printer, if you can believe that. There's a nice basement, and I've already started moving some of my woodworking equipment into an old garage in the back. By

Thanksgiving, I'll be making toys for your kids," Will said, as Amanda's phone buzzed for the second time.

"Daddy . . . I don't have any children," Amanda said, wondering if her father's mind was starting to get old along with the rest of him.

"Exactly! Work's important, but you need someone to help you through the hard times, and I'm not talking about a dog. Girl, somebody's trying to get hold of you, real bad. You might as well answer that thing."

Amanda sighed, as she removed her cell phone from her back pocket, and turned it on.

"Oh crap, it's my boss!"

"Watch your language, child. Your momma still knows how to use a switch," Will said, and laughed as he remembered how his wife would tie a switch to her apron as a warning when the kids were misbehaving.

"Yes, Ms. Davidson," Amanda said, as she answered the call.

"Agent Langford, the CIA gives you a cell phone for a reason, and it's not so you can ignore calls. Am I understood?"

"Yes, ma'am . . . Ms. Davidson, what can I do for you?" Amanda asked, as her father chuckled.

"Go turn on the TV and find out what's happening. Where are you, out in the woods, or in the middle of a field picking berries?"

"Yes, Ms. Davidson, checking right now," Amanda said, while running into the house.

"Amanda, if something is going on around here, it will be on WRAL. Put it on Channel 3. Selma, you better come in here. Something is going on," Will said, as Amanda picked up the remote.

"There, it's on WRAL," Amanda said, as she sat down between her parents on the living room sofa.

. . . .

"This is Gilbert Gomez with Breaking News. I'm broadcasting live from the intersection of New-Hill Holloman Road and SR 1135. This is as close as the Highway Patrol will let anyone get to the Shearon Harris Nuclear Power Plant. We have it from numerous reliable sources that the nuclear plant has been taken over by

182

suspected terrorists. You can hear the sound of sirens as first responders of all types are converging on the area around the plant. I have been told that there are no indications of a radioactive release at this time. Despite that claim, evacuation sirens have been sounded, and police are going door to door inside the 10-mile EPZ. They are requesting that people leave the area immediately. We will be staying live with this story for the foreseeable future. This is Gilbert Gomez, WRAL Breaking News."

. . . .

"Holy crap!" Amanda said, as she jumped off the sofa.

"Young lady, I did not raise you to use such language," Selma said, as Amanda ran outside to the porch.

"Director, this looks bad. What do you want me to do?" Amanda asked, while pacing on the porch.

"First question, have you recovered enough from the explosion to be functional?"

"I'm fine. What do you want me to do?"

"The NRC has declared a General Emergency at Harris. The security force has been taken out, and they can't get in touch with the Main Control Room. The President has declared a National Emergency. The military will be taking action soon. The State of North Carolina will be activating their EOC in downtown Raleigh. Get down there and find out what they know. I'm sending a team down there, but I need information right now. Stay in touch and answer your damn phone!" Janet said, and hung up.

"Momma, Daddy . . . I have to go. You two need to pack some bags and leave the area. The Chinese that I told you about, they've taken the Harris Nuclear Plant. Harris is the biggest nuclear waste repository in the Southeast. They've been storing spent fuel there from four different plants for decades. These men have a nuclear bomb. This could get really bad. Daddy, I want you and Momma out of this house in 15 minutes. Do you still have that cabin in the mountains?" Amanda said, as she ran back inside, grabbed her backpack, car keys, and ran back out the door.

"It's still there, just west of Asheville," Will replied.

"You and Momma get on Highway 40 and head there until you hear from me. I'm not asking, Daddy. I'm telling you that unless you want to die, you have to leave now," Amanda said, as her mother began crying and hugged her.

"Momma, I love you both, but I have work to do. You go pack some clothes for you and Daddy. Daddy, take your pistol with you, and some canned food and water . . . ten minutes. Daddy, I have to go," Amanda said, as she held back tears, and ran for her car.

CHAPTER 47

Headquarters
2nd Brigade Combat Team
82nd Airborne Division
Fort Bragg, North Carolina
August 2, 2310 hours EST

"Lieutenant Colonel Thompson, thank you for getting here in an expedited manner. It would seem that we have a national emergency. The President has requested our services, and your battalion is on call. I'll cut to the chase. I trust that you are familiar with the ongoing situation with the rogue Chinese Special Forces operators within the United States," said Brigadier General Alcott, commanding officer of the 2nd Brigade Combat Team at Ft. Bragg, North Carolina.

"Yes, Sir. Intimately familiar, Sir. When I was assigned to the Pentagon, one of these bastards murdered my pregnant wife," Lt. Colonel Anthony Thompson said.

"I've read your file. I know that was a horrible time for you. My question is this: can you maintain your objectivity as a battalion commander? This can't become a personal vendetta. Do you understand me, Lieutenant Colonel?" General Alcott asked.

"I'll be honest with you, General. I hate these bastards with a burning passion, but I'm a professional soldier. I'll operate within the mission parameters, as determined by the Army and our civilian leadership," Anthony said.

"Good answer! Here's the latest information that I have from the Pentagon, and it's ugly," General Alcott said, as he picked up a document from his desk.

"At approximately 1900 hours today an assault team, comprised of an unknown number of rogue Chinese Special Forces operators, attacked the access post at the Harris Nuclear Plant and killed three guards. They then proceeded to the Security Building at the main entrance to the plant, and subdued the security personnel located there. Based on the timing, the security staff, approximately 30 individuals, were conducting turnover from day shift to night shift. The majority of the personnel would have been in a single meeting room. The site also has six gun towers. It seems that they were able to take control of these locations, also. One call was received by 911 operators from a woman on site who identified herself as the Site Vice President. The call ended abruptly, and there have been no other calls from the plant. Attempts to contact personnel inside the plant have also been unsuccessful," General Alcott said, then paused, looking up at Lt. Colonel Thompson.

"Based on the best information available, it is likely that these individuals are in possession of the last missing nuclear device from the Chinese plot. The device is projected to be in the 30 kt to 40 kt range. Analysts from various federal agencies have concluded that the terrorists intend to detonate this weapon inside the Fuel Handling Building. Duke Energy records show that over 3000 spent fuel bundles are stored in pools located in the building. If the weapon is detonated inside the building, the effects will be catastrophic. And that, Lt. Colonel Thompson, is about as bad as it gets. Any questions?"

"A few, Sir. Are we going to have any air cover?"

"Son, you're going to have air cover from 500 miles up, down to treetop, and everywhere in between."

"Excellent, Sir! When do we leave and what's our mission, General?"

"Good . . . I want your Stryker battalion on the road in two hours. Your destination is the Harris Nuclear Plant, up near New Hill. By the time you're ready to move out, you'll have all the contact information you'll need to get there and execute your assigned mission. You'll be heading straight up Highway 203 to 401. From Fuquay-Varina, you'll be on Highway 55 until you turn toward the plant. Local law enforcement and the Highway Patrol will clear all civilian traffic from your path . . . and Lt. Col. Thompson . . . you will have to remain flexible. The mission parameters could change rapidly. The initial mission is containment, but I can envision a direct combined arms assault on the plant as this situation develops further."

"One other thing, your battalion won't be the only unit involved in this operation. As things develop, you will receive additional information. Good luck, Lieutenant Colonel Thompson," General Alcott said, rose from his chair, and saluted.

"Thank you, Sir. My battalion will be ready," Anthony said, saluted, and left the office.

CHAPTER 48

2555 Beard Road
Fayetteville, NC
August 2, 2310 hours EST

"Damn, Colonel, this place is sweet! Kind of an odd time to have us drop by for a beer," said SFC Ancellis York, as he and the four other operators of C/A 1A (Delta Force, Charlie Squadron/Alpha Troop/Assault Troop 1A) walked into the entry way of Colonel Mike Jankens' home on the outskirts of Fayetteville.

"First of all, you're late. I said be here at 2300 hours. Second, no beer until this mission is completed. Come with me," Colonel Mike Jankens said, as he turned and walked down a long hall into the home's great room.

"Well, well, better late than never," said SFC Brian Mays, while sitting in the room with the rest of team C/A 4A.

"Damn, the 'back of the bus' team. I hope this isn't anything serious, we might come up a little light," SFC York said, as he and SFC Mays shook hands and bumped shoulders.

"Gentlemen, listen up, this will be the most significant op you'll ever undertake. If I told you that the fate of the entire country was riding on this mission, I wouldn't be exaggerating," Colonel Jankens said, as the 10 warrior brothers greeted each other.

"Well, that's different. Usually we're just taking out some pogue that the government wants to transport to some virgins in the next world," said SSG Bennie Clay, as he plopped down on the sofa.

"Shut up, Bennie. Colonel, what's the deal? You don't usually play with this 'end of the world' stuff," said, SFC York.

"Everybody, sit. This is gonna be quick. I don't have time for a long, detailed, formal brief. There will be no mockups, no walkthroughs or practice jumps. You're going to go into this cold with minimal intel," Colonel Jankens said, while pointing at a 6' by 6' satellite pic of the Harris Plant mounted on a side wall.

"We all know the crap that's been going on in the country with these 'imported' nuclear weapons. We've had teams spread around the country to help collect these devices and the people who were guarding them. There is only one weapon left unaccounted for, and now we know where it is. At approximately 1900 hours today, a dozen or so Chinese Special Forces operators from the Siberian Tigers took over the Harris Nuclear Plant. They attacked the plant at shift change, so most of the guards on both shifts were at a turnover meeting," Colonel Jankens said.

"Daaaaamn, I'm smart! You owe me $20, York. I told you that was the way to do it," SSG Clay said.

"Shut up, Bennie, and listen to the Colonel," SFC York said, while opening up his wallet and handing Bennie a $20 bill.

"That's why you're here, plus your availability. I know you're familiar with Harris," Colonel Jankens said.

"Sir, we've practiced on most of the nuke sites in the Southeast. SSG Clay commented during that particular evolution that turnover was the perfect time to hit the Harris plant. 'Almost all the eggs in one basket' was the phrase he used, as I remember. We included that as part of our after-action report. I guess they ignored it," SFC York said, as he and SSG Clay fist bumped.

"Harris was one of the stronger plants we tested. These Chinese guys must be pretty damn good. The plant probably had 30-40 guards on site when they struck. Have we heard anything?" asked SFC York.

"The site VP called 911. She said that the 'guards' were killing everyone," Colonel Jankens said.

"Which means they were dressed as Harris guards," SFC Mays said.

"That was my assumption. At about the same time, 911 got another call from a woman who said her home had been taken over by Chinese soldiers. Her husband is a guard at the plant," Colonel Jankens said.

"Daaaamn, that's another $20," SSG Clay said.

"Shit!" SFC York said, while reaching for his wallet.

"The only way a team that small could take out the whole security force is with inside info, Colonel. Take the family hostage,

189

and force the husband to cooperate. I'd do the same thing," SSG Clay said, while pocketing the second $20 bill.

"Now, the bad part. They are in possession of a 30 kt nuclear device. Best guess, they're going to place the device in the Fuel Handling Building and blow up 6,000,000 pounds of spent fuel," Colonel Jankens said.

"Shit! That would make a big mess!" SFC York said.

"The intelligence wonks say it would be like a volcanic explosion and contaminate the whole Northern Hemisphere, maybe the whole planet," Colonel Jankens said.

"Any threats or demands?" SFC York asked.

"None, no communication at all. We think that their intent is to destroy the US, so China can take over the world," Colonel Jankens said.

"That's bad. These guys are like jihadists. They have a higher mission, and they don't care if they live through this," SFC York said.

"Well then, I guess we have to drop in and kill 'em all," SSG Clay said.

Colonel Jankens then briefed the ten Delta Force operators every detail that the Pentagon and CIA had provided to him.

"So, they've got one guy in each armored tower, that's six. The others are probably scattered across the plant site or moving the weapon into the Fuel Handling Building," SFC Mays said.

"What other assets do we have?" SFC York asked.

"A Striker Battalion will be leaving Bragg in about two hours. Their mission is to seal the plant and then start pressing in," Colonel Jankens said.

"Good, we'll need a diversion. This looks like a HALO insertion. The roof on the Fuel Handling Building looks like you could land a C-130 on it. We can drop one team on this building, and the second team on this other one. What's this one called?" SFC York asked.

"The Waste Processing Building," Colonel Jankens said.

"One problem. They'll be waiting for us. We have to remember who we're dealing with. These aren't a bunch of thug gunmen working for a drug lord, or fanatical butchers trying to set up a caliphate for the Mahdi. The Chinese Special Forces have based their training and tactics on us. They study our missions. They would know this is a vulnerability for them. They'll have men on the roof waiting for this," SSG Clay said.

"Gunships?" SFC Mays asked.

"That's a possibility, but we're short assets," said Colonel Jankens.

"If you do that, we might as well drop the 82nd on top of them. They'd get shot up, but they'd be over them like a bunch of fire ants," SFC York said.

"Maybe that's what we should do . . . blunt force trauma," SFC Mays said.

"That was considered by the Pentagon, but there's not enough time. That's why they called me, and I called you," Colonel Jankens said.

"Your op, gentlemen . . . how do you want to proceed? I have my ideas, but I want to hear yours," Colonel Jankens said.

"The diversion will be the Striker Battalion. That will draw their attention to the perimeter. While they're defending the perimeter, we hit the roof," SFC Mays said.

"Then what? We'll hunt down the bad guys, but what about the nuke?" SSG Clay asked.

"I've got the answer to that one. You'll be bringing a civilian specialist with you. She disarmed the first device found in San Francisco and several others across the country," Colonel Jankens said.

"She? Colonel did you just say that some female civilian will be making a HALO with us? Sir, with all due respect that's a little . . . chancy," SFC Mays said.

"She's a parachutist and has free fall experience . . . and . . . she's also 51 years old," Colonel Jankens said.

"Great! We strap her to a rocking chair and pop her chute at 500 feet," SSG Clay said.

"Kiss my ass! I've made over 600 jumps and have a 'D' License. I've made over 50 night jumps," said Kate Williams, as she walked into the room from the kitchen.

All eyes turned to the tall, red-haired woman with cold blue eyes.

"This is Kate Williams. She's a contractor for the National Nuclear Security Administration, Accident Response Group. She owns a company that specializes in this type of work," Colonel Jankens said.

"Don't worry, boys. I won't slow you down. All you have to do is get me to the device in one piece, and I'll take care of the rest. All of these devices have been modified the same way. They built a five-minute timer into the weapon that's hardwired. I don't think the Chinese operators will dare to change it. They might risk activating the timer. I disarmed a big one near DC with the timer running. I made it with five seconds to spare," Kate said, while walking up to the large satellite pic on the wall.

The teams parted like a wave.

"So, here's the plan. After landing on the roof, we'll rappel down the north end of the Fuel Handling Building and enter through the railcar entrance. I'm a certified Alpine Climber by the International Climbing and Mountaineering Federation. So that won't be a problem. If we can't get in that way, there's a side door on the East side, that you can blow open, if it's locked. Then we go up the stairs to 286' and find the device. I disarm the device, and we all go have a cold one down by the lake," Kate said.

"Damn! I like this woman. I bet she can shoot, too," SSG Clay said.

"The timing will have to be perfect. Once the perimeter is hit, they may start the timer. That only gives us five minutes to reach the weapon and disarm it," SFC York said.

"The timing is my job. The grunts will be in position by 0300. You need to be wheels up and over the plant by 0330. I'll forward all updated info to you as it happens, both prior to the jump and after you're on the ground," Colonel Jankens said.

"Granny, you may not have five minutes. Can you disarm it in one or two minutes?" SSG Clay asked, as he walked up beside Kate and stared at her.

"Well, I wouldn't mind being a grandmother. But if you call me that again, I'll punch you in the face. You can call me Kate," Kate said, as she looked up at the hulking man.

"Yes, I do like this woman, but answer the damn question," SSG Clay said.

"Don't mind him. He's all bark," SFC York said.

"Like I said, all you boys have to do is get me there. You kill the bad guys, and I'll kill the bomb. I've refined this down to 150 seconds. The equipment I need weighs 19 pounds. It'll drop with me," Kate said.

"SFC York, you are mission lead. You know the schedule. Ms. Williams is yours. Get her fitted up to jump. Call me when you're in position at Simmons Army Airfield," Colonel Jankens said.

CHAPTER 49

North Carolina State Emergency Operations Center
1636 Gold Star Drive
Raleigh, North Carolina
August 2, 2310 hours EST

She could put up with the bruised ribs and the scrapes, but the headache wouldn't go away. It felt like someone was driving a nail into her temples. Amanda knew that if she took any more painkillers, she'd just fall asleep, and this wasn't the time for that.

She picked up her cell phone as she exited off Wade Avenue onto Blue Ridge Road, and called her father.

"Pick up, Daddy, you and Momma better be heading out of town by now," she said, as the number rang.

The phone answered, and it was her mother.

"Hi, Amanda, we've almost left the house. Your father is turning off the gas. I'm packing a cooler. Are you sure this is necessary? WRAL isn't evacuating the station on Western Boulevard."

"Momma, you and Daddy get in that damn car right now and head for the cabin. If you don't, I am really going to be pissed with both of you," Amanda said, as she turned left onto District Drive.

"Young lady, there is no need for you to use such language. We raised you better than that."

"I'm sorry, Momma, but you two need to get out of this area right now. If nothing happens, then you can lecture me all you want. I look forward to a big 'I told you so'. Until then, you head west on I-40 until you reach the cabin."

"Honey, we are moving as fast as we can. We'll be out of the house in just a little bit. Your father just walked in. He wants to talk to you," Selma said, while handing the phone to her husband.

"Amanda, it's your Dad. Now stop talking and listen to me. You take care of yourself, and don't do anything foolish. It would kill us both if something happened to you."

"Daddy, I'll be fine. I'll try not to do anything stupid. I just wanted you to know that I love you both very much. Please, do as I ask, and leave town now. Just think about it as a summer trip to the mountains. Just get to the cabin and wait until the government says it's safe to go back home," Amanda said, while wiping tears from her eyes.

"We're ready to go. Your Momma just nodded to me, and she has her suitcase in her hand. Amanda, remember what I said earlier. Work is fine, and it's an important thing, but life can be real hard when you go through it without someone beside you. Promise me that you'll find that someone special."

"I promise, Daddy. Now you and Momma get moving. I love you both, bye," Amanda said, as she reached the entrance to the State EOC.

North Carolina State Emergency Operations Center
2315 hours EST

Amanda reached for her CIA ID as she pulled off District Drive and approached the entrance to the NC State EOC. Two Raleigh Police officers were inspecting each vehicle prior to allowing access. As she lowered her window, she could hear the mournful wail of the Harris emergency sirens in the distance.

"*I feel like I'm in a movie and bad things are getting ready to happen*," she thought, as the officer shined her flashlight in the window and inspected Amanda's ID.

"Take the second left and find a parking spot. It's filling up fast. The main entrance is on the other side of the building," the officer said, while inspecting the back seat of Amanda's car.

Amanda parked the car as directed, and began walking toward the brightly lit main entrance. The sirens could be heard more clearly now. Two National Guardsmen stood at the entrance.

"*They're nervous. I can see it on their faces. This isn't a drill. I wonder how many people with assigned duties will just flee with their families,*" Amanda thought, while presenting her ID once again.

"There are emergency staff members inside who will tell you where to go," the soldier said.

Amanda nodded and entered through the glass doors. The wailing of the sirens disappeared, along with the stifling humidity of the summer night.

"Hello, Agent Langford. My name is Sheila Warren. I'm one of the Liaison Specialists. We got a call a while ago to expect you. We help people who aren't part of the state emergency organization get acclimated. You know . . . directions about where to go, where the bathrooms are, food, communications . . . whatever you need," Sheila said, as they rode the escalator down to the next level.

"Thank you very much. I need to talk to the director or manager . . . whoever is in charge of the facility."

"Well, he's real busy right now. We request that observers just watch for a while as things develop. We're still setting up and all the emergency positions aren't filled yet."

"I understand, but I need you to take me to whoever is in charge . . . now. If you can't, then I'll find him myself. I need information and I need it now," Amanda said, as they exited the escalator.

"Okay . . . since you insist, I'll take you to Emergency Operations Director Madison. He can update you on what we know at this time," Sheila said, somewhat put off by the tone in Amanda's voice.

"Thank you! That would be appreciated."

They walked into the Command Room. It was almost silent. The people who were talking were communicating in hushed tones, as they set up their stations and assumed the various emergency positions. The front of the huge room was all glass. It overlooked a larger room ten feet below . . . the room they called the Pit. It reminded Amanda of the old NASA Control Rooms, where dozens of people sat at their consoles monitoring data as rockets leapt into space. The wall on the far side of that room was one large video display, split into dozens of screens. They displayed national news, local news, weather, satellite views, CCTV of areas near the plant, live scenes of Harris and drone cameras. One man stood alone at the window observing the organized chaos below, in the Pit.

"That's EOD Brian Madison. He's in charge of everything," Sheila said, as she turned and walked away, glad to be rid of the pushy young woman.

Amanda worked her way through the various state agencies represented in the Command Room. She could tell by the layout, that the area was designed to funnel information in one direction, toward the Emergency Operations Director.

"Director Madison, I'm Agent Amanda Langford. I'm here from the CIA, and I need an update on the emergency," Amanda said, as she stepped up beside him, presented her ID, and began studying the various monitors on the far wall.

He turned his head, first looking at her, and then her ID, before saying, "We've had drills for just about everything you can imagine. Hurricanes, tornadoes, earthquakes, riots . . . we've done it all. A General Emergency at Harris was, of course, high on the list. But a terrorist takeover of the plant, and a threat to blow up the plant with a nuclear bomb . . . that wasn't on the list of possible occurrences."

"I didn't know that particular piece of information had become common knowledge."

"After the President's speech the other night, it doesn't take a genius to read between the lines. Besides, the NRC representative from the plant was in here talking to me ten minutes ago. We've started countywide evacuations. Upwind evacuations are trickier. Luckily, the weather patterns are predicted to be stable for the next week or so. To further complicate things, I have a number of staff members who have decided to evacuate with their families rather than come here and fill their assigned positions. I can't say as I blame them, but that's slowing things down," Director Madison said, as he turned, and began studying the monitors again.

"At least the public is taking this seriously. This late at night, and the roads are starting to fill up. We haven't expanded our primary road system for 20 years. A lane here, a lane there, but nothing significant. The population, that's another matter. Wake County has over a million people now. When I was a child, there were only 150,000 people. That was before I-40 and I-95, but those were federal projects. Now I have to figure out how to get a million people out of the county in the middle of the night. Do you think that they're going to blow the plant up, Agent Langford? Would any sane human really do such a thing?"

Amanda hesitated before saying, "I think . . . that you need to get all these people out of the area as quickly as possible. But right now, I need to know what actions you've taken around the plant, and what you know about what's going on inside the fences."

"The Highway Patrol and the Wake County Sheriff's Department have the plant isolated. All the access roads are barricaded, large or small, even a few dirt roads. Drone footage shows no activity on the plant site. One drone that flew near the Turbine Building was shot down. That shocked a lot of people. After that, we've stayed away from the guard towers and out past the perimeter fence. We received a call a few minutes ago that the 82nd is sending troops up here from Ft. Bragg. They're supposed to be at the plant in a few hours. When they're in place, we'll back off the law enforcement personnel and turn over control of the area to the military. The President declared a national emergency an hour ago, and then went to the Supreme Court. They just ruled that under 18 Code US 831, the Posse Comitatus Act doesn't apply. It's Martial Law now. The Pentagon is in charge of this emergency. We're here to support them and protect the people. Agent Langford, I'll ask you one more time, and then I'll let it be. Do you think these terrorists are going to blow up the Harris plant?"

"I think that you should do what you said. Protect the people. Because . . . I think they're going to need it. I just left my parents' house in Raleigh. They're headed for a cabin they have up in the mountains. I told them not to come back until the government says it's safe."

"Agent Langford, I know you can't say anything, but I'll take that as a yes."

"Director Madison, does the military have a representative in the building yet?" Amanda asked, trying to change the subject..

"Yes, he's with the NC National Guard. They're in the back left corner. Brigadier General Dave Moore is in charge," Director Madison recalled, while pointing toward the area.

Amanda walked away, trying to focus on her mission. But she was very afraid that her home, her family, and her state would never be the same after this night was over.

"General Moore, my name is Amanda Langford. The EOD referred me to you," Amanda said, presented her ID, and reached out to shake his hand.

"Lady, I'm trying to coordinate the evacuation of a million people, set up road blocks, and escort a Stryker Battalion up from Ft. Bragg. I don't have time for another bureaucrat," General Moore said, with a comm link in one ear and a cell phone on the other. He ignored her outstretched hand.

Presenting her ID again, Amanda bent over, pulled the cell phone from his ear, and said, "General Moore, I work for the CIA, and I need some damn information. I can get you replaced in 30 minutes with one phone call, but neither of us has time for that. Take some time now, and answer my questions. Then I promise I'll get out of your way."

"Central Intelligence Agency, huh? So what do you want?" General Moore said, while studying Amanda's ID.

"What's the military plan for Harris?"

"Lady, I don't think you have the clearance for . . ."

"Thirty minutes, maybe less, and your career's over. What's the plan?" Amanda asked, while pulling up a chair and sitting beside the frazzled officer.

"The 82nd is sending a Stryker Battalion from the 2nd Brigade Combat Team up to Harris. That's almost 1000 men and over 70 armored vehicles. They're taking over perimeter security. What happens after that is beyond my pay grade."

The unit sounded familiar to Amanda, so she asked, "Who's the battalion commanding officer?"

"Umm, I've got it here somewhere," General Moore said, while looking through a stack of printouts.

"Lieutenant Colonel Anthony Thompson and they're supposed to be up there and in position by 0300. After that, the civilian law enforcement will pull back."

"Then what happens?"

"What do you think? All hell breaks loose and they start kicking somebody's ass."

CHAPTER 50

Harris Nuclear Plant
5421 Shearon Harris Rd
New Hill, North Carolina
August 2, 2330 hours EST

Radwaste Control Room

"Listen, Cornell, I know you're the only one with combat experience, but you're 62 years old. I know you've got bad feet, bad knees, and a bad back. Stay here and protect Kay. Tommy and I'll go check things out on 286'," Chris said, as the three of them discussed their next move.

"He's right. Kay's asleep on Steve's old cot. I'm amazed that she could sleep after everything that's happened. Now is the time to go, before she wakes up," Tommy said.

"And when she does wake up, she's going to be pissed . . . at me for letting you two go without us. Hell, I'm more scared of her than the Chinese dudes," Cornell said.

"Come on, Cornell. Like you said, you're a combat veteran. She's just a woman," Chris said.

"Yeah right . . . just a woman. She's sleeping with that weapon cradled in her arms," Cornell said.

"Come on, Tommy, let's get moving," Chris said, while reaching for his rifle.

"Shit! Remember what I told you two. Keep low, keep your finger off of the trigger until you need it, and watch your backs. You've got no business going up against these men. They took out the guards, and most of them were combat veterans. These guys are deadly. Are you sure this is what you want to do?" Cornell asked.

"Hell no, I want to go home to my wife and kids. But that's not going to happen while these guys still have the plant. Cornell, there isn't anyone else. We don't have a choice. We have to try," Tommy said, as he shook Cornell's hand.

"You take care of Kay . . . and good luck when she wakes up. You're right, she's gonna be pissed," Chris said, as he picked up his weapon, and headed for the stairs leading out of the room.

Fuel Handling Building 286'
2330 hours EST

"Listen to me, Chonglin. Quit arguing with me. I know what I'm doing. When I lift the hatch, I'll set it down by the stairs. You unhook the cables. Then, I'll lower the cables through the hatch, and we'll attach them to the bomb," Jian said, from 30 feet above, while sitting in the control cab, suspended below the overhead crane, at the north end of the building.

"I showed you how. Slip the shackle inside the cable. Then insert the shackle pin and tighten it. Slip each shackle onto the hook, and spread them out evenly," Jian said.

"I've got it. Just shut up and let me work," Chonglin said, as he inserted the first pin and tightened it.

Jian leaned back in the crane operator's seat and thought about what they were doing.

"*This isn't sanctioned by the Chinese government. They are our true commanders, not the Lieutenant. He is a fine officer and leader, but he is just a Lieutenant. General Kung may have been wrong. What if we are wrong in following his orders?*" Jian thought, as Chonglin began yelling in his earpiece.

"It's ready! Lift the damn hatch!" Chonglin yelled, as he stepped back from the big red hatch that separated the refuel floor from the railcar bay.

"I'll lift enough to put tension on the rigging and free the hatch. Then I'll stop. Make sure the load is level and nothing is twisted," Jian said.

The hatch was heavy steel plate. It was stenciled with its weight: 3150 lbs., but the crane was rated at over 50 tons. It had taken

Jian hours to figure out how to return power to the crane, and then more time to figure out the controls.

Jian tapped the up lever and felt the crane respond. The main cable began to move ever so slightly.

"How does it look?" Jian asked.

"All four cables are straight and tight. Lift the damn thing," Chonglin said.

The red hatch squealed as it broke free and began to rise into the air. Jian stopped the lift when the cable readout indicated that he had raised the load almost two feet.

"That's high enough. Swing it over to the side," Chonglin said.

Jian paused, studying the controls.

"*Trolly over? Is that the whole crane or just the body that hangs down between the girders?*" he asked himself, while studying the labels on the controls

"Hurry! What are you . . ." Chonglin began, then paused, having heard something other than the noise of the crane.

"I thought I heard something," Chonglin said, over the comm link.

Jian looked up from the controls, and down the 300-foot length of the Fuel Handling Building floor.

"Two men just entered through a door at the south end. They both have weapons. They aren't dressed like guards," Jian said, as he released his controls and reached for his weapon.

Then he remembered that he had left it at the base of the ladder before climbing up to the crane cab.

"Chonglin, I left my weapon down below. You'll have to take them," Jian said.

He glanced down and to his right. Chonglin was already moving down a narrow walkway on the left.

"I can't see them yet. Where are they?" Chonglin asked, while kneeling and sighting through his 4X power scope.

"There are pools at the far end. They separated. One went to the east, the other to the west. You should have a straight shot down the east side," Jian said.

Chonglin settled into a kneeling position and studied his sight picture. The walkway on the east was crowded with electrical panels mounted on the wall. A figure had just entered the walkway at the other end.

"The wall is on one side. The railings run the length of the building to keep you from falling into the pools. Once he enters the walkway, he's trapped between the wall and the handrails," Chonglin said, over the comm link.

"Good, wait a bit, and then take him down. I'll keep an eye on the other one.

Fuel Handling Building 286'
2359 hours EST

Tommy and Chris had split up as they entered through the security door on the south end of the Fuel Handling Building. Tommy had started down the west side. Chris had crept over to the other side of the building and was beginning to make his way down the east side.

Tommy looked down the length of the building. He could see taught cables hanging from the 50-Ton Crane. He stood upright and could see the red hatch dangling a few feet off the floor.

He tapped the railing on his right twice with his rifle barrel. Chris stopped and glanced over at him. Tommy pointed at the far end of the building. Chris stood upright to look, ducking behind a protruding electrical box. The sound of a bullet ricocheting off metal echoed across the vast floor. Chris threw himself backwards and began crawling back the way he'd come. Tommy ducked behind a rolling tool box, raised his weapon, and began shooting at the control cab mounted under the 50-Ton crane, over 100 yards away.

. . . .

August 3,
0003 hours EST

"Shit, I should have just shot him in the leg. He ducked behind a panel," Chonglin said, as he rose and began rushing down the east side.

Jian ducked as bullets began pinging off the cab. He was spun around as one round struck him in the chest, and another in the right arm. He began cursing in Chinese as he slumped to the floor of the cab and lay on his back.

"Chonglin, I'm hit," Jian said, while grabbing his upper right arm. The other round had been stopped by his body armor.

Jian could hear at least one weapon firing in short bursts. More rounds were pinging off the cab.

"I'm still taking fire, Chonglin," Jian said, while reaching for a first aide pouch on his web gear.

. . . .

"Shit . . . shit . . . shit!" Chris said, as he turned at the end of the east walkway, and began running for the door they had entered through.

Tommy was standing beside the Bridge Crane that was parked at the south end. He was firing three-round bursts at the cab on the 50-Ton Crane at the other end of the building. Bullets were pinging off the wall and the steel of the Bridge Crane, as Chris ran up beside him and crouched behind the steel structure.

"I glanced back and saw a guy moving down the east side. He must be the one who shot at me," Chris said.

"Yeah, I know. Now he's shooting at both of us," Tommy said, as he ducked behind the crane to reload his weapon.

Tommy stuck his head up, and then back down, as several more rounds bounced around them.

"He's halfway down the east side. He'll be on us in less than a minute. I don't think I want to get in a shootout with this guy," Tommy said, as he and Chris huddled behind cover.

Chris nodded in agreement and glanced at the exit. They both headed for the door without exchanging any more words.

. . . .

0010 hours EST

Jian was sitting in the cab's operator chair tightening the bandage on his right arm.

"Damn, we can't reach the Lieutenant from in here . . . the building is too thick. He needs to know that there is still armed resistance in the plant," Jian said.

204

"Chonglin, Chonglin, did you get them?" Jian asked, but received no answer.

Then he glanced down at his chest where the other bullet had hit. His comm set had been in a pocket on the outside of the vest. As he pulled on the line attached to the comm set, the wire came loose. The bullet had shattered the threaded connection.

"Maybe the transmitter still works," Jian said, as he removed the comm set and switched between modes.

"Chonglin, did you get them?" Jian asked, and released the transmit button.

"No, they ran back the way they came. I'm going hunting."

Jian looked toward the other end of the building from his high vantage point, and saw Chonglin at the south end.

"No, the mission is priority. I'm hit in the right arm. I need you to reposition the cables so we can get the weapon up here."

Chonglin said nothing. Jian could see him open the door at the far end and then close it. A dull thud told Jian that Chonglin had tossed a grenade into the room on the other side, and then closed the door.

"Chonglin . . . no!" Jian said, as he saw Chonglin open the door and rush into the room.

. . . .

The small room outside the south entrance to the 286' refuel floor was a vestibule, only 12 feet on a side, but it had three doors. One led into the Fuel Handling Building, another to the stairwell that Tommy and Chris had used to access the floor. The third door exited onto the roof of the Common Area that connected the Waste Processing Building to the Fuel Handling Building.

Tommy and Chris ran across the roof, and around the outside of the Reactor Containment Building. Chris paused as they neared the Main Steam Dumps where Steve had been killed. The roar of the steam dumps seemed even louder than before.

"Check your phone. See if you can get a signal!" Chris yelled.

"No, same as before. We're surrounded by three different buildings. It's like being in a valley," Tommy said, as he crouched down, and faced back the way they had come.

"So, we climb out of the valley," Chris said, while pointing to his right.

They both stared at the caged ladder that was mounted on the side of the Reactor Containment Building. It was a scary climb, but it led straight to a circular walkway built into the outside of the containment building. It was where the cylinder shape of the building ended and the curved dome began. The only higher point on site was the cooling tower.

"I'll cover you from down here. When you get to the walkway, you cover me while I climb up," Tommy said.

Chris nodded, loosened the sling on his weapon, placed it across his back, and began climbing.

. . . .

Chonglin opened the door to the vestibule outside the south end of the Fuel Handling Building and paused, waiting for the smoke from the grenade blast to clear.

"Two more doors, which way did they go?" he asked himself, while stepping inside.

He opened the door on the left, and saw a stairwell leading downward.

"*They would have gone to hide somewhere,*" he told himself, while glancing at the other door.

He walked through the door leading to the stairwell and proceeded downward.

. . . .

Walkway on the side of the Reactor Containment Building
0020 hours EST

"God, I hate heights," Chris said, as he lay on the concrete walkway outside the containment building.

The walkway was narrow, only three feet wide. A handrail was on the outside, and the curved surface of the dome on the other. The dome rose another 60 feet above them. Another ladder hugged the curve and led to the peak of the dome.

"Beats getting shot at," Tommy said, while lying on his stomach, face to face with Chris.

"Try your phone. I'm too tired to move," Chris said, while rolling onto his back and staring up at the night sky.

"We have to get a signal up here," Tommy said, while calling 911.

"9-1-1, what's the emergency?" the operator asked.

"Holy shit, I got through!" Tommy yelled.

"Quiet, somebody might hear us. You don't know where that guy went. He could be right below," Chris said, while rolling on his side and looking down at the base of the ladder.

"I repeat, 9-1-1, what's the emergency?" the operator asked.

"My name is Tommy Borders. I work at the Harris Nuclear Plant. The plant has been taken over by terrorists. We think they're trying to move that nuclear bomb the President talked about into our Fuel Handling Building. We just had a shootout with them. We had to run, me and Chris Baardsen. We're hiding on the side of the Reactor Containment Building. We need help!" Tommy said.

"Mr. Borders, please hold on the line while I transfer you," the operator said.

"Holy crap . . . now I'm on hold," Tommy said, as Chris rolled back over and stared at him.

"I didn't see anything down below. I think we're safe up here," Chris said.

Over a minute later, a different voice came on the phone.

"Mr. Borders, my name is Brian Madison. I'm the Emergency Operations Director at the North Carolina Emergency Operations Center. Just so you know, another half dozen people from various agencies, including the FBI, are listening to this conversation. Are you calling from the Harris Nuclear Plant?"

"Yes, Sir!" Tommy said, and proceeded to give his full name, social security number, date of birth, address, and home phone number, in rapid succession.

"Mr. Borders, what position do you hold at the Harris plant?" Director Madison asked.

"I'm a Senior ALARA Technician in Radiation Control. I've worked here since 1985," Tommy said.

After another pause, Director Madison said, "Mr. Borders, we believe you. Now tell us everything that's happened to you this shift."

Tommy told him everything they had seen and experienced since they had come to work that night.

"Mr. Borders, we want to get a visual on your face. Some people here think that you are a diversion. I've been told that there is a ladder near your location that extends to the top of the dome of the containment building. We have drones in the area and want to verify your identity. We would send the drone to you, but that would give away your location."

Tommy put the phone against his chest, and said, "Chris, now they want one of us to climb to the top of the frigging dome. They think I might be Chinese. They've got a drone around here, and they want to ID my face."

"What? The hell with that! Don't do it, Tommy. I can't believe I climbed up here to begin with. I hate heights."

Tommy lay back against the concrete and wiped the sweat from his face. Then he looked at his phone and said, "Okay, I'll climb up there, but I'm not staying up there long. It's too exposed."

"Mr. Borders, I'll let you know when we have verified your identity. Then you can go back down."

Tommy looked at Chris, laid his rifle on the walkway and stared at the ladder.

"Great, no cage! Just a straight frigging climb on a curved ladder. I'll be right back, cover me, dude," Tommy said, as he tucked the live phone into a shirt pocket, and began climbing the ladder.

Chris nodded, as he crawled on his hands and knees along the curved walkway toward the southeast side of the plant. The wind had shifted. There was a strong wind blowing from the southwest. The plume from the main steam dumps had flattened out. Chris saw a man walking on the Tank Area Building roof.

"*That's the guy. He's the one who shot Steve,*" Chris told himself, while tilting his head downward.

He could see Steve's body still lying in the open area outside the steam dumps. His blood was a dark stain on the roof. The stain snaked off to the right, ending at a floor drain in the roof.

"So his life ends there, just running down a drain."

Chris could feel the anger and the hatred rise, as he slid the stock of the M-16A2 into his shoulder.

The wind shifted again. The steam rose and blocked his view of the man on the other roof. Chris could hear the sound of thunder.

He looked up at the horizon as the storm clouds in the distance lit up. He remembered listening to the news as he was driving to work. Right before he got out of his car, the weather report said that thunder storms were probable during the night.

"Great! They're never right about the weather. Tonight they have to be right," Chris said, as he settled into a prone shooting position.

"I'll wait for the wind to change," Chris said, as he stared at the movement of the clouds, revealed by cloud-to-cloud lightning.

Chris had vague memories from Navy boot camp of qualifying with an M-16. Unlike Tommy, he wasn't a hunter. He hadn't shot a rifle in well over 20 years. A pistol was more his style.

"I can hit this guy. That's got to be less than 100 yards," Chris told himself, as he pulled the weapon tight into his shoulder and formed a sight picture.

"Look through the peep hole in the rear sight. Put the front sight post in the middle. Look through and find the target. Line it all up," Chris said, remembering how awkward it had all felt back then.

He moved the selector switch from 'Safe' to 'Semi' and thought about what he was getting ready to do.

"*They'll know we're outside and armed. They may hunt us down and kill us if I shoot this guy . . . but he murdered Steve. They've murdered everybody but us. Damn . . . I'm getting ready to shoot a man. Screw that, he wouldn't hesitate to kill me for one second,*" Chris thought, as he regained the sight picture, and began to squeeze the trigger.

"Center of mass. That's what the instructor always said. Don't try a head shot . . . just center of mass," Chris said, held his breath, settled on the man's back, and felt the weapon jump in his hands.

Tank Area Building Roof
0040 hours EST

Renshu was knocked to the ground as the bullet struck him. His body armor had stopped the round, but he still felt like someone had kicked him in the back. He jumped to his feet and began zigzagging across the roof of the Tank Area Building. He felt another bullet whiz by his head as he turned toward the plant and began firing.

"It's Renshu! I'm being shot at from the northwest! I'm leaving the roof now," Renshu yelled into the comm link.

Renshu ran for the caged ladder that was the only way off the Tank Area Building roof. One bullet skipped by near his feet. He felt another zip by his head. He turned, and began climbing down the ladder. He never felt the bullet enter his right temple and exit from his left eye He fell three rungs, catching one leg in the cage, and then an arm. He hung there, 20 feet off the lower roof.

. . . .

Chris stared at the man hanging inside the caged ladder. The wind shifted once again, and the man disappeared as the steam blocked his view. He could feel his heart pounding and was nauseous.

They always seem happy in the movies when they kill the enemy. Why don't I feel happy?" Chris thought, as he closed his eyes and laid his forehead on the warm barrel of his weapon.

Outside the Security Building
0042 hours EST

"Renshu, come up!" Aiguo said, for the third time.

There was no answer.

"Sergeant Davies, do you have any cameras pointing toward the center of the plant or the Reactor Containment Building?" Aiguo asked, over the comm link.

"We have adjustable cameras all along the perimeter. There are also cameras on the 314' level of the Turbine Building. What am I looking for?"

"The last time I visited you, we saw Renshu take out the individual who ran out of the steam cloud. Now Renshu seems to be missing. You know where he was. Look for him and anyone in that area . . . and Sergeant Davies . . . remember your family," Aiguo said, and closed the comm link.

"Bingwen, have you finished your deliveries?" Aiguo asked, over the comm link.

"No, two left, these damn things are heavy. Guan's bastards are making me carry them up to the top of the guard towers."

"Something has happened to Renshu. He's not answering. The last thing he said was that he was taking fire. I want you back here now!"

"I'm on the other side of the plant. I'll drop the missiles at the base of the stairs up the towers and head back your way. I'll be there in less than ten minutes."

"This is Sergeant Davies. I found your missing man. I think he's dead. He's hanging inside the caged ladder coming off the TAB roof," Jonathan said, over the comm link.

"Then find the shooter, Sergeant Davies. Find the shooter and call me back," Aiguo said.

Aiguo stood outside the Security Building, staring at the elevated position that Renshu had held. Steam still billowed in the background, shifting as the wind changed from moment to moment. He lifted his rifle and used the 4X scope to scan the area known as the Power Block. From this angle, the various roof lines of the multiple buildings crisscrossed and intersected. The only one that was different was the dome of the containment building.

"Why would Renshu abandon that position? He had elevation. That means the shooter had higher elevation."

Aiguo lowered his rifle and stared at the dome. The steam kept shifting and obscuring his view. He thought he had seen something or someone. He lifted the rifle to his shoulder and rested the barrel against the side of the Security building to steady is aim.

"There's a man up there on the top of the dome. All I can see are his head and shoulders. That's a perfect sniper position," Aiguo thought, as he relaxed, leaned against the building, and focused on the target 300 yards away.

Top of the Reactor Containment Building Dome
0041 hours EST

Tommy lay on the curved ladder at the top of the containment building. He wasn't exactly afraid of heights, but he didn't seek them out either.

"Okay, I'm at the top of the RCB. Can you see me?" Tommy said, into his cell phone.

"The drone is at the plant boundary, Mr. Borders . . . right in front of you. Wave your hand," Director Madison said.

Tommy stuck the cell phone up in the air with his right hand and waved. The bullet struck his forearm. He screamed, and watched the cell phone tumble down the side of the dome, bounce once, and skip through the rails on the platform below.

He slid to the right, holding onto the ladder with his left hand. His feet began skidding on the concrete, as he lifted his right arm and stared at the rip in his forearm.

"Jesus, I just got shot!" Tommy said, as he began to feel dizzy.

He hugged the side of the dome as his left hand loosened from the ladder, and he began to slide down toward the narrow walkway 80 feet below.

Chris was still staring at the limp body hanging in the ladder cage when he heard Tommy scream. He scrambled to his feet, and began running back toward the ladder that led to the top of the dome. He heard or felt the bullet that caromed off the concrete dome to his left. As he rounded the curve, he saw Tommy slam into the walkway ahead. A smear of blood ran up the side of the dome.

Waste Processing Building 236'
0045 hours EST

Chonglin found himself back at the stairwell by the elevator, and knew that he had walked in a complete circle.

"This place is a maze. There must be a thousand different rooms and cubicles. They could be anywhere, and I've checked every room I've passed . . . except one," he said, then walked past the elevator and through a set of double doors.

"*A boundary . . . portal monitors? I walked past here and all the way around this area. There's something in the middle,*" he thought, while approaching the magenta and yellow boundary rope and signs. A sign said 'RCA Exit to the Radwaste Control Room'.

"The rats have a nest," Chonglin said, as he reached the boundary.

He stepped through the portal monitor and cursed when it alarmed. When he opened the door on the other side, he saw a set of

212

stairs leading upward. Voices told him that he had found his prey, and that one of them was a woman. The door shut behind him with a loud click, and he paused, listening. The talking above him had ceased.

Chonglin smiled, and rolled his shoulders to loosen the tension in his neck. He could smell the woman's perfume as he crept up the stairs, his weapon trained on the area at the top. He stopped before his head cleared the floor, and loosened a grenade from his harness. He pulled the pin, counted to three, and tossed the grenade high into the room above.

He heard a man scream 'Grenade!' just before the detonation. Two seconds after the blast, Chonglin ran up the stairs and began firing into the haze left by the explosion. A man rose from behind a fallen desk and began firing and cursing at the same time. Chonglin was struck twice in the chest and once in the arm as they exchanged shots from 20 feet away.

Chonglin was wearing body armor. The man in front of him was not.

Cornell was thrown against a wall and sagged to the floor. Kay began screaming as she stepped from behind a wall locker, pointed her M-16 at Chonglin, and pulled the trigger. Nothing happened. She squeezed the trigger again and again, as the man began laughing at her.

"The eyes, the eyes tell everything. The old black man was a soldier when he was young. His fear was controlled. He was already wounded by the grenade before I killed him, but he waited for me to appear. Only a soldier has that kind of control. But you . . . you don't even know how to fire that weapon. You are shaking like a leaf. A woman should know her place," Chonglin said, grimacing at the flesh wound on his left arm.

"I will have fun with you before I kill you," Chonglin said, as he set his rifle aside, rolled his shoulders, and slowly slid his knife from its sheath.

Kay pointed the weapon at him, and pulled the trigger again and again. Then she remembered Tommy telling her about the selector switch. The man was ten feet way and walking toward her when she slid her thumb onto the selector switch, moved it, and felt two clicks.

Chonglin saw the motion and rushed toward her with the knife extended.

A three-round burst struck him in the chest and knocked him backwards. He screamed through the pain, and turned back toward her as another burst struck him in the left side. One bullet shattered his upper arm and spun him around. Three more rounds tore into his legs, causing him to collapse onto the floor. The knife tumbled from his hand as he reached for his handgun.

"Know my place, my ass!" Kay said, as she blew his head apart with another three-round burst.

Kay stared down at the man as his life poured onto the carpeted floor. She fired the weapon again until it clicked. Her heart was pounding in her chest, as she began to shake. Then she thought about Cornell. She threw the weapon aside as if it was a snake. Then ran behind the desk and knelt by his body. His chest was riddled. His eyes stared at nothing . . . and everything.

"Oh, Cornell, I'd be dead if you hadn't thrown me behind the locker. Why did you have to go and die? Now I'm alone," Kay said, as she rested her hand on his chest and began to sob.

Walkway around the Containment Building
0045 hours EST

Chris jumped over Tommy's still body, and knelt by his head as he rolled him over.

"Tommy . . . Tommy, shit, you've been shot!" Chris said, as he looked at Tommy's forearm.

"Flesh wound, the bleeding has almost stopped. I'll bandage it later. Now wake up! Aww, please don't make me give you CPR," Chris said, while checking for a pulse at his friend's neck.

"God, that hurt! I think I broke my ribs," Tommy said, as his eyes popped open and stared up into Chris's face.

"I got one of them, Tommy. I shot the bastard who killed Steve!"

"Great! And another one shot me. They know where we are. We have to get out of here or we're dead," Tommy said, while rolling onto his side.

"What did the guy on the phone want?" Chris asked, as he stepped back over Tommy, and looked over the side at the roof down below.

"I don't know. He was just starting to say something when I got shot. I always wondered what it felt like to get shot. It hurts like shit, and I just got grazed. It feels like a really bad burn," Tommy said, while looking at his forearm.

"Do you think you can climb down?" Chris asked.

"Dude, I think that's a bad idea. Where would we go? That's a trap down below. We're vulnerable when we climb down. No, I say we stay up here. They can't get above us. As long as we stay low, they can't hit us, we're too high," Tommy said, while pulling himself along the walkway toward his rifle.

"What about the bomb? I thought we were going to go after the bomb?" Chris asked, as he settled down on the walkway, trying to stay as low as possible.

"We tried that. That's why we're up here. Now we wait and see what happens. If the police or the military attack, then maybe we'll try again. Right now, I need to rest," Tommy said, as he slid as far away from the railing as he could go.

The rumble of distant thunder became more frequent and louder as the minutes passed. Chris could feel the air grow cooler as it swirled over and around the containment building.

"Tommy, when the storm hits, we'll make a run for it."

When Tommy didn't answer, Chris grabbed his best friend's arm to feel for a pulse. Snoring, and a strong pulse, told him that Tommy was just fine.

"Damn . . . he gets shot, and then decides to take a nap. Damn!" Chris said, clutched his rifle tight to his chest, and closed his eyes.

CHAPTER 51

1-130th Attack Recon Battalion Headquarters
Raleigh-Durham International Airport
Raleigh, North Carolina
August 3, 0230 hours EST

"This is it? Where the hell is everybody else?" Captain Allison Wills said, while pacing across the front of the briefing room at the headquarters of the 1-130th Attack-Recon Battalion.

"We're lucky we got this many to show up. This evacuation has scattered everyone. None of us have families. If any more pilots show up I'll be surprised," said Captain Malcomb DuBose.

"If I don't see at least four more aircrew in the next 30 minutes, I'll have somebody's ass," Major Antoine Bouchard said, while standing in the doorway.

"Attention!" yelled Captain Jessie Porter.

"At ease! Where do we stand with air crews?" Major Bouchard asked.

Captain Wills looked around the room, "Sir, we've got enough for six flights, but that's if we mix and match. My gunner isn't here, and we're missing some pilots."

"Then you may have to fly alone. Think you can handle that, Captain Wills?" asked Major Bouchard.

"No doubt about it, Sir! What's the mission?" Captain Wills asked, as she thought about flying and fighting her AH-64D Apache helicopter by herself.

"I think we all know about the President's speech and the threat to the nation. That threat is here, and by here, I mean in North Carolina. The Chinese Special Forces operators, who the President talked about, have taken over the Harris Nuclear Plant," Major Bouchard said, and paused to let that settle in.

"That means that they have a nuke with them?" Captain Porter asked.

"That's the assumption. We're part of a task force that's going to take the plant back, and prevent these bastards from blowing up the nuke," Major Bouchard said.

"Why us? Why isn't the 82nd Combat Aviation Brigade providing support?" asked Captain Porter.

"Because the mission requires Apaches, and the CAB's 1-82 Battalion is in Afghanistan with all their Apaches. We're the 'B' Team. The mission is ours. Any more questions?" said Major Bouchard.

"So, Sir, what is our mission?" Captain DuBose asked.

"Ground forces are coming up from Ft. Bragg. Delta is involved in the op, but I don't know the details of their mission. That's above my pay grade. Our mission is to take out six armored security towers on the perimeter of the plant at precisely 0400," Major Bouchard said.

"Let's do it, Sir! Let's light 'em up!" said Captain Wills.

"Outstanding! Here's the plan . . ." Major Bouchard said.

CHAPTER 52

Highway 401
25 miles south of Fuquay-Varina, North Carolina
August 3, 0300 hours EST

"Sir, we need to slow down. We've already lost six Strykers to mechanical problems," Captain Blake Jackson said, over the battalion comm net.

"Negative, Captain Jackson, we keep pushing. I expect the after action report to reflect those responsible for inadequate maintenance of those vehicles," Lieutenant Colonel Anthony Thompson said, from the lead Stryker vehicle.

"But Sir, I've got two more vehicles that are overheating. These vehicles aren't designed for sprinting at 60 miles per hour," Captain Jackson said.

"They are if I say they are. Keep going!" LTC Thompson said, and cut the link.

"Sir, with all due respect, he's right," said Sergeant Major (SGM) Davis Jones, as he sat beside LTC Thompson inside their Stryker vehicle.

"I know that, Sergeant Major, but we can't slow down. We have to be there in 60 minutes, and we're behind schedule. If we lose some vehicles, then we'll make do with what we have left," LTC Thompson said, as he reviewed the latest data from the Pentagon on his laptop.

"It looks like the plan to surround the plant and relieve the cops has changed, Sergeant Major. We're going straight in. We've been ordered to assault the plant entrance at 0400," LTC Thompson said, as he looked across at SGM Jones.

"So what's the plan, Sir?"

"Hey diddle diddle, right up the middle, Sergeant Major . . . just like your football days at Michigan State. We'll need to reconfigure the lineup. We'll need max firepower up front," said LTC Thompson, as he began relaying orders to his company commanders.

CHAPTER 53

The White House
The Situation Room
Washington, DC
August 3, 0300 hours EST

"Mr. President, all our forces will be in position by 0400. The only complication is the weather. Forecasters are predicting a thunderstorm and heavy rain over the plant. It will provide excellent cover for the assault, but the Delta teams are going to have a hard time landing. The Fuel Handling Building roof is huge, but not that huge. Crosswinds could exceed 40 mph," General Munford said.

"Why don't we just drop them in by chopper?" President Miller asked.

"Sir . . . a little complication there. After 9/11 all of the nuclear power sites in the country were hardened to one extent or another. Harris is probably in the top ten for added capabilities. One of those capabilities was surface-to-air missiles. The plant was provided with six FIM-92D Stingers. As far as we know, they still have them. They also have a couple of FM-148 Javelin anti-tank missiles. We have to assume that the terrorists have located these weapons."

The President just stared in disbelief.

"General Munford, those men . . . and the specialist they are taking with them . . . have got to get on site in one piece. How that happens is up to you, but the success of this entire mission is based on her disarming that damn bomb."

"We do have a backup plan. Ms. Williams recommended two of her assistants. They have worked with her during the process of disarming all the other devices that we've located across the country. We've staged her assistants with the North Carolina National Guard at the State EOC in Raleigh. We can forward stage them to the area outside the plant, and link them up with the Stryker Battalion coming up from Bragg."

"Make it happen, General. Everything comes down to the success of this mission. Failure is not an option . . . whatever the cost. Am I understood?" the President said, while looking around the table at all the high powered representatives of various federal agencies.

"Understood, Mr. President!" General Munford said, as he pulled out his cell phone and left the table.

CHAPTER 54

NC National Guard
North Carolina State Emergency Operations Center
1636 Gold Star Drive
Raleigh, North Carolina
August 3, 0310 hours EST

Amanda had never seen a soldier come to attention while sitting in a chair, but that's exactly what happened after Brigadier General Dave Moore answered a call from an outside line.

"Yes, Sir . . . yes, Sir, I'll have them moving ASAP. Right now . . . yes, Sir, I understand the urgency," General Moore said, then slowly set the phone back in its cradle as if it was a bomb.

Then he picked up his cell phone, keyed in a number and asked, "Major Talton, do you still have eyes on those two civilians who came in after midnight?"

"Yes, Sir! We're sitting downstairs in the cafeteria."

"Good, I need them escorted to the access road at Harris. They need to be there by 0400 at the latest, understood?"

"Understood, Sir! I'll get them there!"

"What just happened?" Amanda asked, after General Moore slid his cell phone into his shirt pocket.

"That was the Chairman of the Joint Chiefs, General Munford. Two civilian nuclear bomb specialists showed up a couple of hours ago and said they were told to report here and wait. General Munford wants them at the plant site by 0400. I don't know all the details, but I think things are getting ready to happen."

"Where are they?"

"They were in the cafeteria. They'll be heading out the front door in two minutes. Major Talton has a Hummer parked out front. The Highway Patrol will clear a path for them."

"I'm going with them," Amanda said, while jumping up and running out of the EOC Command Room.

CHAPTER 55

Harris Nuclear Plant
August 3, 0330 hours EST

Fuel Handling Building 286'
Refuel Floor

Jian lay against the side of the 50-Ton Crane cab suspended high above the refuel floor. His right arm was throbbing. He had stopped most of the bleeding, but his arm was useless. His boots felt sticky from the blood that had settled into the base of the cab. He had wedged his injured arm inside his shirt, and injected himself with a low dose of morphine to deaden the pain. He had begun to drift off when he heard his name being yelled over the comm link, and sat upright.

"Jian, here. What is my mission?"

Jian . . . it's Aiguo. My friend, we're almost finished. The weapon is attached to the crane. Lift it and trolley over to the middle of the building. Set it on the floor, and then you can rest. We will have accomplished our mission. China will be supreme!"

"Understood, Comrade Lieutenant! The mission, above all," Jian said, as he forced himself to sit upright and stare at the controls.

"Up lever . . . lift it up until it clears the floor . . . then move to the center," he told himself, as the cab jolted and the cables began to move.

The load had just cleared the floor, when he passed out from blood loss.

"Jian, that's good. Move the load to the middle . . . Jian, move the load!" Aiguo yelled into the comm link, while staring up at the dangling bomb from inside the Railcar Bay.

"Heng, can you operate a crane?" Aiguo asked.

"I'm not trained, but I can try," Heng said, while staring up at the device hanging above their heads.

"When you have moved the weapon, and lowered it to the floor, contact me. I'll come up and activate the device. I have some other things to check on," Aiguo said, while turning and running out of the Railcar Bay.

It was beginning to pour. The temperature had dropped, and the smell of ozone was in the air. The sky to the south was alive with electricity. Aiguo knew that a great storm would soon break upon Harris.

Walkway around the Containment Building
0340 hours EST

"Tommy, wake up! It's raining, and the lightning is getting really bad. We've got to move," Chris said, while shaking Tommy.

"Aww, shit! What happened to me? I really hurt," Tommy said, as he awoke, and pushed Chris away.

"I know. I feel like shit too, but we've got to go. We've got to get inside. This storm is getting worse," Chris said, as lighting flashed overhead, followed by a crashing boom.

The rain came like God had opened a faucet in the sky. Even more water was rolling down the side of the dome and cascading down the side of the building like a wave.

"I'm awake! Quit shaking me," Tommy yelled, as he grasped the handrail and threw up over the side.

"This is our cover, Tommy. Remember, we have to go back and stop them from moving the bomb onto the refuel floor," Chris said, as the lightning flashed again.

Tommy blinked again and again, as his mind began to clear. The cool rain ran down his face and soaked his body.

"Yeah, we need to climb down and go back inside," Tommy said.

"Your rifle, get your rifle!" Chris said, as he steadied Tommy while he stood.

"Tommy, look at me. Are you okay?"

"Yeah, let's go get this done," Tommy said, while tilting his face up into the rain.

CHAPTER 56

717 South Main Street
Fuquay-Varina, North Carolina
August 3, 0340 hours EST

Christine Marks had lived in Fuquay-Varina for the last 40 years. She had raised three sons and two daughters. A year ago she had buried her husband of 44 years. When the mandatory order to evacuate had come, she had ignored it. This was her home, and she was willing to die there.

It had been a hot summer evening, but she knew a storm was coming. She could feel it in her bones and smell it in the air. When the thunder and lightning woke her at 3:30 AM, she knew the storm was going to be a doozy.

She sat in the small living room of her white, wood frame house, drinking coffee and watching the light show outside her front window. The glare and flash of the storm reminded her of taking her family to Fuquay-Varina High School many years ago to watch the fireworks on the 4th of July. Those had been good times. Now her kids were all gone, with families of their own. Then the ground began to shake like it did when a big construction truck drove by her house.

"Three o'clock in the morning, and it's raining cats and dogs. Who in their right mind is out driving in this mess?" she said, as she rose from her sofa, and walked over to the window.

The rumbling continued, and then intensified, as she stared at a continuous procession of huge tan vehicles flying down Main Street. She knew they were military vehicles, but couldn't remember their name.

"Johnny would have known. He was interested in things like that," she said, as another ten vehicles flew past her window.

"I don't care what they're doing. Don't they know that the speed limit is 25?" she asked herself.

.   .   .   .

Sergeant Martin Gomez was driving the lead Stryker as the 1st Battalion, 2nd Brigade Combat Team, raced up Highway 401, and into downtown Fuquay-Varina. He was following a string of flashing lights as the Highway Patrol led the way.

"I sure hope they can see better than me, 'cause I can't see shit," Sgt. Gomez said, from his hatch-down driving position.

All he saw was a little town flashing by at 50 mph. A minute later, he slowed down as the cops turned left and drove over a bridge crossing a railway. The next left was even sharper, as they turned onto a four-lane highway and accelerated. He floored the Stryker as the Highway Patrol vehicles roared up the highway.

"Five minutes, then a hard left again, Sgt. Gomez. Then ten more minutes to our destination," he heard over the vehicle comm link.

"Loud and clear, Sir!" Gomez said, as he pushed open his hatch, and raised his seat. The rain started pouring in, but at least he could see.

Raleigh-Durham International Airport
0340 hours EST

The six Apache AH-64D Longbows took off together, turned, and formed a string behind Major Antoine Bouchard. The weather was bad and getting worse. Winds were gusting at 30-40 mph.

"All Longbows, 15 minutes flight time to Harris. Remember the sequence. Longbow 6 peels off first onto the No. 6 security tower. I peel off last onto tower No. 1. Maintain distance of 300 meters from your assigned tower. Fire only on my command. Is that understood?" Major Bouchard said.

He nodded, as five confirmations were returned. Then he began monitoring his flight systems and weapon status. His weapons operator had failed to arrive at the airport as ordered, but that was a problem for another day.

"Mark 230 Chain Gun, active-safe, 300 rounds 30mm M789 HEDP. The tower will look like swiss cheese after a few bursts. One each AGM-114 Hellfire missile, just in case, but I shouldn't need it," Major Bouchard said, as he went down his checklist.

"Bouchard to Longbow flight . . . our attack on the towers coincides with an infantry attack on the main entrance. They're in Strykers, but we don't want any 'friendly fire' incidents. Take out your assigned tower, cease fire, and back off to 1000 meters unless ordered otherwise. Is that understood?" Major Bouchard said.

Once again he received five confirmations.

C-130 Aircraft
5,000 feet above Harris
0348 hours EST

The C-130 was bouncing through the air like a ping pong ball. The rear ramp was still secured. The pilots had refused to lower the ramp until 30 seconds before the jump. The roar of the aircraft engines was drowned out by the fury of the storm that surrounded the plane.

"Nice of you to come along, Colonel, but we're used to operating without adult supervision," yelled SFC Ancellis York, as his stomach lurched for the tenth time, as the aircraft dropped a few hundred feet.

"I figured I'd come along to make sure you guys jumped over the right target. Left to your own devices you'd wind up landing on some bar, and assault that rather than a nuke plant filled with Chinese Special Forces," Colonel Jankens replied, as they both started laughing.

Kate Williams stared at both men sitting across from her. She was focused on not throwing up on her feet. She had been on some wild flights in her life, but this was like being inside a washing machine.

"Two minutes to drop," came the announcement from the cockpit.

"Remember, winds gusting at 40 mph from the southwest. We're jumping lower, only 5000 feet, but we're still opening at 500 feet, so this could be a rough landing," said SFC Mays, over the comm link.

"Could be? I'll wind up with my ass around my shoulders," SSG Clay said, while slapping Kate on the knee and laughing.

She felt too sick to come up with a response. She just wrapped her arms around the satchel that was strapped across her chest. Everything that she needed to disarm the device was packed into the satchel. They had no reserve chutes. There wasn't a reason to carry one. If the main chute failed to open at 500 feet, you were dead. She kept going through the disarming sequence for the nuclear weapon to take her mind off her stomach.

"Ms. Williams, you still with us?" Colonel Jankens yelled.

"No problem, I've jumped in worse," Kate lied, as she put on her best fake smile.

SSG Clay leaned close to Kate, stuck out his right hand and said, "Lady, I'll bet you $1000 that when the pilot lowers that ramp, and you see what's waiting for us outside, that you chicken out."

"One minute to drop, lowering the ramp," came the announcement from the cockpit.

"You just lost $1000, SSG Clay," Kate said, and shook his hand.

"Verify auto-opening settings at 500 feet," Colonel Jankens said, over the comm link.

Kate verified the setting with a glance, and then lifted the flap on her glove to check the time . . . 0355 hours.

"Charlie Squadron, Teams 1 Alpha and 4 Alpha . . . on your feet," Colonel Jankens ordered, as the rear ramp began to descend.

He stood with the teams, holding onto a bin welded onto the side of the aircraft.

The red light on the right side of the opening began to flash. Team 1A formed a stick, ran toward the ramp, and jumped into the howling tempest. Team 4A, including Kate Williams, was three seconds behind them.

Kate fought for control, as she felt her body whipped one way, then the other. She felt herself slam into another body and stick.

She glanced to her right as a voice said over the comm link, "Relax! Arch your back, legs together, feet together. I've got us at the right descent angle. I'm letting you go in 3 . . . 2 . . . 1 . . . released," the voice said, as they separated.

Kate struggled as the free fall continued, but then recovered. The turbulence required constant, subtle adjustments. She struggled to remember every trick of executing a controlled free fall that she had learned over the years. The sky above her flashed, and she saw the first team 1000 feet below her. They were all within 50 feet of each other in a V formation, angling downward. She was last in her group, but could see the others grouped tightly just below her in a similar V formation. She was the outlier, trailing behind them all.

The lightning flashed again, and she looked past the two teams. She could see the brightly lit plant below. They were coming in from the southwest.

"It's too far, we're too low. We'll land outside the fence," she said, over the comm link.

"Negative, stay the course. The wind will carry us onto the target once the chutes open," a voice said.

The order was garbled with static. She would never learn whose voice it was.

Intersection of State Road 1134 and Shearon Harris Road
0355 hours EST

"Move, move, move . . . get in the damn vehicle and sit down!" Sergeant Major Jones yelled, as the three civilians scrambled through the downpour, up the ramp, and into the back of the Command Stryker.

"Sit down and shut up. This is a military operation and you are baggage," SGM Jones yelled, while hitting the button to raise the ramp.

Nathan O'Malley and Alan Parkins were both soaked as they settled into the hard bench on the left side of the Stryker's spartan interior. Both were loaded down with bagged equipment. Amanda sat across from them, wiping her sodden hair away from her eyes.

"Sir, civilians on board. We're ready to move!" SGM Jones yelled.

LTC Anthony Thompson didn't look up at the additional passengers. He only nodded, and spoke into his comm link, "Captain Harker, move your four MGS forward and execute Phase 1."

"Roger that, Sir! Execute Phase 1!"

Four M1128 Mobile Gun System Strykers leapt from the intersection and headed down Shearon Harris Road. They separated and formed line abreast as the road widened into a parking lot around the Security Shack.

As each vehicle came into position, the order to fire was given. The four 105mm guns opened fire as one. The guard shack disappeared. At 0400 hours, the assault on Harris had begun . . .

CHAPTER 57

The Assault on Harris
August 3, 0400 hours EST

The Apaches

The last Apache AH-64D Longbow pulled away from the stick and settled into a firing position 300 meters from Security Tower No. 6. One by one, the other five aircraft duplicated the maneuver and hovered. Each pilot had to fight the shifting winds and the pounding rain to hold their positions.

"Longbow flight, confirm positions and readiness to fire," Major Bouchard said.

The first three confirmations came in when Major Bouchard heard, "Missile . . . missile . . . missile . . ."

Then he saw the flash of an explosion on the other side of the formation, as Longbow 3 was struck by a Stinger missile. The airframe buckle as the craft surged inwards toward the plant, the rotors aiming toward the long building on the western side of the plant.

"*He was too close, 100 meters . . . what the hell was he doing?*" he thought, as chatter exploded over the comm link.

"Longbow flight, proceed with the mission. I repeat, proceed with the mission," Major Bouchard ordered, as he stared at the launch of a missile from the No. 1 Security Tower, directly in front of him.

He switched his weapons systems to live and began firing his Mark 230 chain gun at the tower. The missile drew closer. He jinked left, then right, in an effort to draw the missile off target. The chain gun continued to rattle as it threw explosive rounds at the guard tower. He knew he had seconds to live.

"One chance," he told himself, as he fired the Hellfire missile.

The two missiles impacted each other 100 feet from his Apache. The concussion and the shrapnel tore into his aircraft. The airframe shuddered as one rotor was struck. He knew that he was going to crash.

Delta
0400 hours EST

The two Delta teams were at 3000 feet, and plummeting downward, when the shooting began. Explosions lit the eastern side of the plant, indicating that the ground troops had begun their assault on the plant entrance. Flashes of light, and small explosions on the perimeter, indicated that the Apaches were taking down the guard towers.

SFC Ancellis York glanced at his altimeter, and braced himself as his MS-260 M4 chute opened at 500 feet. He was 100 yards outside the plant perimeter fence, and moving almost horizontally in the howling winds.

"We'll make it, but the landing is going to be rough," he told himself.

He was steering for the south end of the Fuel Handling Building roof, when he was cut in half by the rotor blade of Longbow 3.

Kate was still plummeting toward the ground. A glance at her altimeter showed 1500 feet. She watched in horror as the damaged helicopter spun toward the plant from the west. The chutes of Delta Team 1A and 4A had just opened. The men were steering toward the Fuel Handling Building when the helicopter swept through them from behind. She saw at least eight men disappear as the helicopter crashed into the south end of the huge building and explode.

Outside the Fuel Handling Building
South End
0402 hours EST

Tommy had struggled while climbing down the ladder from the containment building walkway. The rain had made the rungs slick. He had slipped more than once. His wounded arm was throbbing, as were several abrasions from his slide down the concrete dome. The impact of hitting the walkway hadn't helped his ribs and right shoulder.

"Dude, I'm hurting. The only thing that doesn't hurt is the bottom of my feet," Tommy said, as he leaned against the handrails on the stairs leading up to the Fuel Handling Building south entrance.

He and Chris looked at each other as the storm above them seemed to intensify. The sounds were different, even more chaotic than before.

"I know you're hurting, but we have to get this done," Chris said, then jumped as the sky above them exploded into a fireball.

"Move, move, move . . . into the building!" Chris yelled, as fire and debris began to rain down on them.

As they slammed the door shut behind them, they felt a sharp bang, as if something large had just struck the heavy steel security door on the outside.

"That wasn't anything from this site. I looked up and saw a fuselage, or something mechanical, like a helicopter," Tommy said, as they both leaned against the steel door.

"Was it landing on the roof?"

"Yeah, but it was in pieces."

They could hear the dull echo of thunder or explosions, as they rested in the vestibule leading onto the refuel floor.

"I think the military's here. They're attacking the plant. Maybe we can just sit this one out," Chris said, while removing his slung rifle from around his shoulders, and sagging to the floor.

"Dude, if I sit down, I won't get back up. It may take a while before anyone else gets this far. The Chinese will try to set off the bomb now . . . maybe right now. We have to stop them or we're dead, no matter what anyone else does," Tommy said, while staring down at Chris, and unslinging his own weapon.

"Hey, if you can keep going, so can I. It's just like hanging lead shielding during an outage. You just have to keep on going until the job's done," Chris said, as he pushed himself up off the concrete floor.

The two friends stood together in front of the door leading to the refuel floor, and stared at each other. They both knew that another shootout was inevitable.

"You know, we'll probably be dead in the next five minutes," Chris said, as Tommy grabbed the handle to pull open the heavy security door.

"Fuck it . . . gotta go some time," Tommy said, as he yanked on the door and groaned.

"Should have let you open the door," Tommy said, as they both stepped through the doorway.

"Nub!" Chris said, and laughed.

The Strykers
0402 hours EST

Two MGS Strykers charged past the remains of the guard shack and roared up the road toward the second objective. As they rounded the crest of the hill, they stopped side-by-side and lowered the muzzles of the 105mm rifled tank guns mounted in turrets on top of their vehicles.

The concrete and steel road barrier was raised. It was designed to stop any bomb-laden truck filled with explosives that was intended for the plant. It was not designed to resist a full frontal military assault.

Both gunners fired at the same time. The auto-loaders were able to insert a fresh round every two seconds. After five cycles, they ceased fire. The massive barrier had been reduced to debris scattered over 500 square yards. The two vehicles drove over the rubble, separated, and drove into the parking lots on either side of the road. They were followed by the other two MGS Strykers and the remainder of Alpha Company. The rest of the battalion followed close behind. They all headed for the Security Building and the main entrance into the Protected Area.

Security Command Center
Overwatch
0404 hours EST

Jonathan began pounding the table in glee as he watched multiple camera views light up with the sight of numerous explosions.

The vehicle barrier had been blown apart. Armored vehicles were storming up Shearon Harris Road, past the cooling tower, and toward the Security Building.

"Your happiness will be short lived, Sergeant Davies," Aiguo said, as he placed the muzzle of his 9mm pistol against the back of Jonathan's skull.

"Looks like you found the Stingers," Jonathan said, as the image of an Apache helicopter being struck by a surface-to-air missile appeared on one screen.

"Yes, you neglected to tell us about the heavy munitions in the armory. They were a nice addition to our inventory. As you can see, we're putting them to good use."

"Just get it over with, asshole!"

"Ohh, Sergeant Davies, I know you were hoping for a happy ending to all this. Isn't that the way all American action movies end? The hero battles against terrible odds, kills the villain, and goes home to his adoring wife and children. Isn't that what you hoped for, Sergeant Davies?"

Jonathan felt each breath, each beat of his heart. His eyes were filled with the faces of his two daughters and his wife, as Aiguo shot him in the back of the head. His blood and brain matter scattered across multiple screens, as he slumped forward onto the desk.

"Fitting end for a traitor," Aiguo said, while flicking a piece of skull off his sleeve, and holstering his pistol.

He stared once more at the images of the ongoing battle, turned, and ran toward the stairwell.

"They better have the bomb in position," he said, while running down the stairs.

The Strykers
0410 hours EST

LTC Anthony Thompson stood in the open hatch of his Command Stryker. The heads-up display on his visor showed him the location of every vehicle as they streamed up Shearon Harris Road and onto the plant site.

He switched to the vehicle comm channel, and said, "Sgt. Gomez, pull off to the right side and halt."

They pulled off the paved road, even with the mid-section of the massive cooling tower on their right. Anthony glanced upward at the 50-story structure, just as the sky above erupted in nature's light show.

He switched back to the command channel to monitor chatter, as Alpha Company continued down the road past him and toward the Security Building. Bravo Company had turned left, and was circling the Switchyard. They would emerge on the south side of the plant, and ensure that the three guard towers on that side were down. If not, they would complete that part of the mission, and then breach the fence line. Charlie Company was circling the cooling tower on the north side to ensure that the two guard towers on that side were no longer in service. The third breach of the Protected Area fence would occur there.

Anthony glanced over his left shoulder at the burning wreckage of an Apache helicopter. He could see a man staggering away as onboard munitions began detonating.

"Captain Rigsbee, bring up a Medical EVAC Stryker. There's an injured pilot on the left side of the access road, just past the barrier," Anthony ordered.

"Roger that, Sir! On the way!"

Anthony turned back toward the battle just as a rocket was fired from the roof of the Security Building.

"Shit! . . . Gomez, hard left . . . accelerate!" Anthony yelled, and ducked down in the vehicle as the missile streaked toward them.

The Stryker lurched, its wheels spinning in the sodden grass, and then spun to the left as the missile detonated on the road just in front of the vehicle. The 20-ton Stryker was tipped into the air, and spun 180 degrees before crashing onto its side on the asphalt road.

"Command down . . . command down! AT gunner on security building roof . . . engage, engage! Medivac Stryker needed left of the cooling tower," came the command over the comm net.

Alpha Company CO, Captain Blake Jackson, was the ranking Captain in the battalion, and took over command when he saw the battalion commander's vehicle flip over. His Stryker had been 50 yards in front of the Command Stryker. The missile had streaked by his vehicle at the height of his head.

Three MGS Strykers turned their 105mm guns and began obliterating the security building and the nearby guard tower. Another 20 vehicles began pouring 50 cal rounds into any building in front of them. The Admin Building on the left front of the plant was torn to pieces by high caliber rounds and explosive projectiles.

Soldiers began stumbling out of the damaged Command Stryker. LTC Thompson was carrying SGT Gomez, who was unconscious and bleeding heavily from facial lacerations. Anthony stared at two male civilians and a female who were standing beside SGM Jones. The SGM and the woman were yelling at each other as another Stryker pulled up beside the wrecked vehicle.

"Listen, lady, I don't give a damn. I've got injured men. The first thing I'm going to do is get them help. Then I'll see to your needs," SGM Jones said, as he knelt down and inspected the injuries of an unconscious soldier.

"You don't understand. These men have got to get to the back of the Fuel Handling Building!" the woman yelled, as LTC Thompson walked up, and laid SGT Gomez beside the other wounded soldier.

As he stood up, Anthony stared down at the young woman standing in front of him. Her hair was sodden and plastered to her head. She had a scrape on her forehead that was bleeding down the side of her face, but she looked familiar.

"Agent Amanda Langford, how did you wind up in the back of my vehicle?"

"Escort duty. These men are nuclear weapon EOD specialists. We have to get them to the device ASAP. They know how to disarm it!" Amanda said, as she grabbed him by the front of his web gear.

He remembered the last time she had grabbed him like that.

"You should have let me kill him," Anthony said, recalling the day when they had been together in Vola's Dockside Bar & Grill in Old Towne Alexandria.

Anthony had been standing over the wounded Chinese Special Forces Operator who had murdered his pregnant wife. He still remembered the Aiguo's defiant words as he pointed his .45 between the man's eyes.

"Maybe, but the SWAT team would have killed you. I didn't want that . . . to happen," Amanda said, as she clung to his web gear.

"A lot of people have died because of him. A whole lot more might die tonight," Anthony said.

"That's why I have to get these two to the device . . . like right now!" Amanda said.

LTC Thompson looked up at the Stryker that had stopped beside him and said, "Staff Sergeant, unload one Fire Team. I need room in the back, and I'm taking your vehicle."

The Apaches
0410 hours EST

Captain Allison Wills had taken longer than expected to topple her assigned target, Security Tower No. 4. Once that was completed, she turned her aircraft toward Tower No. 3. She had seen Longbow 3 spin out of control after it was struck by a surface-to-air missile. Her instinct had been to turn and run. The pilot, Malcomb DuBose, had been a close friend. He was a real estate developer. She, and her husband Paul, had bought their home in Cary from him. Her two young sons had evacuated with her husband, as mom "left for work".

She thought about her husband and children as she turned her Apache AH-64D toward Tower No. 3 and closed in.

At 300 yards, she began firing short bursts from her chain gun. She only had 150 rounds left. She could see the silhouette of a man standing outside the tower by the railing. He was raising a weapon to his shoulder. She knew it was a Stinger. She pushed the throttle forward and charged the tower while keeping the chain gun's target reticule locked on the tower. The Stinger had a minimum range of 660 feet, and she intended to stay much closer than that.

At 200 yards, the missile fired. The man began to dance in her sights before coming apart. She could see arms and legs scattered in different directions as the explosive rounds shredded the armored tower. The rocket flew past her, detonating far behind, as she flew through the debris and fire of the destroyed tower.

Fuel Handling Building
Refuel Floor
North End
0415 hours EST

Heng had been fighting with the crane controls for over 30 minutes. Without Jian's guidance, he was struggling. Despite Heng's best efforts, Jian had bled out. An artery in his upper arm had been severed. It was too high on the inside of the arm for a tourniquet to work.

Heng had experimented with the controls, but the best he had managed was to move the load away from the open hatch. Now it hung a foot off the refuel floor, and he couldn't figure out how to raise the load any higher. All the spent fuel pools on the floor were surrounded with handrails over three feet tall.

"Four feet . . . all I need is four feet up. Then I have to figure out how to move to the middle of the building," Heng said, as he continued to try one control after another.

"Stupid Americans! Why can't it just have a joy stick? All I want is UP/Down and Left/Right . . . something simple," Heng said, as he threw his hands up in frustration.

. . . .

Tommy and Chris had crept down the west side of the refuel floor. They stepped off the walkway beside the first spent fuel pool and onto the huge concrete floor area between the two main spent fuel pools. The area was 50 yards long and the width of the building.

"Stand up and don't move," Tommy said, as they reached the middle of the building.

The 50-Ton Crane was 70 yards away. Tommy stood behind Chris and rested his M16A2 on Chris's shoulder. He slid forward until the magazine rested against Chris's back.

"Hold your breath and close your eyes. Do not move!" Tommy said, into Chris's right ear.

"Oh, shit!" Chris said, as he held his breath.

. . . .

Heng stood up from the operator's chair and began cursing in frustration. He turned and rested his hands on the cab's safety rail. He raised his head and saw two men less than 100 yards away, standing in the middle of the floor.

The first two bullets struck him in the chest on his body armor. The third one entered just under his chin, severed his spine, and blew out the back of his skull. He fell back into the crane operator's chair, and twitched for almost a minute as his blood drained onto the deck plate floor, blending with Jian's.

"Just like shooting a buck. Always best to shoot from a rest, keeps the rifle steady," Tommy said, while lowering the weapon, and patting Chris on the shoulder.

"Damn, boy, you drilled him! I bet that's the bomb hanging from the crane. Let's go check it out," Chris said.

They both began walking toward the north end of the floor, when a man rose from the stairwell on the east side. He braced his elbow against the rail and began shooting at them with a pistol.

Both Tommy and Chris fell to the floor as bullets whizzed by their heads and skipped off the floor.

"Get him! Shoot the bastard!" Chris yelled, as he pulled his weapon and began shooting on automatic.

"Shoot at him! Don't spray and pray!" Tommy yelled, as he settled into a prone position and took careful aim.

"Shit, the handrails are in the way," Tommy said, as he struggled into a kneeling position.

. . . .

Aiguo ran from the stairwell and toward the nuclear device. It was suspended from the crane, a foot off the floor. Blood was dripping from above, onto the concrete beside the device. He walked through large splatter marks as he stepped onto the oversized steel pallet. It began to sway as he slipped a thin chain out from under his shirt, and inserted a key into a padlock. He threw the lock away, as a bullet passed near his head. More rounds pinged off the device. Another clipped the sleeve on his shirt. He ducked behind the device, and flipped open the cover that protected the device's controls.

"One of them can't shoot. The other is very precise," Aiguo said, as he slipped out of his body armor, stood, and lifted it in front of him.

241

The armor was stiff enough that it provided a barrier between him and the shooters. It jumped as rounds struck the other side, but it was the cover he needed.

"Five minutes! Once it's set, they're done. This country ceases to exist. I may die, but China will live. China will rule this planet. A statue of me will be erected in the Great Hall," Aiguo said, as he stood and entered a 16-digit activation code that allowed him to detonate the device manually.

"It accepted the code. It's over," Aiguo said, as he placed the tip of his right index finger on the button labeled with the Chinese character for 'Enter', and pressed.

He felt a subtle click, and then looked at the timer. It began counting down from 15 minutes. Aiguo began cursing. He had forgotten to reset the timer from the 15-minute default.

"Five minutes! Five minutes, you idiot," he screamed, as the body armor shield was knocked over by the impact of two more bullets.

He ducked behind the device and reloaded his pistol. Then he glanced at his watch . . . 0432.

"It's all right. Everything will be all right. They can't do anything in 15 minutes. 0447 . . . that gives me time to get out of here. I can still live through this. I'll return to China. They'll realize their mistake. I can still be the hero, just like in the American movies," he said, then dashed for the stairwell while firing at the two men in the distance.

.   .   .   .

Tommy fired at the man as he sprinted down the stairwell, but missed.

"Come on, Chris, we've got to get that thing out of here," Tommy said, as he rose to his feet and began running north toward the suspended package.

Chris followed on Tommy's right, keeping his weapon aimed at the stairwell that the man had used to escape.

"Do you know how to operate that crane?' Chris asked, as they ran.

"Yeah, I worked on the Spent Fuel Team for years. The 50-Ton Crane was used to move spent fuel casks from the railcar down below up to the Unloading Pool," Tommy said, as they reached the stairwell.

Both men walked around the open stairwell with their weapons pointed down the stairs.

"I think he split. Now what?" Chris asked.

"You cover the stairs, and I'll take a look at this thing," Tommy said, while walking over to the pallet carrying the nuclear device.

"Oh, shit! Dude, we're screwed. This thing has a timer, and he started it. We've got 14 minutes and 12 seconds before this thing goes off," Tommy said, while staring down at the timer.

"Can you turn it off?"

"All I see is a timer and a panel for entering some type of code. Everything is in Chinese."

"Then what do we do? We gotta get out of here!"

"No, we have to get this thing out of the building, and as far away from the plant as possible before it goes off," Tommy said, as he ran over to a yellow gang box on the western wall.

"We don't have enough time. You'll have to climb up to the cab and then move it. As I remember, that thing is as slow as shit," Chris said, while running over to the device and staring at the timer.

"They didn't know about this," Tommy said, as he lifted a large rectangular instrument from the box.

"Remote control, baby! The mechanics got tired of dressing out and climbing up to the cab to operate the crane. So they bought a remote control," Tommy said, as he turned the remote on, and began lifting the device higher off the floor.

"You know how to operate that thing?"

"No Qual Card, but yeah, I can operate this crane. One of the mechanics owed me a favor and showed me how to use it. He also told me that if I ever moved the crane, he'd break my arms," Tommy said, while grinning at Chris.

"Okay, we still have to get rid of that thing," Chris said, then stared at the stairwell.

"That's right, buddy, you have to go down to the Railcar Bay, make sure our pal isn't down there, and see if there's a vehicle. They used to keep a forklift down there," Tommy said, as he moved the load over the hatch opening.

"Can't that thing go down any faster?" Chris asked, as he walked over to the stairwell and began looking down.

Fuel Handling Building Roof
0420 hours EST

Kate regained consciousness as her head banged against one of the handrails that ran the length of the roof. She felt a sharp tug and opened her eyes. Lightning, thunder, and the sound of gunfire told her that it wasn't a bad dream. Another tug, and she looked forward. Her chute was extended out past the west side of the Fuel Handling Building. It billowed in the fierce winds, and was trying to drag her off the roof of the ten-story tall building.

"Shit, the mission," she said, as she struggled to get out of her harness.

"What's wrong with my legs? I can't feel them. Why won't they move?" Kate shouted, as her senses began to awaken.

The rain still poured from the sky. She was soaked and beginning to shiver from cold or shock. She wasn't sure which. Her head ached and her vision was blurry. The chute was pulled so taut by the wind that she couldn't get out of it. She pulled a knife and began cutting the nylon cords away, then fell back to the roof as the chute flew away in the wind. Her head and right shoulder had been wedged against the upright section of the railing; otherwise, she would have been dragged off the roof.

Kate stared up into the sky and thought, "*Where is everybody? Why can't I move my legs?*"

She pulled herself up against the vertical rail and stared down at her legs. They wouldn't move. She noticed that she was at the far end of the roof, 30 feet from the north end.

"Damn, I broke my back in the landing," she told herself, hoping that she was wrong.

"The last thing I remember is the helicopter crashing below me. The teams . . ." she said, and looked to her left, down the 300 foot length of the roof.

She saw numerous piles of men, equipment . . . and parts of men. A few chutes still blew up into the sky like kites, pinned to the ground by corpses. The southern end of the roof was still engulfed in flames, despite the wind and the downpour. Bent rotor blades reached up into the sky, pleading with a greater power to live again. She saw one man rise, backlit against the swirling flames, and walk toward her.

SSG Clay limped up and knelt beside her. His hands were covered with blood that the rain was rapidly washing away.

"That was a righteous fuck up! That damn chopper just about did us all. Can you move?" SSG Clay asked.

"I can't move my legs. I'm numb from the waist down. I must have hit something. By the way, you owe me a $1000 bucks," Kate said, and tried to smile, but couldn't.

"I don't carry that much on me, but I'm good for it."

"So now what?" she asked.

"So we continue with the mission. I'll rig a harness out of rope and lower you off the end of the building. Then I'll follow you down, and we disarm the bomb," SSG Clay said, while he began examining Kate for other injuries.

"My bag broke loose. I'll need all my equipment," Kate said, while looking around the roof.

"There, at the end of the roof. It slid over there," Kate said, and felt herself begin to lose consciousness.

"Oh, no, can't have you falling out on me," SSG Clay said, while reaching into a med-kit pouch on his waist.

"This injector has a little pain killer, and a whole lot of stimulant. It's a special cocktail provided by Uncle Sam, just for us," SSG Clay said, as he removed the cap and injected the drug into Kate's neck.

"Oh, shit! What's in that? I want a prescription," Kate said, as she became fully alert.

"You don't want to know, but it's worth a fortune on the black market," SSG Clay said, as he finished his inspection of Kate's injuries.

"Lady . . . your back is broken at the 3rd or 4th lumbar vertebrae. I can feel the displacement. So it's a bad break. You're paralyzed from the waist down. Nothing else seems to be broken, no internal injuries that I can find. The good news, you're just fine up here," SSG Clay said, while tapping the side of her helmet.

Kate closed her eyes, and began breathing deeply, trying to control the sense of panic that was threatening to overwhelm her.

"You still willing to go through with this? I shouldn't move you with that injury."

Kate nodded, trying to focus on the mission, and not on being paralyzed.

"I'll set everything up for the rappel. Then I'll come back to get you," SSG Clay said, as he turned, and began running toward the north end of the roof.

As he looked down off the end of the building, a man dressed as a security guard ran by below, and jumped into a brown truck parked a few yards past the building.

"*Truck . . . bomb . . . security guard,*" all flashed as rapid thoughts in SSG Clay's mind as he raised his weapon, and leaned his elbow on the upper handrail.

The first two rounds took out the left rear tire. As the truck swerved to the left, two more rounds took out the front left. A man leapt from the passenger side and began running for the fence line. SSG Clay dropped him with one shot. The man lay on his face, and didn't move.

Railcar Bay
0435 hours EST

Chris stood in the Railcar Bay below the open hatch. Tommy was looking down from above, as Chris signaled him to keep lowering the nuclear weapon. One more foot, and it would be resting on the concrete floor. Chris had already positioned the forklift. He had a plan, but he was desperately racking his mind for another one.

"Oh, this sucks, this really sucks. I don't want to do this. I really, really don't want to do this," Chris said, as the load landed, and he began removing the lifting cables.

"Crap! 0437 . . . ten minutes. That's all we've got, ten minutes," Chris said, as he threw the cables to the side, and climbed into the cab of the forklift.

Next, everything seemed to happen at once. Tommy came running into the Railcar Bay. An older woman with long red hair, dressed like a soldier, dropped out of the sky, landing right in the open doorway leading from the building. Five seconds later, another soldier landed right beside her. Then, a US Army Stryker roared up right beside them and parked, blocking the exit. The soldier on top had a .50

cal M2 machine gun aimed directly at Chris's chest. Soldiers and civilians began swarming out of the back of the vehicle and everyone began talking at once.

Chris glanced down at the timer, and began shouting over and over, "9 minutes and 30 seconds . . . 29 . . . 28 . . . 27. Get out of the damn way!"

"Sir, get out of that forklift right now, or I will shoot you," SSG Clay said, as he pointed his weapon at Chris and began walking toward him.

"Asshole, do we look like Chinese terrorists? We've been fighting them all night. Where the hell have you been?" Tommy said, as he jumped down into the Railcar Bay from an elevated walkway, which he immediately regretted.

"9 minutes and 20 seconds . . . and then we're all dust. So if you want to shoot, then go right ahead," Chris said.

"Hold on, Staff Sergeant. Let these men look at the weapon," Anthony said.

Nathan and Alan were both kneeling beside Kate. The conversation was heated.

"We can still do this. I disarmed the device in Alexandria in less than five minutes," Kate said.

"I read your report. That device wasn't set up like the ones we dealt with on the West Coast. It didn't have the internal tampering net. The electronics were simpler . . . more straight forward. They hid the weapon inside a diesel generator. That was the protection, the camouflage. This is like one of the West Coast devices. It will have the same internal anti-tampering protections. There is no way to disarm this device in less than an hour. We've got 9 minutes," Nathan said.

"Will all of you shut up and listen. If that bomb goes off in here it will take the spent fuel with it. If you can't stop this thing from going off, then we have to move the bomb as far away from here as possible. That's all we can do and we don't have time for a discussion," Chris yelled, while pounding on the steering wheel of the fork lift.

They all looked at Anthony. He looked at the three civilian experts.

"Can you disarm it in time? Yes . . . or no?" Anthony asked.

They all looked at each other, and then shook their heads.

Anthony looked over at the Stryker, and signaled the driver to back the vehicle out of the way.

"How much time?" Anthony asked.

"8 minutes and 50 seconds," Chris said, while starting the forklift's engine and sliding the forks under the pallet containing the bomb.

Tommy stood beside him and said, "Chris, this is crazy. Let one of the military guys do this. This isn't our job."

"Tommy, haven't you been saying all night that this was our plant, our responsibility . . . our job. I know how to drive this thing. They don't. When I leave, get them all inside. Get downstairs and wait out the blast. Then, you can go back upstairs and exit down into the Waste Processing Building. You'll be shielded the whole way. You know how to protect them," Chris said, as he and Tommy shook hands for the last time.

"Dude, we were supposed to live through this, and go drink beer at the Aviator Brewery. We were going to give Kay and Cornell a hard time for hiding out while we were out doing all the hard work," Tommy said, while choking back tears.

"I know . . . I know . . . drink one for me, and tell Kristie how much I love her," Chris said, as he turned away, and lifted the pallet off the floor.

"I will . . . brother, I will," Tommy said, as Chris pulled the forklift forward, and began driving across the asphalt toward the Protected Area security fence.

Large sections of the fence were gone. The Strykers had taken care of that. He could see military vehicles fleeing toward the south as fast as they could go. A brown truck was pulled off to the side of the road as he passed through the fence. As he drove by on the left side, a man rose from a crouched position on the other side of the truck.

. . . .

Aiguo took careful aim at the forklift driver's head sticking up above the seat as he drove past.

"You will not rob me of this victory. I will see this country brought to its knees. My statue will stand beside one of General Kung in the Great Hall of the People," Aiguo said, as he raised his 9mm pistol, and slowly began to squeeze the trigger.

Fired from behind him, the .45 caliber bullet shattered Aiguo's right shoulder. The 9mm round fired from his pistol caromed off the side of the forklift, as it continued down the gravel road, away from the plant.

This wound hurt much worse than the earlier shot in the left side of his back. The sound of the weapon seemed familiar, Aiguo thought, as he fell to his knees and sagged backwards against the truck bumper. His legs crumpled under him as he began to lose consciousness. Then he heard the sound of boots crunching on gravel to his right. A man in uniform walked past him, then turned and squatted down in front of him.

Anthony said nothing as he stared at the dying man in front of him. He had seen this face in his dreams many times over the past few months.

"I still win. I took your wife . . . now I'll take your country," Aiguo said, while bloody spittle foamed from his mouth.

"No . . . you still lose. I have her in here," Anthony said, as he tapped his chest with his left hand.

"The United . . . States . . . of America . . . will survive. We always do. We always will. But your country . . . something tells me that the President is going to make China pay for this day," Anthony said, as he raised his .45 in his right hand, and shot Aiguo between the eyes.

Aiguo's head slammed back against the bumper of the truck. His body slid slowly down into the dirt. Anthony stared at the corpse for a few seconds, and then glanced at his watch.

"4 minutes, time to go," he said, as he stood and turned to look at the road heading north. He could just see the forklift heading into the woods. He turned and began sprinting back toward the Fuel Handling Building.

North of the Harris Plant
0443 hours EST

Chris ran the forklift up the paved road that paralleled the railroad tracks leading to the Fuel Handling Building until he got to the small helipad. Then he turned left, passed through an empty security check point, and headed west down a dirt road. He leaned over and stared at the timer on the bomb.

249

"*4 minutes . . . I've got to get as far away as possible,*" he thought, as he sped through a sharp right hand turn that headed north.

He turned on the small headlights on the fork lift as he got further away from the bright lights of the plant. He passed some small houses, and hoped that the families that lived there had evacuated. He knew this road. Tommy had gotten permission to hunt back here a few years ago. It was in the Fall. Tommy liked to hunt deer from a tree stand. Chris remembered that they hadn't seen one buck, and that he had frozen his ass off while sitting up in a swaying pine tree. He smiled at the memory as the forklift bounced down the dirt road.

Chris thought about his early life, and a father who had been so hard on him. He thought about the Navy, and where that had led. Marriages and children, vacations and parties, the houses and the places, all the friends he had known, everywhere he had lived. Then he thought about Harris. He had worked here while the plant was owned by three different companies. But it hadn't mattered. Most of his friends in Radiation Protection had worked with him for over 20 years. Management had changed, but they had stayed together. They had grown old together. When the plant had first started up, they talked about the plant softball league, raising kids, bowling, drinking and women. Back then, those were the normal things that young men talked about. Now it was grandkids, retirement, insurance policies, and which doctor's appointment or surgery you had scheduled next.

"2 minutes . . ." he said, as the trees closed in and it grew very dark.

The storm had paused, as if catching its breath, leaving behind a fresh coolness. He could hear tree frogs and other night creatures out looking for food before the next onslaught. Small branches covered the road. He hoped that he didn't come across a large tree blocking his path.

He slowed, as the forklift crossed the railway tracks, and kept going. The road was straight for another mile. Chris knew he'd never reach the next curve. He looked up, and saw that the sky had cleared for just a moment. He breathed deep, reveling in the sweetness of the night air. Then he stared at the stars as tears began to fall down his face.

Chris looked down at the timer, one final time, "1 minute . . . I'll miss this life," he said, as he breathed deeply once more, and drove on into the darkness . . .

CHAPTER 58

The Detonation
August 3, 0445 hours EST

They rushed down the north stairwell of the Fuel Handling Building, as Tommy led them deeper into the plant. Anthony had wanted to join his troops on the other side of the site, but Amanda had convinced him that his troops were as safe as possible, considering the circumstances.

On Anthony's command, a warning of an imminent nuclear detonation had been sent to brigade headquarters. Then the battalion had rushed toward the massive set of concrete buildings that plant workers called the Power Block. The plant had been built after the accident at Three Mile Island and was built like a modern day fortress. The walls of the major buildings were high density concrete, reinforced with dense layers of steel rebar. The outer walls were at least four feet thick. The Reactor Containment Building had been designed to resist the impact of a Boeing 707 at terminal velocity. The Fuel Handling Building was almost as strong. A thousand soldiers flowed into the Waste Processing Building like ants, searching for cover.

Ground level at the plant was 261' feet above sea level. The lowest level in the plant was 190'. Concrete, steel and dirt were everything. They were shielding from the blast and radiation. Shielding was survival.

The Pentagon had been notified of an imminent nuclear detonation near the Harris Nuclear Plant. The NC State EOC had been notified next. Within minutes, alerts had been sent to emergency organizations across the nation.

. . . .

Tommy opened the door onto the 216' elevation of the north end of the Fuel Handling Building. Seventeen people followed behind him as he shut the door and glanced at his watch.

"90 seconds!" he yelled, as he thought about Chris, and what he must be thinking.

Kate groaned as they placed her on the cold concrete floor. SSG Clay rushed over to her side and looked into her eyes.

"I think you need some more meds," he said, as he reached into his med kit.

"No . . . I want to remember this. I want to feel it as it happens," Kate said, while grabbing his wrist.

SSG Clay nodded, sat beside her, and leaned back against the concrete wall.

"You know, I've been through some wild shit, but this takes the cake," he said, while injecting himself with the potent mixture of pain killers and uppers.

"Each to their own," she said, as she looked around at the others trapped below ground awaiting the detonation of a nuclear weapon three times as powerful as the Hiroshima weapon.

Anthony and Amanda stood a few yards away, in a corner, away from the others.

"I'm a Nuclear Engineer and I've studied these things, but I have no idea how this is going to end. If he gets the device far enough away, we might survive. This building is strong enough to survive a blast, but it all depends . . ." Amanda said, as she stared into the eyes of a man who had lived in her dreams for months.

"Let me bandage your head. You're still bleeding," Anthony said, while reaching into the med kit on his web gear.

"We might die in the next two minutes, and I have to tell you how I feel," Amanda said, as he began cleaning her wound.

"Later, now isn't the time. Let's live through this, and then we can talk," he said, as he discarded the alcohol swab, and placed a bandage over her torn brow.

. . . .

The first thing they felt was a deep shudder, as if the entire earth had shifted on its axis. Next, a deep boom that seemed to wrap them in its intensity, followed by a prolonged rumble that went on and on. Then the building began to vibrate and shake. The lighting in the room went out as the shaking continued.

Tommy's Electronic Dosimeter began to alarm. It was mounted on his company ID Badge right below his TLD. He had completely forgotten about it. He pulled it off and activated the backlight. Someone else turned on a flashlight.

The others stared at him as the alarm and the shaking continued. He removed the ED, silenced the alarm, and switched from dose, to dose rate. He marveled as the number rose to 2 Rem per hour. They were 50 feet below ground, and the dose rate had risen from 0.001 Rem per hour to over 2 Rem per hour, despite all the dirt, concrete and steel.

"What does the alarm mean?" asked a soldier standing nearby, the fear evident in his voice.

"We're safe down here. It just means that the bomb has gone off," Tommy said, as he wept, and began to pray for the soul of his friend.

CHAPTER 59

The White House
The Situation Room
Washington, DC, USA
August 3, 0500 hours EST

"Mr. President, we've received notification that a nuclear detonation has occurred at or near the Harris Nuclear Plant," said Chief of Staff Roger Yost, as he walked into the Situation Room.

"Oh, God . . . so the mission failed? They detonated the bomb in the Fuel Handling Building?" President Miller asked, while rubbing his tired eyes.

"Mr. President, as you know, satellite visibility has been minimal due to thunderstorm activity in the area, but reports prior to the detonation lead us to believe that the weapon was removed from the building prior to detonation. We had comms from the ground forces that they were ordered into the main structures, en masse. They were ordered to abandon their vehicles and flee indoors," said the Chairman of the Joint Chiefs, General Munford.

"Sir, it must have been to shield them. Their commanding officer must have known that the device was about to detonate. He ordered his troops inside to shield them from the blast," said NRC Chairman Carol Wisnicki.

"What about the evacuation of the surrounding area? Casualties? Fallout projections? Will more evacuations be needed?" the President asked.

"Mr. President, the only benefit of this storm front has been the rain and the extended duration of the storm. Our projections show that the fallout will be effectively limited to a narrow plume around 100 miles long and 12 miles wide. Most of the fallout will be washed out of the sky. Of course, the impact on those areas will be magnified, but most of those areas are sparsely populated. The exceptions are Apex, Cary, and large portions of Raleigh, in North Carolina. They were directly upwind from the blast. They'll be uninhabitable for years," the NRC Chairman said.

"Mr. President, we've received confirmation that the blast occurred outside the Fuel Handling Building. We have video from a news helicopter that shows the Harris Plant intact. I repeat, Sir, the major buildings on site are shown to be intact. The video was taken from ten miles away, downwind from the blast, but it shows the plant intact," said the Chief of Staff, as the short video was displayed on one of the large screens.

"The cooling tower is gone. That's a long-term problem," said NRC Chairman Wisnicki.

"You aren't advocating that the plant should ever start back up, are you?" asked Attorney General Delores Bull.

"No, of course not! But Harris was running at the time it was taken over. We have to address two problems. First, keeping that core covered and cooled, or we have the potential for a Three Mile Island type accident where the core melts down. Second, we still have a massive amount of spent fuel in the pools in the Fuel Handling Building that needs constant cooling. We can't just walk away from the plant," Chairman Wisnicki replied.

"As of right now the dose rates on site will make the area unapproachable. It's probably over 1000 Rem per hour. But, within 72 hours, the dose rates will probably be closer to 10-20 Rem per hour. That's still high, but volunteers can work in that environment for short periods of time. We have to reestablish cooling to the reactor core and the spent fuel system, or the problem could get much worse," Chairman Wisnicki said.

"How can things get worse? We just had a foreign power detonate a nuclear bomb on American soil. What are we going to do about that, Mr. President?" asked Vice President O'Quinn.

"One problem at a time," said the President.

"What about my soldiers? When can we evacuate them from the site?" asked General Munford.

"They should be trained to operate in that environment. They're going to have to find places deep in the plant that have the lowest dose rates, and wait it out for a few days. As long as they don't panic, and leave those massive concrete buildings, they'll live through this. After that . . . they'll require medical care of varying levels for the rest of their lives. It will depend on their total exposure and how much radioactive material they have ingested," Chairman Wisnicki said.

"Back to China! Mr. President, we have to respond to this attack. The American people will demand vengeance," the Vice President said.

"Harold, I'm not in the business of vengeance. They will pay for this, but this wasn't a direct attack on the United States by the government of the PRC. You know that. This whole incident was caused by one rogue general."

"True, but they went along with it. Or have you forgotten your conversation with General Secretary Li, when he tried to blackmail us into leaving Asia and abandoning our allies in the region? Nothing has been done about that," the Vice President said.

"So what do you want, Harold? Do you want me to blow China off the face of the Earth? Is a nuclear war the answer?"

"Mr. President, you are now aware of the full capabilities of the United States military. We don't have to use nuclear weapons to 'de-fang' the Chinese military," the Joint Chief said.

"We just had a nuclear detonation on American soil. Tens of thousands of our fellow citizens are either dead, or going to die within the next few days. The financial markets across the globe are going to go into free fall, starting this morning. Riots will probably break out in every major city in the US. We're going to have to deal with millions of frightened citizens up wind of this blast, and you two want me to go to war with the People's Republic of China?" the President asked, as he stared at every person sitting at the table.

"The problem with China will be addressed, but not today, and not this week. Right now, we take care of our own. Right now, we help the American people recover from this disaster. The full weight of the American military will not fall on China. It will be utilized within our own borders to assist our fellow citizens. Local law enforcement will be overwhelmed in some areas. I may have to declare martial law, but the United States of America will survive this," the President said, while rising from his chair.

"Now. . . it's 0530. I'm going to go get two hours sleep. Then I'm going before the American people at 0800 to reassure them, and the world, that we have survived this terrorist assault on our nation. That is what I'm going to emphasize. This was a terrorist assault . . .

not an attack by the People's Republic of China," the President said, as he turned, and left the Situation Room.

Everyone stood as the President and his Secret Service escort left the room. Vice President O'Quinn approached the Chairman of the JCS.

"He's wrong, General. This was an attack by the People's Republic of China. They went along with General Kung's plan when they found out about it. The only reason that we prevailed was the black projects that you boys have been hiding from us for decades," the Vice President said.

"Mr. Vice President, I've thought about that over the last few months. We were wrong to have done that. We've all sworn allegiance to the Constitution and the elected officials that represent the people. What we've developed is amazing, but it shouldn't have been kept secret for so long," General Munford said.

"General, we both know that if the Pentagon had told the Congress about the 'Dory' and the 'Kraken', the information would have leaked within 48 hours. Then the Chinese would have started infiltrating the program to steal the tech. Some things have to be kept hidden. That's why the Chinese are always a decade behind. We have to ensure that it stays that way," Vice President O'Quinn said.

"I understand that, Mr. Vice President, but I won't cross him. He's the President, and I have sworn allegiance to him," General Munford said.

"Incorrect, General. You've sworn allegiance to the Constitution. He never said that you couldn't make contingency plans to address the problem with China. That's what you guys do, isn't it? You make contingency plans for multiple eventualities. So make some plans, General. We'll just wait and see how things develop over the next few months. Once things settle down, the American people are going to be pissed. They'll want their revenge," the Vice President said, as he turned and walked away.

CHAPTER 60

Harris Nuclear Plant
Fuel Handling Building
216' North
August 3, 0530 hours EST

"Listen, Mr. Borders, I appreciate what you're saying, but I have to find out what happened to my battalion," LTC Anthony Thompson said, as Tommy stood in front of the door leading out of the area known as 216' North Fuel Handling Building.

"Colonel, you're not listening. We're 50 feet underground. There is probably 20 feet of concrete between us and the outside. There's an area monitor on the wall over there, and the dose rates in here are 100 times normal. Once we leave here and start heading up the stairs to the refuel floor, they'll be 10,000 times higher, maybe more. We need to wait down here for a day at least," Tommy said.

"Do you want me to move him, Colonel?" SSG Clay asked, as he walked up and stood beside Anthony.

Both men towered over the technician, but he stood his ground like a pit bull.

"Tommy, your name's Tommy, right?" Amanda asked, as she pushed both men aside.

"Radiation Protection is your specialty. I understand that, but we have to get out of here. That woman over there needs medical help. I'm guessing that there are first aid supplies, maybe a small clinic of some sort inside these buildings. She needs some help or she's not going to make it," Amanda said.

"There's a first aid room in the Waste Processing Building, up near our offices. But that's near the outside of the building. There are doors to the outside near there. Those doors are two inches of steel, but they might as well be made of paper. The gamma radiation will go right through them. We need to stay behind concrete, lots of it. The plant ventilation has shut down, but the airborne contamination will start filtering into the building. We'll need respirators, or the ingestion will kill us," Tommy said, as the two men started closing in again.

"Tommy, can we leave here and get her help?" Amanda asked.

"Yes, but you have to follow me and do as I say. We have to move fast and stay away from any openings to the outside," Tommy said, as he started planning a travel path in his mind.

Waste Processing Building 236'
Radwaste Control Room
0530 hours EST

It had been almost an hour since the building had stopped shaking. The lights were out, and Kay sat huddled in a corner with her mag light for company. She had cried until she didn't have any more tears. Then her electronic dosimeter alarmed and caused her to jump to her feet.

"That was the bomb. The bomb must have gone off. But I'm still here and the building is in one piece. If it had gone off inside the Fuel Handling Building the whole plant would have been torn apart. So it must have been outside," Kay said, reassured by the sound of her own voice.

"Okay, so what do I do? What are the dose rates in here?" she asked herself, and then remembered that the operators had their own private stash of radiation survey instruments in the Radwaste Control Room.

She broke the seal on the wall locker, and saw protective coveralls, booties, hoods, respirators, and survey instruments. Five minutes later she was completely covered from head to foot in protective clothing. The respirator was tight, which made it harder to breathe, but she found the confinement somehow comforting.

She removed a Teletector from the wall locker and set it down on a desk. Then she loosened the strap on her M-16 and draped the weapon in front of her. She picked up the Teletector again, and walked down the stairs from the Radwaste Control Room.

"Let's go see what's out there," she told herself, as she turned on the Laurus 6112M Teletector.

"Wow, 10 mRem per hour in here. Normally, it's less than 0.01. No wonder my ED alarmed," Kay said, and then began laughing for some reason.

Waste Processing Building 261'
Exit Door from the Fuel Handling Building
0540 hours EST

Kay screamed as she exited the stairwell from 236' onto the 261' elevation. The automatic weapon was aimed at her head. She instinctively pointed the Teletector at the man, and then began cursing when she noticed Tommy standing beside the soldier. Tommy was laughing while he asked the huge man not to shoot her.

"Tommy Borders, you scared me almost to death," Kay yelled, her voice muffled by the respirator, as she ran up and hugged him.

"This is Kay Snaps, she works with me," Tommy said, as the group exited the stairwell behind him.

"Kay, where's Cornell?" Tommy asked, as he grabbed her by the shoulders and stared at her face through the respirator.

"One of them came after us . . . found us in the Radwaste Control Room. He killed Cornell, and I killed him," Kay said, as she patted her M-16.

"You killed a Chinese Special Forces operator? Are you sure he's dead?" SGG Clay asked, as he walked up beside the pair.

"I shot him in the legs, shot him in the arms, and took most of his head off. I'm pretty sure he's dead," Kay said, while fighting the urge to throw up.

"Well, damn!" SSG Clay said, as he backed up and looked at the woman encased in protective clothing with an M-16 draped across her chest, and some strange, telescoping, radiation detection device in her hands.

"Where's Chris?" Kay asked, as she looked past Tommy at the collection of strangers.

Tommy shook his head and said, "He drove the bomb offsite on a forklift."

Kay just looked at him, fresh tears welling up in her eyes.

They all jumped back, as the double doors leading into the forward office areas of the building popped open. Four soldiers were aiming automatic weapons at them.

"Colonel . . . Hey guys, it's the Colonel. We thought you were dead, Sir. The last we heard, your vehicle got hit up by an AT missile. After that, things went to shit. We tore up the front of the plant, and killed everyone who wasn't wearing tan. Then we were ordered to exit our vehicles and evac inside here. Then the bomb went off," said First Lieutenant Billy Powell, as he stepped forward and saluted LTC Thompson.

"Somebody found a survey meter back there in the offices. They turned it on and said it pegged. We're getting everyone deeper into the building. We're not sure where to go," Lt. Powell said.

"How many men made it in here?" Anthony asked.

"Most of the battalion, Sir. We're backed up tight behind me," Lt. Powell said.

"Where can we take them?" Anthony asked Tommy.

Tommy thought for a few seconds, and then said, "Kay, take them down to 211', and then come back up here. We've got to go get some medical supplies."

Kay nodded, opened the door to the stairwell she had just come from, and said, "Follow me."

"Lieutenant, follow that woman and get a head count," Anthony said, as Lt. Powell followed Kay down the stairwell.

"Yes, Sir," came the reply.

"Now all we have to do is survive until help arrives," Anthony said, as he glanced at Amanda standing beside him.

She leaned against him, reached over, and squeezed his arm. Neither one of them wanted to move.

CHAPTER 61

Central Military Commission Headquarters
August 1st Building
Beijing, China
August 7, 1830 hours CT

The 16 men who formed the power base of the People's Republic of China sat at a long rectangular table deep below the August 1st Building, headquarters of the Central Military Commission. Ten senior officers sat opposite five politicians. Each group talked quietly amongst themselves. Party General Secretary Li Xibin, the man to whom all had sworn their allegiance, sat at the head of the table.

"General Fan, what is the latest information?" General Secretary Li asked the Vice-Chairman of the CMC.

"There has been a nuclear detonation within the United States, at a location near a nuclear plant in North Carolina. That is in the southeast portion of . . ." General Fan began

"I know where North Carolina is, General Fan. How are the Americans reacting? Have their fleets begun to move? Have they increased the readiness of their nuclear forces? Have there been any sightings of their damned space planes? What are they preparing to do?" General Secretary Li asked, as he thumped the table with his fist.

"General Secretary, as far as we can tell, they aren't doing anything . . . reactionary. We all saw the President's address to his people. They are using their military resources to support recovery within the areas affected by the nuclear detonation. Their only fleet movements have been to move in support of recovery operations. As far as their space planes . . . we still have no way of detecting them," General Fan said.

"Six months . . . it has been six months since I stared at a silent, hovering aircraft with a fluttering red, white and blue pattern. It hovered in the courtyard of the most sacred building in our nation. The American President was showing me that we had nothing. Do you understand me, General Fan? Nothing!" General Secretary Li said, as he began shouting at the military officers at the table.

"You failed to control a rogue general. You allowed him to develop a private nuclear force right under your noses. Then you had the audacity to bring him to me with his insane plan of blackmailing the Americans," General Secretary Li yelled, continuing his tirade.

"General Secretary . . . with all due respect . . . you went along with his plan when it was presented to you," General Fan replied, understanding that his life was at risk.

"Comrades, this is not productive. We all had a hand in this debacle to one extent or another. We can continue to tear ourselves apart, have a few people in this room shot, or we can take action to protect ourselves," said Admiral Wu Yaoyan.

"Admiral Wu . . . despite the fact that we publically laud the achievements and power of the new and modern Chinese navy, we all know that your fleet is shit when compared to the Americans," General Fan said.

"Perhaps, Comrade General, but what we lack in technological advancement, we make up for with brute force . . . and the careful placement of certain hidden assets," Admiral Wu replied.

General Secretary Li sat down and shook his head before saying, "I think we are reverting to our past. You gentlemen are no more than warlords, each with their own private army. Please tell us, Comrade Admiral, what hidden assets?"

"Comrades, I must humbly confess that General Kung was not the only servant of the Chinese people who had plans for our eventual domination of this planet. The Americans may have the high ground, but I have the sea," Admiral Wu began, and then paused as he rose to his feet.

"On October 30, 1961, the Russians detonated the largest nuclear weapon ever developed . . . the RDS-220, also known as the Tsar Bomba. It had a theoretical yield of over 100 megatons. The subsequent explosion was only 50 megatons. Otherwise the aircraft that dropped the bomb would not have been able to escape the blast. The limited weapon was ferocious, and discarded as too unwieldy," Admiral Wu said, in a calm manner, as if he was teaching a classroom of cadets at the naval college.

"The Soviets built a total of three of these weapons. I am in possession of the two that remain. One sits imbedded deep within the island of La Palma, in the Canary Islands. The other sits in the Gulf of California, nestled on top of the southern end of the San Andreas Fault. The first device would produce a tidal wave over 500 meters high that would engulf the entire Atlantic Seaboard. The second device would . . . what is the phrase in English? Unzip . . . that's it! The second device would unzip the San Andreas Fault, and rip the West Coast of the United States apart," Admiral Wu said, while sitting and calmly watching, as the Generals and Politicians all began shouting at once.

THE END

To be continued in 'FIRE AND WATER'

Made in the USA
Columbia, SC
23 June 2019